An Australian Fugue novel

MISSING

Also by Ruth Skilbeck

Australian Fugue: The Antipode Room

Non-Fiction

The Writer's Fugue:
Musicalization, Trauma and Subjectivity
in the Literature of Modernity

An Australian Fugue novel

MISSING

Ruth Skilbeck

POSTMISTRESS PRESS
FuguEditions

National Library of Australia
Cataloguing-in-Publication entry:

Creator: Skilbeck, Ruth, author.
Title: Missing/Ruth Skilbeck.

ISBN: 9780992277956

Series: Skilbeck, Ruth. Australian fugue.

Fugue (Psychology)–Fiction.

Psychological fiction, Australian.

A823.4

This novel is a work of fiction. Names, characters, places, and incidents are the product of the author's imagination or are used entirely fictitiously. Art works, artists, authors, books, films, places and politics are included to create background only. Any perceived resemblance to actual persons, living or dead, events or locales is purely coincidental.

The sources of the literary quotations (including intentional mis-quotations/misrememberings by characters in this novel) are cited in endnotes at the end of the novel.

Contents

Prelude

'I HAVE THE *ART OF FUGUE*. I often listen to it as I'm going to sleep... It's my bedtime music,' she adds suggestively.

She leans over to the CD player beside her bed and touches something.

The first haunting bars; searing profound beauty of a violin shatters the still warm air.

She sits up, leans down across me. The top of her kimono falls open. As she's sitting up, she twists around and kisses me on the mouth. I don't want kisses. Our bodies push and brace against each other. This is the last thing that I want. I wanted the love of my life she stole away from me.

The searing beauty of a violin shatters the still warm air.

Fastening her lips on mine, she kisses me deeply, passionately; crushing me with her perfumed body weight. I'm struggling; my legs kick against the wall, hitting the wardrobe next to the bed, trying to gain solid ground.

And then the doorbell starts ringing.

Ringing and ringing and ringing...

Boring into my brain, alarm sirens. Thunderous noise explodes in my head. Pain. And that's when I saw... That's when everything went—blood red, crimson rage, magenta poison, pink thrills, crashing cerise, ruby red—

Spurting over sheets, gushing, dripping onto the polished floorboards of the immaculate designer dream interior.

Every morning I wake in hope. Have I remembered, in my sleep? I heard of amputees waking and checking the space where a limb was, unable to believe it's not there. They say, you feel an itch when you try to scratch you find there's nothing there. No images, sudden startling revelations. Shake me.

Only the walls are dreaming. They know everything. Bird songs scratch upstretched underarms of dawn. Black, white, traumatic verticals, bars, light. Bars. I watch aeroplanes fly by, frail amoebas. My window to truth and justice, the outside world, is striped. Prison grids it.

And I shall tell Dr Mael. No.

I did not remember in the night.

And I shall move slowly through the day. As all the days, since they brought me here. Three hundred and sixty days, since I was convicted of the murder at the trial. The full moon rises high each month. Drowns me in seductive grief. If I am good, they say, I will be allowed to paint. I am very good. My good work is my offering. I drink expensive French perfume. Voodoo zombies romp in my veins. Mermaid-cult priestesses throw themselves into the ocean in trances. My drum beats to an elusive deity. Tap-tap-tap. Keep on going, as I try to recall, recover what happened in Sydney. Almost two years ago.

The murder I cannot remember.

Tap-tap-tap on the keys of the laptop Hugo brought me, which they let me keep in cell. I am trying to figure out what caused that catastrophe, the time blanked from my mind.

What happened? I lie on the hard narrow bed. The voices will not stop. Spaghetti bolognaise for lunch today, I bet. Followed by a slice of sugar cake. A symphony of English comfort puddings. In London in the kitchen Hugo handed me a wooden spoon. Ouch! I think I can feel a memory coming through my body. Rushing through my blood. Silence. Then the dangerous music.

'Bach was the master of the art of fugue.' 'It's my bedtime music.'

Seething higher, hysteria! Shattering every waking day. An infernal, internal Nietzschean CD track, stuck on Eternal Return.

What happened? I can't remember but I was there! I must remember! Have to remember so that I can forget. Move on, at least, that is, figuratively speaking. To move on out of here, a free woman, would be bliss. Divine. Her violent violin. Lay forever to rest that double ghost. My nemesis. My love. Haunted. Wanted. Swooping and soaring. Flying and falling. Cutting the still air of the Castle into sad motifs. Ribbons and confetti. Dancing music, in a blood red gypsy dress.

They say it's there. Repressed. The blanked-out moments. Of the forgotten afternoon. You'll get it. The missing real-to-reel. Talk up. Talk out. It's a five-dollar-a-minute talking cure, only here, it's on the house. The long-lost bit of me that will or might set me free. The councillors, shrinks, doctors, all say. Think. And you will find. It's buried deep within. Lost behind the couch in the house in Primrose Hill perhaps, which Lady Ode, delightful mother-in-law, used to say once belonged to Oscar Fingal O'Flahertie Wilde. The walls know. But they're not saying. In a box, beneath a bed? Hugo's bed, or Ray's…

If not peace, I want the chance of inner peace.

If not dreamless sleep at least sweet dreams. I want to find the one I am searching for. Bring her back from the other side. What was it Father Aristotle said, without a visible trace of irony, in the prisoners' service, last Sunday? The truth, my sisters, the Truth will set you free…

Murder! I don't remember. Murder! My mind is reeling. I remember going to Australia to collect art for my gallery.

Day Six

Ruby

BANG! Bang

Ouch!

SOUNDS OF INDUSTRY CRASH AGAINST MY hangover. Susan and Ham are fixing up The Antipode Room. Ready for when Hugo and I return from Australia laden with art and artists contracts, if the plan goes according to plan. Fresh blood to inject colour and verve into the Antipodean collection I'm becoming known for.

Oris Chrifili's Madonna with dung... Waste has swamped art lately. Am I the only art dealer craving new life, passion, dreams and visions to inspire us? Although I can't let my view be known in public. I'd never give Hugo the satisfaction of knowing that. Authentic and relevant, or at least cutting-edge and hip though I assure him it is, I'm getting tired of all that ordure...

What was it he said after I hung the current Christmas show, Brenda Bickett's commentary on East End family life, incorporating body fluids?

'Ruby! Why must you exhibit such abjection, my dear?' he boomed. 'Cheer up! Be happy! Celebrate life!!'

It was Hugo's idea we go on this trip. He's been trying to persuade me to go to Australia with him for years, since just after we got together. Finally I've agreed. Going back to Australia, my 'homeland' as Hugo rather teasingly terms it, was not something I thought I could do. Even though I have a lingering idea I am from there. Although I have no knowledge or memory of my real birth family—that was all lost, forgotten after The Accident. I agreed to go because I know it's what the Gallery needs.

It's a good business move.

That's all.

Blearily I pick up pages of photocopied blurb from on top of the pile of papers on my desk. *Beauties Captured in Time…* by Australian artist, Wang Zhiyuan. The image is framed and imprisoned by dense bars of text; an island of tranquillity floating on a sea of words that swims and melts before my eyes. I force myself to look deeply into it, as if it will make me feel better, make the morning all right. The photocopied image is grainy, reduced and condensed, rendered in deathly shades of grey, like a faded memory of itself, but even so, remarkably, its magic still shimmers through. Two oriental women sit next to each other in adjacent panels. One holds a piece of fruit. The forefinger of her companion is pointing upwards. In each panel, accompanying each beauty, a small flying bird.

Who are these women? Are they sisters? Friends? Lovers? Courtesans? What does it mean, they are 'captured in time?' I flick through the pile of papers, pick up, and there they are again, eight panels, this time on the cover in vibrant technicolour. My attention is seized by the vermilion background against which the women's pale skin shimmers translucently.

A colour so deliciously deep I could drink it, I could eat it. I'd like to drape myself in its velvety smoothness, curl myself up and hide inside it. Live suspended, eternally, within it, like the beauties...

A philosopher colleague of Hugo's, who is interested in the art of 'the Third Space,' sent the catalogue for the exhibition in Sydney to me. My eyes travel over the lines of text:

'Zhiyuan Wang is of a new wave of international avant-garde Chinese artists who have left China over the past decade, settling in urban centres such as Sydney. From this Diaspora, a new perspective of visual art, an authentically non-Eurocentric way of seeing the world is emerging which is setting the international art world buzzing...

'The Third Space' is the term used to describe the dreamlike 'space' or virtual moment between cultures in which these individual artists are working...

Art from the Third Space challenges mainstream orthodoxies, it dreams in east and west, it is art in which perspectives shift and boundaries are pushed apart. Its defining conditions are experience of exile and cultural dislocation, coupled with increased freedom of expression...'[1]

My stomach surges threateningly. O God. I lay head in my arms on my desk. Leaning on the Beauties, close my eyes.

Despite the Diazepam I took at breakfast my head is pounding. I'm sure there was a time when I did not feel the need to keep up with Hugo and his cronies, the alcoholic academics, as I (privately) term them. I'd have two or three glasses of wine with dinner, no more. But lately, for some reason, I've been drinking to get drunk, drinking to—almost—keep up with Hugo, and that's a feat. I even get a kick from the following damage, the wasted nausea, and the hammered-brain pain of all-day hangover. For which I've found the best cure is another drink (after work and then it's okay). Another drink and then another, followed preferably by a snort or two or three…until the world is like a crystal prism and I am spinning through the colours radiating from thoughts and everything, every fleeting wisp of dream, seems real, brilliant and true; until you try to stand up and just fall flat on your face.

If I were an artist, not a gallery director, I would have been up painting all last night. I was jittery and restless with a kind of crazy yearning tug in the depths of my being, an unbearable excitement, pulling me to somewhere I have to somehow burst out of. When I came home I couldn't keep still. Racing through the five-storey terrace in Primrose Hill. Rearranging the massive floral display in the hall, straightening paintings on the walls. I even went so far as to begin fossicking through the musty depths of Mrs Fennell's mysterious cupboard beneath the stairs, looking for the vacuum cleaner. But I forced myself to stop. I had to get ready to go out with Hugo!

Changing outfits countless times. Decisions, decisions… My thigh-length leather boots or my Mangles heels—and if so, which ones??

We were dining at Vienna with a couple of Hugo's colleagues from the Think-Tank days, Professor Bear and Doctor Soul. I did not burst out of anything. Instead I stayed firmly in my place, by Hugo's side. I wore a V-VA black dress with elbow-length white leather gloves, purple heels (matching purple lips and nails). Red-blonde hair teased and twisted into a 6-inch chignon. ('Ruby, you're a delight to the eye'—Hugo).

And with an eye to business—sales, the Gallery's reputation—I entertained the all-male company with the latest racy witty theories on art they've all come to expect from me, Hugo River's delightfully outré wife. This time I found myself telling them about the Phi-Love Room... It was half way through the cheese and fruit. In a blur, a burst of colour and noise, I heard my tipsy voice curling archly around the words. Recounting what I'd recently written for *Art Weekly.*

'Phi is a legal drug. Apparently it comes from phenyl ethylamine, which has a chemical configuration similar to ecstasy apparently... It's a stimulant that, apparently, fills the imbiber with feelings of ecstatic love, and heightened sexual energy... A German performance artist, Coller, has made an installation called The Phi-Love Room. Willing participants go to the room, inhale phi, then are strapped in swinging leather 'love harnesses' where they can indulge their phi-love fantasies to their heart's content...' Raucous laughter from the gentlemen. Sir runs his hand up and down my thigh under the table...

'It's true, I heard it from Jasper Jackson so it must be true, apparently you rent out the installation by the hour. He says he's going to try next time he's in Cologne...' Talking on auto, watch me now, here I go...Lately I haven't been able to stop... Drinking, talking, smoking, popping...Spinning like a dizzy top through the social whirl... Openings, dinners, lunches, launches... Laughing over sherry in front of the fire with Hugo in our house in Primrose Hill late last night...

Laughing uncontrollably because I just can't stop, can't stop what I've started...

Acting as if everything is just fine. Under control. Playing the part, of me, in my life here, the successful young gallery director, married to a successful, older, philosopher. Playing the part as if born to be a Gallerist, I convince myself. And,

I think, everyone else around me. Why, I sometimes wonder in my calmer more reflective moments, typified by hangover, like now, sitting at the table in the front gallery, with endless thundering banging of renovations shaking the very vertebrae in my spine, staring out the window at the rain in Harriet Mews, why it is easier to play a part and do it well, so convincingly that people fall at your feet in admiration and respect (or not). Why it is much easier to play a part, than to live life authentically, to be yourself, be real. But then, what does it mean to be 'real'? 'Know thyself,' is the exhortation of the ancient Greek proverb that Hugo told me has driven the philosopher's quest since the birth of western philosophy. I don't get it. How can one know one-self? What does it mean to authentically 'be' oneself. What does it mean to be 'real'? Answer this, Jean-Paul, I ask the ghost of Sartre. But like any living philosopher these days the great dead existentialist refuses to provide any answers. There's only questions, Ruby he whispers in my ear. That's just like him.

But it seems I am good at what I do. Reinvention. Faking it. Whichever way you want to spin it. If you don't know who you are, if at heart you are nobody to your Self, so long as you can keep on living as if you are somebody, it's OK. Who dares, who bluffs best, wins? It's developed into a principle by which I live my life.

The top drawer of the eighteenth-century ladies' writing desk in the corner of the mistress bedroom of the house in Charcot Square contains a folder in which I have gathered photocopies and press cuttings that relate to a mysterious medical condition that fascinates me. At night when I cannot sleep sometimes I get up out of bed, and read them.

In the second drawer of the writing desk are press clippings about me and Hugo from the society pages, and ancient legal documents, our names are writ in bold letters. 'Lord and Lady Rivers.' 'Earl and Countess Rivers Wed in Northminster Abbey.' 'Art Aristocracy White Wedding!'

'Peer Marries Art Critic.'

'Countess Rivers Cuts the Cake.'

In the third drawer are portfolios of art stories. Interviews with artists—Reviews—Articles on the 'global art market'—opening, galleries—scandals, controversies and stunts. Since I started up the gallery I have stopped writing about art as a critic. Now I concentrate on building up my stable, collecting the most exciting conceptual artists I can find—wherever they are in the world. Selling works, judiciously and discreetly, to only the most discerning collectors.

According to (many) media reports we are a perfect partnership. We are one of London's 'art celebrity couples'—the 'young agenda-setting gallerist' and 'philosopher'—a 'pretty man' certain scribes have—charmingly—alluded to as bisexual. An allegation the scurrilous media loves to make. But nobody knows Sir Hugo like I do. And nobody knows who I really am.

Nobody knows about the shadowlands, the phantoms that play inside my head. Last night as I lay awake beside Hugo, in the luxury-hush of our draped and carpeted bedroom, spinning out from the champagne of dinner, my secret after-dinner snorts in the toilets of the Waldorf Hotel. In my mind I saw the shadow of a tidal wave, bigger than a mountain on the horizon, bigger than a dinosaur, than a comet just before it smashes into planet Earth. A tidal wave that rises from the darkness with all the power of everything I have forgotten. Lost—My old life before London—In Australia—the life that I cannot remember. Self I buried years ago. The strange absence, inside me, that keeps this whole thing spinning.

'Antipodes is Greek for 'having the feet opposite.' I'm putting a plaque in The Antipode Room with that information on it, the dictionary definition,' I said to Hugo as I drove him to work this morning.

'But, if 'antipodean' designates a relation, not a fixed place of origin, shouldn't that mean that in Australia, Europe is the antipodes?'

He laughed long and loud as if I'd deliberately cracked a hilarious joke. My head was pounding. I smiled queasily and accelerated through an amber light.

Oh Ruby thou art sick/ the invisible worm/ That flies in the dark/in the howling storm/ Has found out thy bed [2]

I might have known that would come back to me now. That poem's been going through my mind for days. It's worse than having a useless song from the radio stuck in your mind. At least that's a normal hazard of inner-city life. You're in the middle of a marketing web, some of its sticky strands, jingles and jangles, the siren songs of crass commercialism, seductive voices of adverts and pop songs, are bound to sneak their way down your ears and temporarily lodge themselves, irritatingly, in your brain. But having a poem stuck on your mind, now that's a different matter. A poem that's first imprinted itself from—long ago—onto your memory, and then migrated into your conscious thoughts, randomly, on an agenda of its own, has to make you ask, why?

found out thy bed/Of crimson joy/And his dark secret love/

Does thy life destroy [3]

The Sick Rose. The rain, the banging, the dark December sky; it all pounds on around me. The dull detached perceptual overload of a diazepam-soothed hangover. I took a tablet after I got to the gallery and I still feel numb and removed from the morning, as if I'm in a bubble, a blood-temperature cocoon.

This morning I sold two paintings. Received a cheque for a healthy sum in the mail. As usual business is going well, very well. We're expanding. We're collecting. We're making a profit in difficult times. We're about to go to Australia... I have absolutely nothing to worry about. Everything to feel happy about, to celebrate. As Sir Hugo so often reminds me. But he's right. Hugo has always been right. His ancestors founded the political Party. Unlike me, Hugo was born Right.

Susan walks towards me, staggering under a box from the back room. She dumps it beside me on the floor and we go through it together. Sorting the papers accumulated over the six years I've had the gallery. Catalogues, submissions by artists and agents, résumé statements, photos, articles. Clippings of openings...all has to be sorted, filed, cleared, disposed of, to make room for the expanding collection of antipodean art.

'File, chuck, file, file, chuck,' I say to my shaven-headed employee as she holds up items to my scrutiny.

Then.

'What about these?' She holds up a dusty photo lab envelope that suddenly looks shockingly familiar. 'Let me see.' I hold out my hand as she passes over the envelope. I pull out the photos. Mon Dieu. What is this? Who are these people? What are they doing here? The numbing effect of the tranquillizer evaporates instantly. I bite my lip resolutely, force my shock into cynicism. Pull out the first photo staring at it with a willed immunity.

The sky is radiant dazzling blue. High summer in the high country. In my trembling fingers I am holding a young woman. She is dancing around the side of a wooden farmhouse in a black silk slip dress, laughing, holding out her skirts at both sides in a parody of a country girl. Heidi of the Alps posing for her goatherd. Even more ridiculously, she is wearing an old homemade beekeeper hat encircled with a long green muslin veil as a sun hat. I turn to the next photo. A close-up. The same dark-haired young woman peeping with an intentionally ironic expression from under the beekeeper's veil, towards the camera. At the viewer. Her long dark eyelashes frame her eyes seductively, mouth pouts in a deliberate Mata Hari moue. Playing a game, she looks lusciously provocative. Surprisingly provocative. I peer at her and am staggered by the refined lines of her features, her heavy-lidded deep blue eyes, those long black lashes...Her large, full-lipped mouth, without lipstick, all the more sensuous for being naked like the rest of her face.

I select the third photo. The same girl in the farmhouse kitchen. Playing a violin. Still in her black silk slip.

Fourth photo. A young man with wild red hair. Standing with a young woman who looks disturbingly familiar. They are on the steps of the farmhouse verandah. The girl is on the top step; standing under the overhang of the roof, hair swept away from her face in a ponytail. She looks young and unsophisticated, natural, a girl from another world. Her shadowy profile turned away from the camera is dark, cool, brooding. Eyes half-closed, unfocussed, gazing into some private realm of inner space. In contrast, the young red-haired man, on the step below, is caught in the full glare of the midday sun. His sharp-featured face is radiant in the light. Old canvas back-pack slung over his bare shoulders, the clear rims of his glasses held together by sticky-tape. Beneath a flat brimmed straw hat, his head is tilted at a rakish angle. He is staring at the camera, the photographer, with an inscrutably blank expression on his face.

My memory whirs uncontrollably, failing to catch. Could he be setting out on a bushwalk? A sketching expedition perhaps? In his backpack could be watercolours, sketchbook, and inks... Was he an artist?

'Bloody hell.' I utter the words, and hear the sharp tone of voice, the choice of expletive, as if the words are coming from someone else's mouth. Bloody hell is a phrase many people use habitually but not me. I fan the photos together and put them back into the envelope.

'Throw these out.' Susan looks at me curiously, squatting on the floor beside me in her trendy baggy pants and top (like a skinhead coolie in a rice paddy or a chemotherapy survivor). Why she'd want to adopt the Auschwitz refugee look in the middle of an English winter is beyond me, but some people's propensity for masochism is never-ending. As marriage to Hugo has taught me.

'Is everything alright?' she asks, as if she can sense my alienation.

'Yes. No. It's nothing. I don't know what these are or where they came from.'

I tuck in the envelope flap, and hurl the photos with force into the rest of the junk, 3D C.V.s, the taped bios, P.R. hype, the wasted hopes and dreams of other people's lives. The ones who didn't make it into the gallery. The ones I throw out with easy power. Flick of the wrist. Forget. Erase. Disappear. Bury.

Without a further thought. As if it were that easy.

Outside rain hisses and spits against the big plate glass windows, the walls of glass that protect me from the street, from the cold, the noise, hunger, greed, the needs of people who look the way I used to look—and feel—cold and hungry on the streets in the rain, when I came around on the train on the Northern Line. Re-born like a character in a Laurel and Hardy movie joining the Foreign Legion, 'to forget.' Before I made another life, my new self, and met Hugo.

O Ruby thou art sick...

I sit up in my chair, and look at my watch. The diamond studded antique watch Sir Hugo gave me for my birthday, last year. The birthday that—he doesn't know—I decided upon. The 8th of July 1968.

It's twelve-o-clock. In three-quarters of an hour I am meeting my Professor for lunch in a restaurant approximately half way between the Gallery and Kings.

Lunching at Sprouts every day when we are in town, has become one of our healthier routines. Probably our only healthy habit. Apart from the slow Sunday afternoon constitutional on Primrose Hill, over the road from our house. The occasional strolls farther afield through Regents Park, along the canal. To 'shake out the cobwebs,' as Hugo puts it. Move the booze and nicotine through the blood stream a bit faster would be accurate, especially on Sunday afternoons. My husband's capacity for fine wine and good tobacco is quite awe-inspiring. He loves to get out of it, although he'd never take illegal drugs. Hugo likes to stay firmly within the limits of the law, and as the Ethical Adviser to the Conservative government, like his ancestors, he's well rewarded for his love of authority—which I know intimately.

When I first started going out with Hugo I was intrigued, amused, quite carried away by the sense of power of being his Lady. He was wealthy, well connected and well dressed in his three-piece Edwardian gentleman suits, so well read and well heeled. Well, I thought. A philosopher. Aristocrat. A peer. And all I needed to do was look at him and he filled with slavish adoration. Being his lover was a role I enjoyed, an indulgence, a challenge, distraction, until—what? This existential sense of there must be something more than this, the *thing-in-itself* set in. He hasn't stopped. It's been three years (at least). And now I don't know what it is but I feel like something's got to break round here. The gold egg has lost its shine. And I can hear it starting to crack.

Susan turns on her brogue heel and walks towards the back room, her arms full of papers to file. Pale floorboards shake beneath her footsteps. Through the open doorway I can see her talking to Ham; the muted buzz of their voices drifts into the gallery. A fat lady in green is peering intently at the series *Nuclear Family, Still Life With Mushroom Cloud*. My state of hung-over torpor, sustained through the morning's deals, has disappeared totally, replaced by an edgy sense, of agitation, and restlessness. *The invisible worm/ that flies in the night/ in the howling storm...* Those photos have disturbed me, unsettled me. The thought of going back to Australia, so soon now, is making me nervous, so jumpy that I've been developing a coke-and-diazepam habit, on top of Sir's endless wine and cigarettes to try and deal with it.

Back in that landscape of beauty and terror...
In only six days time... It seems impossible to believe...I

tell myself it's just another business trip. Every month I make international trips for Ruby Love. There's no difference, just because it's 'Australia.' It must be five years since I've been there, for Christ's sake. It might as well be another country, a Republic, a Dictator State, Shangri-La, anything else by now for all the effect it will have on me. Anyway, I'm going to be so busy, there won't be time to do anything except business as I keep trying to explain to Hugo, who insists on seeing the trip as a rather special sort of 'holiday.'

From the corner of my eye I see the rubbish box. I can see the photo envelope, which fell open when I threw it down. An edge of startlingly blue sky...The shining silver farmhouse roof... My fine resolve starts to waver. I want to look at those photos again. I want to scrutinize them in private. In my office. Interrogate the past at my leisure. This is ridiculous, crazy. I've thrown them out. Dealt with it. Ruby, get on with your work. I'm good at that. Admonishing myself. And getting on with my work. That's how come I'm here now, sitting in the Director's chair. To me the practice of efficiency is thrilling. I get off on its vital charge. At least I try. Getting things done, getting down to it, an interesting etymology. Glamourizing and fetishizing the mechanics of work, the business of business, from designer make-up to smart suits, not to mention the charge of discovering new talent, doing deals and making money, is the only way I do business. There has to be a pretty strong incentive for me to get out of bed in the morning. It would take more than just tending the house, and overseeing the staff, meeting with girlfriends, chatting with the gardener, whatever else I'd be doing if I wasn't working at least ten hours a day. To stay strong, powerful, in control, to wield that whip, to be a Director (not to mention Countess), I have to work.

Hard and relentlessly.

Ruthlessly and unflinchingly.

Trying to make myself feel efficient, I turn to the information on the table before me.

Ret Felix. Diana Shaw. Arnold Grainger. Three Australian artists showing in Sydney. 'Bad artist', 'bricolage-designer,' and a 'new landscape' painter, according to P.R. blurb. Three artists that I hope to collect on our trip. I stare at Shaw's sculptural goddess wrapped in an Aboriginal flag, Grainger's hot chromatic landscape. On another day I might feel inclined at this low ebb before lunch, to browse through my collection, fall into the images of beauty like dreams, objects of desire, irresistibly seductive. Objects I can hold within my gaze, own in a way in which it's impossible to ever possess a real lover.

Getting into art deeply, a flattering form of engagement... Always energises me up for the rest of the day, puts that spring in my step, winning sparkle in the business patter. That sexy power-polish Hugo adores. 'Talk to me Ruby, show me Yoon's prints.' Handing me the file with a look of ironic entreaty on his large handsome yet florid face.

But this morning, despite the success of my deals, instead of feeling efficient, in control, I just feel dizzy. Head spinning. Heart racing. And there's a high-pitched ringing in my left ear.

Is my eardrum bursting? O God, panic surges through my veins. I press the nub of my thumb to my ear to block it, stop the ringing, but all that happens is the high pitched sound that at first appeared to be coming from somewhere above and beyond my left ear, maybe connected to the renovations, now appears to be inside my head, instead. It's hardly an improvement. Ruby, you're panicking, baby, that's it, that's all it is. Recently these panic attacks have been becoming more frequent. That's what Doctor Mael calls this sense of racing dissolution, this end of the world mortal terror, that grabs me onto it black back and bolts with the wind down an unknown track, to swerve on a curve of calamity, the end. 'Panic attacks'. He tells me to put a paper bag over my mouth and breathe deeply, 'It'll stop you hyper-ventilating, then the dizziness will go away.' Remembering this, and the absurdity of the image that comes to mind, makes me feel calmer, controlled. I stare down at the brochure, glossy colours, tangle of lines. I silently chant 'Ohm,' on each out-breath, focusing on my breathing, as I've learnt in yoga class.

Gradually the adrenaline ebbs from my veins, the ringing in my ear abates. The whirling vortex slows and coalesces into solid images. Now I see what it is I'm looking at, make sense of it. I put my face in the palms of my hands and my body shudders. What the hell is happening to me? In the howling storm.

I stand up slowly, carefully. A few minutes ago I was a nervous wreck. Now I feel calm enough to set off for the restaurant. My new ankle-length black faux-leather coat with the black faux-fur collar is hanging on the hook behind my office door. I slip into its enveloping folds, pick up my umbrella.

Looming hugely in my field of vision is the rubbish box. I just can't seem to get it out of my sight. Very soon, whilst I am at lunch, the box will be disposed of in the bins in the parking yard behind the gallery. Tomorrow no doubt it will be floating down the Thames in a barge of rubbish. Seagulls, the rats of the air, will circle and swoop, pecking at stinking cargo, sharp orange beaks scattering confetti of slimy decomposing things, shredded scraps of photographs...

I pick up my purse. Looking at the box, looking at the girl playing violin. What was it she used to play? A ghostly, ethereal music that obsessed her.

Her face quivers with that expression of sweet intense private pain that she always has when she plays violin alone. I hover in the shadows of the old French doors in between my room and the balcony-kitchenette. Inadvertently spying on her, like one of those dark-eyed family girls in a painting by her favourite artist. Those intense, huge-eyed little girls whom she adores. She doesn't notice me, she's way too far gone. Swooping and soaring on high-pitched waves of baroque sound. She hits a discordant note. Patiently, obsessively, flicking back her locks she starts again.

Forget it, I tell myself, but then something else takes over. It's crazy, compulsive, like snorting five lines in a row instead of going for a good long bracing walk, and it will probably be as self-destructive. The ringing in my ear is starting up again, is it the tranquillizer? but then the weirdest thing happens. The ringing intensity and pitch increases until my head feels like it's going to burst, but instead of my head bursting, the ringing bursts into music, the sweetest wildest most high-pitched music I've never heard; like an angelic choir. The photograph image and memory of that fugue fuse together in a swoon of violent longing.

I bend and snatch the photo envelope from the rubbish box. Just as I'm straightening up, photos in hand, Susan walks back into the space. She pauses, fixing me with an expression I do not care to interpret. I feel cavernous eyes burn into me as I slip photos into my purse, trying to look cool. Fumbling, dropping some. I pick them up. She is still looking at me. This is ridiculous. Remember who's the Director; I tell myself frantically, reaching for a tissue to blow my nose, cover my temporary confusion.

'I'm going to lunch, Susan,' I say, giving her what I hope is a commanding gaze, struggling to regain control.

'Okay, boss,' she says, looking me straight in the eyes with an enigmatic smile twisting the corners of her lips. It's as if she can see through me. But that's the problem I have these days, I never know who to trust.

I manage to open the entrance door and walk out without anything terrible happening. Without falling into a quivering heap on the floor. Or detouring into the bathroom for a secret snort of angel-snuff.

And now, at last, I can put up my umbrella and walk, for a few minutes of freedom through the cold shiny streets, protected from the pouring rain.

Hugo

Professor Rivers, Room 508, Princes College

I have been magnetically attracted to Ruby since the moment I first saw her. At introductory drinks for first year students on the evening course. She arrived more than half way through. Or should I say, she made her entrance.

The small room in the Philosophy Department building was crowded. My eyes swung across the sea of bodies, faces, like the needle of a compass meeting its master point. North. She was standing in the doorway; and her physique filled that portal. Long golden tresses cascaded over her shoulders. Her face was remote and proud, as she surveyed the room with an almost disdainful expression that made my knees quiver. She radiated a vitality, a fascinating mysterious energy, and miracle of miracles; she was wearing a real fur coat.

In an age of Save the Whales, Meat is Murder, she stood out like Wanda von Dunajew in *Venus im Pelz*—beautiful and awe-inspiring amongst her peers in parkas and sensible shoes. I found her nerve extraordinary.

When our eyes first met it was with a flash I registered as instant recognition. I did not have an intuitive understanding of the meeting of souls before that moment—but the strong sense of recognition I felt when I looked at Ruby, made me sympathetic to Plato's notion for it was indeed extraordinary and materially unaccountable. My eyes held hers for what seemed like an eternity. It's a moment I remember now with a pang, a kind of longing. Very soon it seemed she was right in front of me, having woven gracefully through the milling throng. She was holding out a plastic beaker towards the bottle of champagne that I, in my role of welcoming professor, was jovially dispensing. Laughing with a charm that made me feel years younger.

I did not, of course, mention her fur coat on that evening, but later as the year progressed and we became intimate, she confided in me that she had bought it in a second-hand shop because it was cheap.

'Only seven pounds, can you believe? It was twice as much for dirty old raincoats that looked as if they'd come straight from a flasher's back.' One of things I appreciate in my young wife is her sense of cultivation, her refinement. Unlike many young women in my experience, she always knows how, and when, to stop. Never goes far into areas of tastelessness, rudeness or, even worse, vulgarity. She's as restrained, as perfectly self-controlled, filled with decorum as an Indian princess. The type of splendid woman I read about in books on Tantra in a serenely elevated consciousness. And, of course, if she lacks energy, sometimes, that suits me. After all, the old physique is not what it once was. Our shared faith in and devotion to the good old Protestant work ethic, to which one sublimates baser desires, suits me fine in a young woman. I find it admirable. And I want to reward her with lavish presents for her sense of duty.

The more than commendable way in which she plays the game. Every night with the accessories I give her for the masquerades. The masks behind which her eyes glitter radiantly, terrifyingly. Cold hard precious jewels. Emerald for eternity.

The first time we made love she was wearing her fur. I asked her to put it on. Underneath she was naked.

Every time I saw her in it after, I remembered that moment of blissful union, merging of bodies and souls. After which I asked her to be my wife, and with sweetly lowered eyes, such touching modesty, she agreed.

She wore the coat for quite a while. She wore it everywhere.

Despite taunts and jeers of small girls on the streets who followed her, asking if she'd kill a mink, a fox, her pet dog... She told me that she simply turned and pointed out, quite sensibly, that they were wearing one hundred per cent leather school shoes, carrying real leather satchels. She hadn't slaughtered the beasts, for goodness sake, or anything else. And anyway she'd bought it in a second-hand shop and couldn't afford to buy anything else. She couldn't even afford to buy one of their leather satchels!

Not afraid to be herself, my Ruby Love.

She stopped wearing the coat when she could afford to buy

something as warm, but less controversial. Leather and stylish tweeds. The flayed skin and wool as well as furry hide off the back of the beasts who serve us. But she'd certainly made her point with me.

I rescued the coat a year or so ago. She'd thrown it out. I cleaned off the scraps of food, dusted it down and brought it back inside. It's in my gentleman's wardrobe now. Hanging at the back, concealed behind a row of suits. Every now and then I take it out, stroke the fur. Sometimes I even put it on, wrap it around myself and stare fetchingly at my reflection in the wardrobe mirror. One day I'll surprise her. I'll take it out and insist she wears it like she did the first time.

Ruby

When I'm walking to lunch it comes back to me. The grief I could hide. I could tell myself I felt all right. I could forget the ward. The sensation that as I went under there was an angel behind my shoulder; she'd been there for several weeks. And when I emerged from the fog, the angel had gone. It was just I, too alone. I could forget all that. But I couldn't forget the flow of blood; heavier, a subterranean display of physical solidarity with my buried emotions. I couldn't escape the pain or prevent the fainting fits.

I remember when I 'came around' in London I moved into a rented room which never caught the light, in a houseful of female students in Camden Town, which I'd seen on a health food shop notice board, the day after I came around on the train. I still don't know what I did before that, I think I slept in a park, my clothes were crumpled and unwashed, with bits of grass and twig in my hair. I did find a plane ticket in my bag, which is how I knew I had come from Sydney; the date of arrival on the plane ticket had been three days before. The bag contained documents, a purse full of dollar notes. The first night I spent, in a bed and breakfast in Earl's Court. I moved into the house in Camden Town, and soon realised that the sickness I was feeling was more than a psychosomatic reaction to the shock of my fugue.

I had no friends, no family, and no money, to draw on. No means of support or help. No job, although I'd been thinking of asking for work in some of the small galleries around Camden Town. I'd been too numb and upset to do anything since I'd arrived in this foreign city. On some level I made a decision to forget everything that had happened that had led to my departure. But my body didn't want to forget. My body wanted to celebrate a forgotten love, with the gift of new life. It was deformed from the start.

I had three hundred pounds. It was just enough to cover 'the procedure' until the bleeding stopped. Tears of blood, red rushing river of regret, sadness. It felt like my life was gushing from me in the most ironically yet agonisingly tangible form. The body makes its own metaphors, and my body was sobbing, screaming in pain.

I had to pull myself together. Or else I would disintegrate in that red river, dissolve in that flow of blood. Disappear into the nothingness, the hollow, empty madness of the void, that loss, that triple loss, had left inside me... life, the future, and the child that was not allowed to exist. Which I would not, could not allow myself to think about. That each month I was reminded of with mocking regularity.

Not long after, I watched Fassbinder's *Veronica Voss* and *The Marriage of Maria Baum*. I was fascinated by the pure steel will, the—somehow—erotic work ethic of Hanna Schygulla's role. In her smartly tailored forties suit, stream-lined for efficiency, Veronica stayed up until the early hours with only a coffee cup for company, intent on balancing her books. She was a woman on a mission, to transform her life.

No matter that, as I seemed to recall from a distant Art and Film elective, Voss was supposed to represent Germany under Third Reich. After achieving dubious results from her devotion to business efficiency, she finally blows herself up and her entire apartment block in a misjudged attempt to light a cigarette from a gas ring stove.

I can do that I thought. I can work hard, harder than I've imagined myself. If I do can I escape into a weightless future, escape the past?

I got a part time job as gallery assistant in Body of Work—Contemporary Women's Gallery in Camden, and began writing visual arts reviews and profiles of artists which I published in the beginning in the street press, then as I grew more confident in the listings mags, then the national newspapers. I was just about making ends meet because I didn't have to pay rent. I'd met an Australian girl, Brodie, a singer, in a night-club and moved into her squat, a beautiful run-down Georgian terrace near Regent's Park, where she lived with a shifting population of rock 'n' roll musicians, deejays, cycle couriers, Niles, a merchant banker and his friend Jim, a defence scientist. 'There's thousands of homeless people in London, councils leave thousands of properties empty—it's an invitation to squatters,' she shouted in my ear as we danced to *Venus in Furs*, the Velvet Underground's 60's psychedelic classic.

'It's much cooler than having some slum landlord trying to push you around. Anarchy rules, man.'

Two years after I moved to London I enrolled in a Philosophy degree course to study Aesthetics, and that's when I met Sir Hugo, my first year tutor.

The day before my first tutorial appointment, I passed out in a shop. I'd been walking from the squat to get breakfast. It was the tragic painful time of month. Sudden stabbing pains lacerated my abdomen. Swirling through my back, my guts, and chest. I couldn't breathe. By the time I reached the local fruit shop the world was spinning out, everything was black and white, grainy, disappearing. I was blacking out.

'You alright love?' I only vaguely heard the voice. I begged, 'I have to lie down.'

I heard voices, muted, buzzing.

'There's nowhere...' 'Sit on this stool love.'

'Call an ambulance.'

'A pound of bananas please.'

'The back steps?' A man was standing beside me taking my pulse. 'I have to lie down.'

I was taken to hospital in the ambulance where I stayed for a few hours until I'd recovered, Brodie came to collect me in a taxi. The medical verdict? 'Painful periods.' The middle-aged doctor said peering at me over his pince-nez. Well, I could have told him that.

'It's rare but at the onset of the menstrual period the cervix can actually contract, leading to pain and fainting fits.'

'It's only been like this since I had a procedure two years ago,' I said suddenly feeling desperate.

'I can't help you with that,' he closed his file and turned his back disapprovingly. 'I'm not a specialist.'

Two days later I rang to apologise for missing my tutorial.

'I was taken ill,' I said using an English phrase, in true Darwinian manner. Adapt and survive.

'Oh.' There was a slight pause.

Then: 'Nothing serious I hope?'

His voice was loud and forceful. Somehow, strangely, its volume and velocity was reassuring.

'I passed out in a shop.'

'You've been reading left-wing literature,' he boomed.

'I recommend a healthy diet, a Jane Austen and another tutorial.'

When I saw him next evening, I felt much stronger.

I hung behind as the rest of the class filed out.

'Aha, Ruby!' He approached me carrying a large stack of papers, peering at me over his pince-nez.

Hugo was the kind of person who is often described as 'larger than life.' And I guess he carefully cultivated a certain image. For instance, he always wore a three-piece suit in public. That evening the suit was made of corduroy, leather patches on the jacket elbows. And he was very large. Tall, with a stomach which displayed many years of good living. Very curly black hair flecked with grey flew wildly around a handsome fleshy face creased with humour lines. His blue-grey eyes were sharp, droll. He had a reputation in the right-wing press, and the radical left-wing press. His in-your-face 'Opinion' columns, which I often read with curiosity in the *Deliverer*, delighted in lampooning contradictory lobby positions. The anti-fur lobby; anti-fox-hunting brigade; decline of drawing in art schools… attacks on the countryside…arts censorship… But in the flesh Hugo was a disconcertingly benign, attractive figure despite his stomach.

'Feeling better?' He boomed, twinkling at me.

'Yes, I'm fine now, thank you.' I tossed my hair back. This conservative English aristocrat had better not ask me any personal questions.

'Would you care to join me for a drink?' Hugo asked, 'I'm on my way to the Black Gizzard.'

'Okay, I'll go for a drink,' I stared him straight in the eye. I might have been succumbing to his undeniable and confusing personal charm, but I was determined his famously obnoxious politics would not intimidate me.

I was preparing to fall into a heated argument. But, to my surprise, Hugo didn't mention politics. I brought up university funding cuts, the abolition of rent assistance for students, but he just laughed, quite amiably, and changed the subject to Plato's theory of Beauty.

'Of course Plato held,' he paused. He looked at me. 'That Beauty is a property of objects, that is measurable in reference to their properties of purity, harmony, integrity, and perfection?' he raised an eye-brow. He was staring at me deeply and meaningfully. He drank whisky; I, burgundy.

After chatting about aesthetics we arranged a tutorial two days later at his house in Primrose Hill.

Day Five

Hugo

Princes University College, WC1

FIVE DAYS BEFORE WE LEAVE FOR Australia and I break my arm. Fell off the bike, yesterday morning, negotiating a tricky corner in Bloomsbury. Imbecile opened his car door whilst I was cycling and—thwack! I find myself, beached and gasping on the tarmac, glad for once of the crash helmet Ruby insists I wear. All right apart from the arm; and the bike's got a dent in the front wheel that will have to be fixed when we're on holiday.

Ruby drove this morning. How unfortunately ironic that my car, bought as a young man in the swinging sixties, is now the status symbol of black gangsters and drug-dealers. How I love to see her drive, strong hands with purple nails, competently spinning the steering wheel. Pulling on the handbrake with natural authority. I'd let her drive me anywhere, anytime.

Luckily it's the left arm, so not too difficult 'though dashed awkward, trying to pick up books and papers. Teaching is over for the holidays, so I'm here in the office working away on The Ethics of Desire. Have to keep on calling in young Elena to help me transport leaning towers of literature on all kinds of subjects from the floor and bookshelves to my desk.

Masochism, lesbianism, homosexuality and fetishes...

Depositing them on my desk. Ticky looks on quizzically, eyebrows raised.

Right in the thick of the penultimate chapter Perversions, and it looks like it's shaping into my masterwork. It's a phenomenological British contribution to the challenging philosophical dialogue on sexuality, which has been commandeered by the continentals. Must say I'm pleased with my research for this book to date.

Elena's rather an attractive girl, young, dark, Greek, good secretary although too timid for one's taste. She hands over Sade's *120 Days of Sodom* and almost bolts from the room.

Must say, this whole cycling incident makes me wonder, not for the first time, about the overall wisdom of cycling to work. But, with things the way they are, on top of the gallery and everything else, one can't fully justify the expense of a second car. And, as Ruby points out frequently, exercise is necessary to keep in trim. It was she who got me into this cycling caper.

In the beginning, I used to drive her to the gallery—it's only five minutes from Prince's. Then she became smitten with this fitness urge; that is, an urge for my fitness. But it's worth it, if it makes her happy. And it does that. Only last week she complimented me. 'I'm sure your stomach's shrinking!' she says. I'm not sure if I agree. 'The idea of seeing my toes when I'm standing up straight seems remote as... Zeno's arrow ever hitting its target...' I protest. But I'll take her word for it.

And the slimmer and more youthful my physique for the famed Aussie beach, the better, although the last thing I really want to do is lie around on the beach in Sydney, basting like a side of beef under the great barbecue grill in the sky. But I don't want to let Ruby down. She's reserved when it comes to her own feelings. And that's one of the things I love so much about her. She's too polite and considerate to put her own desires first, the epitome of a lady; she hasn't even mentioned it.

She doesn't have to. I've let her know that I know what she wants. I'll be her outsize pink beach boy. Her ageing but still game Adonis. I'll do the Ernest Hemingway in a Panama hat, and my white flannel suit (that's a surprise from my tailor hidden in my suitcase with a matching surprise for her). Ready and raring to dress up as the gentleman of the colonies, to chaperone my wife around the delights of Sydney Town. Better get over there quick, I've been telling her for a long time while it's still linked in some way to Britain, our poor beleaguered yet still gracious Queen.

I've been reading up on the history of Australian art to give the dear girl some tips and information, slotting it in between the requirements of my typically heavy schedule, writing my columns for the *Daily Deliverer* and the *Accord*, and of course, working on The Ethics of Desire. My time is valuable but it's worth it to me to be able to help her, to educate her. I want to be well-equipped to give her some valuable insights. I'm already giving her advice on what to watch out for. 'You have to be careful,' I told her. 'You're investing your, or should I say *our* valuable time and money, Ruby. Artists always tend to be tricky —but Australian artists, now there's a combination. Pull an arts hoax faster than throw koala on a barbecue.'

I've been keeping up with it. Reading Tristram Tyler, one of our eminent critics who emigrated there a couple of years ago. (Tyler's brother helped my time at school to be distinctly more exciting.) Judging by what he's had to say, the dear girl will have to be very careful that she's not conned. I explained to her what Tyler said about the phenomenon of the Antipodean artists' identity crisis, antipodean wrong-footedness you could call it, which it seems results from the combination of the small population and over-regulation of arts funding institutions. With human nature as it is, Tyler argues, it's inevitable that when you get a system where artists can only survive through sponsorships, grants and bursaries, prizes and scholarships; and where these are awarded according to certain political and ideological agendas that you're going to get the con-artists out in full-throttle... So you've got a situation there where men are pretending to be women, women pretending to be migrant peasants, everyone pretending to be Aboriginal—just to attract the 'politically correct' funding dollar.

I've been filling Ruby in on this. Don't want her to come away thinking she's just signed up some Aboriginal genius unappreciated in her homeland, only to find out in a blaze of adverse publicity down the track that the authentic genius was a blue-collar redneck white man, from a comfortable suburb, with no social conscience. Been so inspired by this, I've written a column: 'The Great Australian P.C. Con Artist.' Brought in a reference to that old Monty Python skit on the sinking of the Titanic. Based on truth, like many ghoulishly humorous sketches are. When it was: 'Women and children first' into the lifeboats as the ship slipped further into the icy sea, increasing numbers of men dressed as women charged the life-boats. In the skit, officers raided the ship's costume party box: 'Women, children, Ukrainian peasant girls, reindeer, Pyrenean mountain dogs— first...'

I thought it might amuse her. I told dear Ruby this story over pre-bed sherry in front of the fire last night. To amuse her further I gave her my ironic non-P.C. rendition: 'Lesbian feminist dwarfs, one-eyed protégées, anyone with an Indigenous great-great-great grandmother by adoption—first...'

Well, maybe my irony was a little childish but I thought it was something she might find funny. I'd hoped to make her laugh, and to bring a flush of life, of humour, to her features. But she didn't laugh. She didn't smile in wan recognition at my effort... She said she'd read my column—and that was it. No further comment. No warmth of shared emotion. No sparkle of adulation, or admiration, in her sea-green eyes fetchingly outlined in kohl pencil. Just a face turned away from me towards the flames in the hearth. I was chilled by the silence of her slim muscular shoulders, her somehow reproving back.

She's been quieter than usual, a bit pale and distant lately. I put it down to the excitement of the impending trip (if not the dreadful contemporary 'art' she's been showing). It will be wonderful for her to see her family whom she misses so much. Poor girl—she's practically an orphan here. As soon as we get to Australia, all the tensions and stresses of preparing for the trip will be over. We'll be able to relax and have a wonderful holiday, as I keep on reassuring her. Although she endearingly insists the trip is for business, I say there's no reason why on earth that should take longer than a few days—after all, she's got me to help her—then we've got the rest of the time to Enjoy! Enjoy! Enjoy! It's what life is for, Ruby, I tell her. I'll make sure we take her sweetly conscientious mind off work. And I've been waiting to meet her family. To find out so much, for such a long time now! Ruby remains such an enigma; such a tantalizing mystery to me—everything about her endears her to me and fascinates me...

And, Christmas with her family, on a beach, my arm still in a sling, what material for a column that will be.

Ruby

I don't know why I thought of Australia as 'home,' Hugo,' I tell him, again, over lunch at Sprouts. 'Home is London, our house in Primrose Hill, the Gallery. It's here...'

I look around the restaurant with what I hope is a brightly optimistic smile.

'I can hardly remember anything...just a few vague things but they don't make any sense.'

He squints at me quizzically, paternalistic, over a forkful of soya casserole. It's a conversation we've had numerous times in various forms.

'But if your family are there, Ruby, you must be able to remember something about them!'

His voice is warm with indulgence. I play along with the game and smile as naturally as I can manage.

'I have a new family now, darling. You are my family.'

'Yes of course you do.' He says, patting my knee under the table.

'Yes, my family.'

Married to Sir Hugo, I'm part of a family net, a close web of ties: quoits and sherry with brother-in-law Perry and my sister-in-law, Yvonne. The occasional tennis match with his sister Binky, phone calls from mother-in-law, Lady Ode, from Violet Hall, the ancestral family seat in Sussex. (Not to mention Ticky, Milo and Clariss, of course).

Hugo is pleased we're going.

'It will be good to be in the South again,' he says. 'What a shame you can't remember anything Ruby. I would very much like to meet *all* your family,' he leans back expansively.

'You're sure they are in Australia, not the sub-continent? We could stay with my Cousin Coddington if they were; do a spot of mountain climbing, Everest...' he continues his bantering tone.

'Mount Everest!' I snort with laughter. 'Yes, that would be nice!'

Using his good arm, he wipes his full fleshy lips with his paper napkin. Behind his head on the other side of the room I spy a dark-haired young man in an army surplus coat. He was in the gallery last month, came up and asked me if we took student work. He had been wearing a red and white bandana, an eighteenth century brocade jacket and jodhpurs. I told him to come back, show me something. Try me. I turned my attention back to Hugo.

'Even if I did have family to visit there we're only going to be in Sydney two weeks...It's hardly even going to be enough time to line up deals with the artists I'm interested in...'

'Oh faff! Ruby girl, we've got to take your mind off work. You're not telling me we're going all the way to Australia without taking in some of the sights of your homeland. And that means doing some shopping, too!' he smiled at me.

As if, by definition, girls just love to shop, and he was as always more than prepared to indulge me. Shopping is an occupation I've never had the nerve to tell him I find, at heart, boring. There's too much at stake. Shopping represents what has become practically a psychic bond between us. You could say it's the natural basis of our relationship. The stocking of our house with goods, the steady replenishing of wardrobes, chiffoniers, chests of drawers, cabinets, with expensive and desirable commodities. There's always something more to buy, something more we need or want; we have to have.

'I'm not coming back to London without a genuine Aussie Dry-your-Bones raincoat and hat,' he smiles at me teasingly with a wickedly triumphant gleam in his blue eyes.

Hugo wanted to go to Australia for a holiday even before we married. He's been before. To an international symposium on the Ethics of Aesthetics. He enjoyed the food, the wine, the sun, the ferry ride around the Harbour, he tells me these facts with an ironic twinkle in his eye and amused smile, I think he's teasing but I'm not quite sure. Although I can't remember how old I am, precisely, the older I get, it seems, the more blurred the outlines of the people I know and meet become.

Who is who they seem to be? What life's taught me is not to trust anyone very deeply. Not to give yourself to anyone. Keep yourself hidden. That way you can be with anyone; you can do anything, if you have enough bottles, as the Brits term it. Gotta lotta bottle, the tag line of a famous British milk ad. London has given me bottle galore.

After eating I go to the ladies. Lock myself into a cubicle; take out my purse and my make-up mirror from my handbag. Shake out the white crystals, chop up with a razor blade, and then snort the line up my nose with a rolled-up fiver. The hit is sublime, divine, carries me straight to cloud nine. As I lean back against the wall an image of Hugo floats into my mind, which cracks me up. The thought of my husband, who never goes out onto the street without a full three-piece suit on, as a tourist in a sun hat with a camera slung around his neck, let alone the idea of Hugo lying on a beach in swimmers, seems suddenly funny to me. And what seems even funnier is what I can't tell him, what I can never tell him, what he will never know, about my life, in Australia before I left, before I came to London.

Sniffing and smiling broadly, maniacally, unable to stop as I walk back to the table.

Hugo looks up at me with a big smile.

'Alright, sugar?' Sugar. Sugar! That sets me off again... Sugar crystals, sugar puff. Sweetness of existence condensed into an essence charging like white horses, white angels, through my red-hot blood. I'm his white-sugar sugar-white girl.

When the Snow Queen in the fairytale kissed Kay he forgot his name, his age, and his family. He forgot his life, he forgot Gerda, the friend who loved him. He climbed up into the Queen's sleigh. She covered him with her ermine mantle. The beautiful deadly cold-hearted queen sped with Kay without delay to her palace of snow and ice on the far side of the world, where he was her slave in her palace of frozen cruelty. Until one day, faithful Gerda, grown-up and lovely now, who had travelled across countries to find him, rescued him from his icy prison and warmed him back to life with her love.

They returned to their hometown where they married and lived happily ever after.

'Yes, I'm fine,' I pronounce the words as if from a distance. If only there was some music in here, to drown out the scrape and clatter of cutlery, the sharp savage implements of the human feeding ritual. I push food aside and watch the beautiful waitresses who might soon be famous actresses gliding around the tables as if on ice-skating blades, carrying trays as if they're on stage.

As we leave the restaurant I almost fall over the feet of the artist in the army greatcoat, but Hugo catches me, holds me upright, almost carrying me out the doorway. Like he carried me over the threshold of his house after our huge social-pages white wedding.

Hugo used to ask me about growing up in Australia. He's given up asking. Of course I couldn't tell him. I never think about it myself. Can't think about it. That time, my life there. It was difficult, though, when we first met. It wasn't long after I 'arrived' in London. I couldn't bear to even hear the word 'Australia' mentioned. This was rather hard in a country that screened Australian soaps not once, but twice, along with a selection of others in the 24-hour TV cycle. Where many people I met seemed eager to chat about kangaroos and antipodean weather patterns.

When we started going out for drinks, then meals together, the biggest social hurdle I had to negotiate was nothing to do with living in a squat, being broke, and, by his lofty standards under-educated. It was nothing to do with being Australian. It was just that I couldn't talk about my past. I didn't want to talk about any of it, anything that had happened to me. Before I arrived in London. I couldn't talk about Australia.

I didn't want to have to try to recreate that life. So instead of telling him about my past I told him about The Accident—imagining an incident to avoid a deep dark truth. The fugue. Who could understand that? What you don't know can't hurt you; I told myself, whispered silently to him under my breath, under my words, my fast and breathless talking.

'I was in an accident after I arrived in London.'

We were sitting in front of the fire in his drawing room. It was the first time he'd invited me in for coffee. We'd been

to the Theatre Royal to see *Les Liaisons Dangereuses*. We were
drinking vintage port in front of a big black marble fireplace.
He was stroking the skirts of my old fur coat, which I thought
a little odd, but endearing. 'I'd just got into a taxi, it pulled
out from the curb, I hadn't put my seat belt on. Suddenly the
taxi swerved to miss a cycle courier, ran into a street sign, my
head hit the window hard and I lost my memory. I was taken
to hospital and stayed for a couple of months.

For several weeks I had no recollection whatsoever of who
I was, my past, then it started coming back, in patches… my
name, age, date of birth. Facts, like facts from another person's
life. There's still a huge amount I can't remember about growing up, what's happened to me…I find it distressing to try and
remember, it just has to come naturally by itself or it can be
very upsetting…'

I gazed into the flames. Hugo was so protective, so sympathetic, I filled with guilt. But my healthy self-survival mecha-
nism empowered me to push it away.

His hands moved from stroking my coat to stroking my
face, and hair. He even carried me into his bedroom. Made
love with a tenderness and intelligence that made me forget all
about the size of his belly, which under other circumstances,
that is if Hugo was not Sir Hugo, and I was being myself, the
real Ruby, I would never have imagined being so close to. But
after that night our romance blossomed. There was nothing
he couldn't, or wouldn't, do for me.

And, with Hugo, for once I felt safe, secure, looked after.

I didn't need to think about the past, about what had happened in Australia. And for what seemed a long time but was
months, maybe a year or two, the past left me alone. I was
free and happy in my new life. Living in the present. It wasn't

until I'd moved into the terrace house with Hugo, not until my new life was well underway that a dark hidden forbidden desire began to haunt and torment me with all the power of a guilty secret.

Curses that try as you might cannot be escaped. Like a worm deep in the juicy heart of a particularly delectable piece of fruit, whose sweetness it will contaminate and poison.

A woman playing a violin. Falling dusk. A darkening room. The first haunting bars of the fugue drift quivering majestically through the warm air, the profound beauty of the melody. Caught in a last ray of sunlight sliding through old French doors, lit up against darkness, illuminated in an otherworldly brilliance, like a martyr painted by Caravaggio. Playing violin, in a black silk slip dress. Standing in the gloom of the room with no windows in the Haunted Castle. Dark locks twitching; moving music sheets with quick flicks of her bow. Head tilts at an angle, anchoring treasured instrument to shoulder. The light changes from gold to white. To black and white. Now she looks like a phantom-beauty from a horror movie. Her pale heart-shaped face. Crimson lips, kohl-lined eyes, soft wraith-like arms. Long strong flickering fingers, compressing, releasing, vibrating the strings. Through Time's prism, I watch the jerky geometry of her bowing arm. The pages of sheet music floating in the dusk like lilies on a pond. Melodic notes drift through the warm air. The music becomes faster, more urgent, transitioning from melancholia to obsession, releasing... A slight figure dressed in black, gilded by the dying sun. Her glowing face transfigured by passion; yet the bow commands release of exquisite expression, as if on the brink of ecstatic revelation. A vision.

Day Four

Hugo

TO AID THE START OF THE new research, I bought Ruby a riding crop. I gave her my gift wrapped in pink paper. When she opened it she told me she didn't go riding. So I explained what I wanted and gave her a potted précis of the chapter. 'In the interests of philosophy, understanding the nature of Sexuality, the very life force of the human race, you have to help me, my darling.' I urged her. 'I hereby invite you to be my research assistant.'

I gave her an account of one of fiction's most delightfully fearsome heroines. I opened up my copy of *Venus in Furs*. (We were in the bedroom, that most inspiring volume was next to the bed, I'd been reading a little each night). Listen to this, I urged her, selecting a passage at random.

> "So love me even when I am cruel?" said Wanda, "now go! – you bore me – don't you hear?"
> She boxed my ears so that I saw stars and my bells rang in my ears."
> "Help me into my furs, slave."
> I helped her, as well as I could.
> "How awkward," she exclaimed, and was scarcely in it before she struck me in the face again. I felt myself growing pale.

"Did I hurt you?" she asked, softly touching me
with her hand.

"No, no," I exclaimed.

"At any rate you have no reason to complain;
you want it thus; now kiss me again."

I threw my arms about her, and her lips clung
closely to mine. As she lay against my breast in her
large heavy furs, I had a curiously oppressive sensation. It was as if a wild beast, a she-bear, were em-
bracing me. It seemed as if I were about to feel her
claws in my flesh. But this time the she-bear let me
off easily.[4]

I was surprised, even, dare I say, a touch disappointed when
the first time Ruby obliged my request, as I lay with my face
in the pillow anticipating the virgin lashes of her whip, I—
quite clearly and distinctly—heard the sound of her laughter,
rising lightly. But then the slashes came raining down.

Ruby

'If I see a dead body pickled in formaldehyde, I swear I'll
scream.'

It's too close to home. Life in a bottle, suspended in limbo.

'I was walking past Mannix Gallery in Soho, when assault-
ed by yet another large mammal preserved in a glass case. A
Shetland pony foal. I almost threw up my latte,' I say to Susan.

Her thin lips twitch remotely in what I read as a sardonic
smile. But which could equally indicate scorn or revulsion.

In my dream, I was at an opening, gazing at a lamb pickled
in a tank. I looked at it and saw myself looking back. It was I
in that bell jar. Pickled like a tortured woman from a poem I
read. My unseeing open eyes, a watery dull green. My naked

body curled up like a foetus. My white raw-fish flesh so soft it looked boneless. My long hair flowing around my body like seaweed, stained nicotine-orange in the preserving fluid. Sir Hugo's favourite, the hand-tooled leather Spanish riding crop, clutched in my white hand. I heard his words: 'Adore.' 'Chastise'… 'Beg you, please…. Oh Ruby…. Please I beg you.' I saw white wobbling jelly beneath lashes. In my bell jar bottle in his favourite red stilettos, the ones he gave me for a birthday. I heard his words: 'My Boadicea. My very own Cleopatra. Venus in Furs, I cannot let you go.' The shoes cosseted my little white feet like his dying wish.

And then I saw Hugo's gigantic hand plunging down into the jar, scooping me out and popping me into his mouth. Yum yum, sushi-girl.

When I woke up, lying next to him in our big soft bed, it seemed like I was still in the pickling bottle. As if I'd met my inner self in my dream.

Now I'm sitting at my desk again. In the gallery. The same old spot. Behind the main gallery. But in my pickling bottle, my very own bell jar, frozen as I am, I dream, I long for more.

I long for a way out, an exit into bliss.

And, if last night's dream was bad; it was a relief. Maybe it was a development. At least dreaming that I was pickled in a jar meant I was not having one of The Dreams. I have been haunted by recurring dreams that return, over and over, in an irregular random pattern.

How many have I had? Couldn't count. Wouldn't want to. Don't want to even think about the dreams. Haven't. Pushed them away.

Back down from whence they came.

Raymond.

Did anyone hear me? The gallery is quiet. I'm sitting at my desk. It's raining in Charlotte Street, again. Presumably in the next street, and the next and the next. Presumably it's raining in all the streets of London. Rain in the city and we could be anywhere. Rain, a soft blur and merge of outline, colour, and form. A thin grey drizzle. Holding together all the streets of the crying city, the crying mind. Did I even speak out loud? My God, got to get a grip. Pull up socks (black, knee-length; The Stocking Top). Tuck in shirt-tails (crisp white, Omani). Adjust mini skirt (forest-green velvet; Eastwood). Go into the store-room and smoke a cigarette, pacing up, down, up and down, until I can't stand it any more, the pressure in my head, and I clutch for the mirror, the plastic sachet, in my Charnel clutch bag. Crystal daze and crystal nights. White sugar crystals of my delight. Shake it out, chop-chop-chop, roll up the five-pound note, carefully, snort a quick ecstatic line.

Our experiences have been committed to eternity nothing can touch our past

A line by Raymond, from a letter he wrote me runs through my mind.

You confuse me but I love it...Long ago. Our experiences have been committed to Eternity, you confuse me but I love it. Our eternities have been committed to experience. You commit me but I experience it. Our commitments have been experienced to Eternity. You love it but I confuse me. Our love has been experienced to Eternity, you confuse it but...

Back at my desk I flip open a manilla file.

Contemporary Aboriginal 3-D. DISPOSSESSED made from bullets. ADDICTED in bullet cases. WHITE SUGAR heaps of shining white crystals, sprinkled with blood. I read:

Images of crystals, surreal fields of a familiar substance in
advertising photographic works—sugar. A colonial tea party
setting with a bowl of sugar on a lace-doiley skull, a sugar bowl
with a skull-topped silver spoon, a bowl of sugar, the bowl is
made of china with blue patterns depicting scenes of Aboriginal people shackled by ankle and neck irons; another bowl
showing a horrific scene of people hung on a tree. Another
shows scenes of women with the word 'Defiled' covering their
broken bodies, another bowl shows a scene of children being
taken by colonial authorities, to place them in missions and
foster homes, with 'Stolen' written in copperplate script.

I read that White Sugar is by Indigenous artist, Buradyara,
the works are her response to finding out the 'hidden history'
of family she discovered in research in Queensland archives,
and oral history. I read that sugar was even laced with arsenic
in rations given to workers on stations when Aboriginal people were being moved off their land, and many were murdered
this way. This work is about a 'hidden history', as much history as art. The work is about the untold numbers of Aboriginal
people shackled by addiction, and murdered. Accompanying
the sugar bowls are tea-cups holding tiny child-size skulls like
eggs in eggcups.[5]

WHITE SUGAR, made from shining white crystals, and
real blood.

So that you can drink your tea sweet, sugar.

From somewhere, I don't know where, hear words tracking

a voice, and the sound of laughter. I have an image of a grandmother, a lost forgotten grandmother that I can't remember,
but I don't know where it's coming from, a nightmare image
of a black fireplace, and two arms reaching out, as if a woman
is imprisoned behind it. Another grandmother, at a table serv-
ing tea, passing the sugar bowl heaped to the brim with shining crystals, I see her hand spooning sugar and ladling it into
her china teacup, she stirs, and the silver-skull spoon and her
refined laughter make a tinkling ominous sound, music from
a horror film echoes in my mind. The *White Sugar* works have
triggered something. I hope that I will see the art in Sydney.

The work is powerful, I would like to bring it back to London, to show in The Antipode Room.

Day Three

Ruby

Ray-dreams Dream—
illuminate the deepest
darkest reaches of my
wanting Last night I
dreamed of you again
the same as all the other dreams
of you

The same but different as
they all are although each one plays out a
different scene the form for each
always
the same

TWO DAYS TO GO. I'M BOILING eggs through a hungover haze. My left nostril feels ragged and stomach nauseous. I'm doing my best to look intelligent and rational. Two qualities that seem suddenly impossible desirable even required attributes in the situation I find myself feeling more out of than in.

'December is such a good time to be going,' Hugo is saying from his seat at the breakfast table as he carefully pours Earl Grey from the pot onto the milk in his teacup.

He is so fastidiously particular when it comes to domestic routines such as the 'right' way to drink tea.

'Christmas!' he continues, heartily, ladling in three heaped teaspoons of white sugar and stirring vigorously. Why he worries about the order of milk and tea— and leaves over teabags and infusions—only to kill the flavour with sweetness, is one of his, many, illogical idiosyncrasies which privately crack me up.

'I'll happily exchange this darkness and gloom,' he takes a noisy sip from his cup and peers through the kitchen window into the shady terrace garden as if he were having trouble with his vision, 'for The Sun! Those Beaches!'

Like everyone I've met in England, Hugo seems to have shares in a fetish for warm climates, which to me seems rather ironically amusing, like an obsession with shopping malls. As if, just because the sky is blue and sun shining, anything is really going to be any different in your life.

I try to smile as I lift the eggs from the boiling water and place them on the Yoons' puppy tea towel on the bench top.

'We'll be back in time for New Year in the country with Mother, but I hope that we will be able to see your family and wish them a Happy Christmas in person for once this year, too!'

Hugo is surely being ironical but seems genuinely pleased by this, and for a moment I feel like a bitch for being so deeply uninvolved. I haven't been in touch with them. Haven't let them know I'm going back. I've been trying to think of a way to let Hugo know I have not been in touch with them. He wants to meet them, and for me to have a family. I plan to let him know when we arrive there. We do not get along.

I was kicked out. Margarita took my place.

As I slice the top of my soft-boiled egg, the images from the night before come back at me in a swirling rush.

I am hurrying down a steep grassy slope towards a pier, or jetty, with a large wooden structure built on it. The sky is clear blue, grass is bright green. The wooden structure is dark and solid, I cannot wait to get there, because I know that he is there. The object of my desire, centre of gravity towards which I can't stop, can't stop myself from falling, fast.

In the beginning, I am always on my way to meet him.

I am almost running now, getting nearer, trying to maintain an illusion of cool control. All I can think of is he. Now I am inside the wooden structure and I can see him. He is on his own, absorbed in his work. Painting. I always find him on his own, working… I walk up quietly, reverently. And now, at last, he looks up; it is as it always was/is. The deepest sense of connection. Of being joined. Part of something so warm and large, he starts talking to me (often in these times, these dreams, he does not talk, our bond is silent). He talks about writing, and I talk writing, and as we talk about my writing, it is as if we become, we are a part of the writing. As if we are in a book of writing, that I have always wanted to, the book about him, about us. It is as if somehow, simultaneously and miraculously, we are being written; and writing at the same time. A secret inner dream narrative. It's the closest, and most powerful connection, deepest I've ever felt for anyone and as the moment settles around in all its intense power, it is broken.

The moment of perfection, crystal prism, is always broken.

She comes running towards us.

Her voice is loud, imperious, abrasive and bossy with her overbearing right. Of course she's in charge. Dominating and commanding his attention. He immediately switches into her realm of focus, a dog responding to its master's call. And I? Shrink away silently. Shrink, cringe, shrivel, and shrink—until I disappear.

In four days, I shall be back, in that *landscape of beauty and terror...* The words track through my head, phantoms disconnected from my thoughts, my feelings.

I am staring at my egg as if I've seen a human foetus curled up in there. I feel as sick. I'm aware of Sir Hugo's eyes on me in concern as I jump up from the table and rush to the downstairs bathroom. I'm retching violently, bringing up bile over the toilet bowl, my head spinning like it's about to fall off.

And Hugo is asking if I'm alright and leading me into the drawing room, to lie me down on the ottoman sofa, with his big calm hand on my brow, feeling my pulse, telling me I can't go to the Gallery today, I must rest, I need to rest.

Day Two

Hugo

'WE WANTED TO HAVE A SPECIAL evening for you and Ruby before you go to the Antipodes!' Yvonne giggled and fluttered her eyelashes flirtatiously. Really. As if we are heading to the ends of the earth for two years, not weeks...But I must say, despite the convenience of modern travel, there is still something ineffably remote, unconquerably distant, about the notion of Australia.

I'm excited about the prospect of being there. Just knowing it's about as far as you can go from England, is quite thrilling in itself. Brings out a boyish spirit of Adventure in me. And Ticky. Clariss says he'd rather stay at home. As a boy I had dreams of travel and adventure aplenty.

My great prep-school chum, Bane-Marlow, and myself.. All the things we were going to do together when we grew up. Become secret agents. Travel to the Himalayas, to capture golden eagles. Ticky says he was going to come too, then, as well. As it was we all had a few real life fantasy adventures, played truly thrilling games together in the dusty attic rooms and secret back passages of Railton College, as youngsters— but that was the end of our adventuring together. Last I heard of Bane-Marlow, from Frobisher at the Club, was that he was one of the pillocks found in the South London gentlemen's House of Relaxation raided by the constabulary, which was one of the sad scandals which did our party no good in the lead-up to the general election. House of Paedophilia and Corruption! The headlines shrieked. Rumoured to have paid a constable's mortgage several times over to have his name dropped off the files. For myself, since sometime in adolescence, I have always considered Philosophy to be the biggest adventure, the pursuit of truth and knowledge; and Aesthetics, search for Beauty... The thrill of asking for oneself the great questions which have no final answers... Making a major contribution to the great ethical debates of our times...And I like to think of my contribution as being not without value. At least in my role of Adviser to the Ethics Committee, in our late P. M.'s term, my thoughts did not go unrewarded…

But it is essential to have contrast, as Plato observed: the Good Man, and the good woman, need balance to thrive. A holiday, an adventure every now and then is just the remedy...

Talking of adventures, as I was saying at dinner last night, look at the history of colonisation. Imagine, two hundred and forty years ago, 'Australia' didn't exist...when Captain Cook set off from Plymouth in his little ship of wood and iron, wind cracking in billowing white sails, sailing across the seven seas to find the rumoured 'Great Southern Land' at the end of the earth. It was the great age of exploration, when the Enlightenment fuelled metaphysical strivings in aspects of art, culture, painting, music, architecture. European minds opening to perspectives of infinity; of an endlessly expanding world... Flat earthers believed the Endeavour would fall off the edge as it disappeared over the horizon, but still he sailed on. His first mission was to Tahiti to view the transit of Venus, and then he was instructed to sail on to find the 'Southern Land' mythological continent, speculated by Aristotle onwards, to exist. After months of gruelling uncertainty, hopes of success, fears of failure, he spots the rim of the land England has been waiting for, hoping for, longing to find, to make her own... Land of Desire and Promise. But promising what? Paradise? Or Hell? The answer to our forbears' prayers and dreams, or their grimmest fears?

He dropped anchor in a natural inlet he initially called Sting-Ray Bay, because of its visible shoals of sting-rays. The name later changed to Botany Bay because of the abundance of many different natural botanical specimens.'

The dear girl looked stricken; stung. I thought she must have swallowed a fish bone—we were eating one of Yvonne's fish soups. 'Are you alright, Ruby?' Yvonne had noticed her state as well.

Ruby took a worryingly long moment to answer. Her eyes looked glazed and distant, her face drained of blood. I was about to hasten to her and slap her back to loosen the fish-bone, when suddenly she appeared to come around with a jolt as if awaking or coming out of a trance state. She shook her head, blinked her eyes, and looked confused.

'I'm fine,' she said. 'I just remembered something...'

She was speaking loudly. As if she were calling to me from the bottom of the stairs when I'm working in my study in the attic. As if she'd forgotten where we were dining this evening. The entire table was looking at her in alarm. And anticipation, waiting for her to continue. She made us wait a few more moments, and then she laughed abruptly, suddenly very bright.

'I'm such a goose. I forgot some research materials from the Gallery—some last minute things I need for the trip. I'll have to go and pick them up later—you don't mind, do you Hugo?' She smiled sweetly. It was a smile that would have brought a frozen cadaver back to life. I smiled at her. That was my Ruby. Always faffing about with business matters.

'Not still thinking about work, Ruby?' I chided her gently. 'Can't you just relax my dear? Forget about work. Relax. Relax! Enjoy the evening! The company! The good food!! Scintillating conversation! The chowder!! Of course we'll go and pick up your little bits and pieces later... But come now, drink up and forget. Here let me propose another toast. To Australia, Land of Hope and Promise!!'

'To Australia.' The others' voices echoed and I was pleased to see Ruby smile again, a smile charming as it was fleeting, flitting like a shadow across her features, as she raised a crystal glass of blood-red burgundy to her crimson lips, and drank.

Ruby

In the middle of the soup, it came to me. In a flashback. Was it imagination playing tricks on me? Was it a fantasy or was it—a memory?? I was in the bush. On top of the mountain. I'd climbed up on my own. To be alone. Margy had set off to read on the banks of the creek. By the platypus pool in the cool of the willows' shade, she'd said. I'd seen her leave in her big black sun hat, emerald long sleeved top and trousers, and pink beaded bag slung over her shoulder.

Ray had wandered off to do some sketching before I'd left the house. It was afternoon. The bush was white and buzzing with vibrating heat, shimmering in a summer haze. I climbed

up the track which Alex, Margy and I had cleared with Harry,
a long time ago. Up the steep wooded side of the mountain,
panting and sweating onto the plateau. My rock.

I lay down on its rough, red surface. And looked out over a
vision of paradise. The plains I secretly called Paradise Plains,
rolled into the drifting mauve horizon.

That's when I saw them.

Two tiny figures, emerald next to black,

walking along together by the creek.

A couple of k's from me.

Margy and Ray, walking together.

They must have met up, I recall thinking.

I thought nothing of it.

Why should I have?

I was pleased to see them—wherever they were.

'The two people I loved most in the world.'

After everything that had happened in the family.

My best friend and my lover.

The image so vivid I was shocked, stunned.

For a few moments the room

around me seemed to

I wasn't quite sure where I was, lost, displaced

from time and space.

A moment of unreality.

Until Yvonne's voice and

Sir Hugo's face swam towards me

And I snapped back into the present tense

Sir Hugo's booming voice

His big face

Pulling me back into

focus

Margarita

Something strange has been happening. A shrieking. It started at around the time the jacaranda on the quadrangle outside my window at work in the university, burst into purple blossom. At about the time summer's scorching promise (white light, white heat, hallucinogenic intensity) slid slyly, then shot violently, into days that had been fresh and clear and sharp, contained by the virginal purity of spring. Summer and its fever pitch, dazzling raze, pulling us all apart, forcing us to dissemble, or carry on, in a welter of sweat, heat exhaustion; drying the land with mocking disregard for human comfort; letting us know in Sydney, in Canberra, in Adelaide, in our modern western cities—with a blaze of bushfires, heatwaves, desert winds—how near the ancient centre, 'red heart' where nothing is as it seems, we really are...

A shrill high-pitched shrieking...Relentless, incongruous, and then the sudden silence, when it stops, is equally shocking. But it doesn't stop, it only pauses, for a minute or two, then resumes its solitary screeching with ferocious gusto.

A lone cicada, like a messenger, a harbinger of summer, has somehow hi-jacked its way into my apartment. And I can't get the sound out.

Every evening as the blue sky empties into the darkening intensity of night, the shrieking starts. God knows where it's come from, or how it can survive here, right in the centre of the city. The nearest piece of greenery is a dusty-leaved plane tree further down the street. I don't have a pot plant. Every evening I try to track down the insistent insect. I walk round and around the large apartment. Open the glass doors which lead onto a narrow balcony. I lean on the railings and the traffic five floors down on George Street drowns out the piercing shrieking. But when I turn and walk inside, there it is again. I've looked everywhere. In the stainless steel cupboards and drawers of the open plan kitchen area. I've looked in the walk-in wardrobe, and behind the fold-up bed in the bedroom. Under Persian rugs. I've found a few cockroaches (even here, in this apartment block) but no cicada.

I stand in the middle of the room trying to pinpoint where it's coming from. Behind, in front. Left or right. It makes no difference. Every time I start to walk towards where I think it is, it switches.

When I saw Ray yesterday I told him about the insect and he cackled. 'Maybe it's in your head. Maybe you're starting to hear things, Mars. Maybe you've been living on your own too long... Maybe you should come back, live with me...'

He was joking but I heard the hurt and anger, in his voice. I looked around at the dirty kitchen where we were sitting, drinking tea. At the peeling paint. Cracked wallboards. A column of black ants marched across the floor, up the rickety table leg, veering through the debris on the table's surface, to swarm in pools of spilt sugar. I smiled firmly and shook my head. It has taken me a long time to achieve my independent status. To finally break free from Ray, and all that held me to him. Now was the first time since I was a kid that I didn't need anybody with desperation which used to terrify and enslave me.

'I can put up with a refugee cicada, Ray,' I said. 'It's not exactly Eraserhead.' The last time we went out, two months before, we'd been to see the cult movie at the Valhalla in Glebe.

He laughed again. 'Maybe it's just the start,' he said. 'Watch out for men with flat tops…'

I knew there was no point in trying to look him in the eye, to make a deeper connection, for a start I didn't know if there was even a possibility of getting through to him, but mainly because I didn't want what might have followed on from being real, open, honest, unguarded. Friendly. Letting him in. I didn't want to shag him. I know that maybe I shouldn't even go round to see him still. And he sometimes asks me, bluntly: 'Why are you here, a charity visit is it?' But despite all the bad stuff that's gone down between us, all the stuff about Ruby, or maybe even because of it, he's still the person I feel closest to.

He's still my best friend.

Eventually I give up trying to find the cicada. Instead I try another tactic. Drowning it out, by practicing. Chopin. Beethoven. Bach. My favourite piece, which I always come back to, these days and nights. The Unfinished Fugue.

Then I get undressed, alone, unwatched, unacknowledged, except perhaps by the cicada. Slip into my purple satin nightshirt and prepare for bed. I pull down the fold-up bed from the wall and climb under the sheet; it's too hot for a duvet.

At night, beyond the small warm pool of peach-coloured-light cast by my reading lamp, large dark shadows loom ominously… I am reminded, momentarily, chillingly, of the flat in Adelaide, the flat that Ruby and Ray shared, until she left, and I moved in. Lying in bed there at night, where she'd lain with him, watching the shadows stripe the floor as the neon street-light flickered and hissed outside…

And then the cicada starts up again. Just as I am drifting into the soft falling lands on the edge of sleep. And as I tumble and start to spin through the speeding shapes of departing consciousness, I am caught again in the golden light, the brilliant glitter, the cicada-shriek of The Farm in summer.

After Ruby's family split up, Ruby and I kept on going down to The Farm. We hardly ever went alone. Ruby always had boyfriends. I didn't really go out with anybody for about five years, and there was my best friend Ruby with her string of admirers like some impossible, smug, princess from a fairy tale where the height of the drama revolves around whom her Highness is going to choose—and all the other female parts go to ladies-in-waiting, wicked witches or step-sisters. Being Ruby's friend meant having to listen to her consorting with one or other of her admirers through the thin partition walls at The Farm. Having to trail along the street with her and the latest love-interest, then having to counsel her about her family, or her boyfriend problems, until I felt like a smouldering combination of all three bit-parts in Ruby's Melodrama: ugly/witch/in-waiting.

But it was always good at The Farm. On winter evenings we sat before huge roaring log fires, drinking and eating and playing scrabble. In the summertime we—Ruby, a boyfriend, me, anyone who happened to be there—sat out on the front porch in the soft heat of the night, drinking red wine as the cicadas screeched and the aroma of the country floated in the stillness under a sky of stars that went on for ever.

When I said that I hadn't been to The Farm since Ruby left that's not strictly accurate. I did go once. But it didn't seem to count. It wasn't long after Ray and I had moved to Sydney. I'd rung Aphrodite, who was still in Glebe. She was delighted to hear from me, she said. Invited me over to dinner to pick up the Farm keys, stay the night with Ray and have a good talk. I hadn't seen her for over a year.

She didn't mind a bit about Ray staying, she said. She was pleased to have him there... He was cynically surprised after what happened the time he stayed at Aphrodite's with Ruby; That was the summer before she left. But Aphrodite made him welcome. I think she was glad to see I had my boyfriend now. Especially since Ruby had left so abruptly. With no one ever hearing from her, apart from the very odd postcard.

I could tell that Aphrodite was concerned. I must be lonely, she said. She'd been deserted too; she knew what it was like. That's the word she used, 'deserted,' in jest, but with a serious edge. 'How do you feel now that she's deserted you?' she asked me sympathetically. 'You were both going over there together, weren't you? That's what you'd always planned.' I didn't bother going into any details. Just smiled and said, 'I'm fine Aphrodite, don't you worry about me.'

But it wasn't a very enjoyable trip, going to The Farm, that last time. Aphrodite drove us down, Ray and myself. She said she'd like to have a look at the place again. We just went for the day.

The grass in the paddock around the house was overgrown. The man up the road hadn't been running his horses on their land, as he usually did. I was terrified of snakes lurking in the grass.

I went into Ruby's old room and looked through coloured panes of glass in the colonial windows that Wolfie had found and installed for her. Through the yellow and purple squares, the willows by the creek looked like distorted fountains. I was feeling suddenly quite queasy. I lay down on her bed, the bed I hadn't slept in with her since we were about fifteen years old, and the best of friends. Lying huddled together for warmth in our duffel coats, under layers of blankets, towels, coats, a weight so heavy we couldn't move, in the freezing nights of the highlands winters. Now it was mid-summer. And it was the heat, which was suffocating.

The heat, a massive hand squeezing the air from my lungs. Pounding against my temples like a hammer.

The shriek of the cicadas seemed to be lodged in my brain, coming from inside me. I didn't have time to sit, I was sick all over her grandmother's heirloom bed-cover.

Raymond

ALCHEMY STUDIOS, MATRAVILLE, SYDNEY

I went to the Farm with Mars after we moved to Sydney. Rube's old lady was driving. She picked us up at the house in Matra, even came in, which I thought was pretty broad-minded of the old doll. Mars kept the place pretty spick, though, not like it is now HA! She moved the doll, part of me latest new little piece, which was suspended from the kitchen ceiling, into our bedroom though, in deference to the old boiler. Just before we were due to leave I had a king-hit of smack in the bedroom, just me alone in there with me sex doll and me spoon—HA! That got me down there, pleasantly numb and detached, at least for the first half of the trip. About half way through I was gettin' rats-arsed, scratching and restless, bones aching, Mars talking to the old boiler, trying to cover up for my despicable state tsk! tsk! Junkie-Ray rolling in the gutter, ripping the skin from his flesh with his disgusting finger nails, not the ideal escort for 'the girls.' I'd brought some smack to smoke, not a great hit but gets you through times of crisis like this, made it to the toilet at the Ompel service station where we were refuelling—whoosh! got my hit on the dunny.

And language, feeling, needs that drive you mad pleasantly ceased. Nodding out like one of those fuzzy wobble-headed dogs people put in the rear windows of their cars when I was a kid, so when you'd be driving along you'd be staring at some imbecilic toy dachshund or poodle's head swinging away. That was me crouched against the rear window of Rube's Ma's car, naked, shivering idiot-dog-head nodding and wobbling as another me in the car behind screeched with joy to see toy dogs antics... yep, I was one of those happy-happy children, setting off on a happy-happy holiday...

Nodding out in one long slow slide-glide, slide-ride, slide show straight into white light, memory-scan-span activating, Rube's eyes, legs, snow-white skin, white as death, softness... enveloping... pictures of... I was always going to paint, works of vision still there in my head...snoozing and wobbling nodding in me wibbly-wobbly doggy head...

Stumbled out behind Mars still babbling doing a convincing impression of a Normal Person to Rube's Ma who didn't seem to notice World War Three had broken out behind my eyes, wasn't paying any attention to me at all, in fact, and I was desperate, I had to get it, get out of it, had to get another fix before the eyes exploded...

All I had was the smoking smack. Smoked a joint of it in Rube's old room. The smell of it made Mars throw up on the rug. Or was it the sight of me, hideous vision of wasted youth, —O horror—her nemesis, sprawled on the floor in the room of our long-lost dear departed one. HA!

'Go on, take a toke, perk you up, make you feel a million bucks. Make you forget about Rube.'

'For god's sake,' she said. 'Can't you do without it just for an afternoon? Can't you at least try to make an effort??' (Well no, Mars, that's what being a junkie means). And that's when she cried Ruth. Technicolour yawned. Strewth. I went Noddy, on the nod, off me noddle, off me noodle poodle.

Ruby

RIVERS CHASE, CHARCOT SQUARE, PRIMROSE HILL

Order
    Control
organise file tidy
    dominate
      get on
   top

If it weren't for Sir Hugo's humble entreaties I'd have my hair cut short as a helmet. I'd clip my nails to the skin. Every hair is painstakingly removed by Miss Pauline in waxing and exfoliation sessions at Beauty Spots in Covent Garden. I don't want anything natural to grow out of me. I want to stay beneath skin, under the surface, lie low, keep the smallest profile, cast slightest shadow. Present my artificial face to the world, painted, glazed, a bowl that holds nothing. My alabaster-pale smooth hairless skin. Perfect mask.

Sir Hugo likes me in a mask, in wigs and disguises. Feathers, velvet, sparkles, leather, studs. He puts his hands over my masked face and drums his fingers rapturously on the textures of disguises, covers. The real me, under wraps, but what Hugo sees, Hugo gets, glad-wrap boy; dreamtime fantasy toy.

Masks that have become me (from the Ruby Love Private Collection).

My black velvet eye mask curving up into sharp alluring

peaks above each eye edged with silver diamanté sequins. The masked ball classic.

My cats-eye mask. Tawny tabby furry pussy stripes. Big cat, prowling through forests of night, *what immortal hand or eye disturbs thy fateful symmetry?* [6] In my cats-eye mask I become big Cat. Panther, lion, tiger, puma racing over wild Savannah, all my muscles rippling powerful and deadly, intent on one thing only, nailing my quarry, with one fatal bound leaping onto his back and plunging my teeth into his neck as talons rip the rough hairy hide of his back into pleasing ribbons, as I pretend to gnaw and rip, slice and chew until beastly hunger is satisfied. And he rolls over purring.

Sir Hugo last night sprawled on our king size sleigh bed, a beached Santa in my pink satin wrap, which covered maybe half of him, imploring me, 'Trample on me, please Ruby, in your red stilettos and furs...please, I beg you Ruby, please... I'll do anything, anything...' I stand back and watch him squirm, helpless as an amoebae on the bed. I smile—suffer, sucker—and then turn on my spiky heel (Mangle) and stalk out of the room...Just as he wants.

For months, our marital bedroom has resembled a scenario from a fantasy bordello. Whips, manacles, riding crops, leather belts, peacock feather masks, and spurs—the lethal-looking ones with the little round spiked wheels which he likes me to dig quite deeply into his flesh. All the accoutrements, the finery and accessories of the 'Ideal Woman' he wants me to play. Boadicea. Cleopatra. Venus. Theatre and ritual have taken over our private life. And I have to conclude that my husband, already much older than myself, is—like me—out of his time. With his particular, very 'English' tastes, he would have been far better suited to living in the fin de siècle of the nineteenth century.

It's been like this since he started 'research' for his chapter on perversions in the book he's writing. Hugo says to me that he is a phenomenologist and it's essential for a phenomenologist to work through the experience of the thing-in-itself.

I have been his assistant.

'You've been writing the masochism section for over two years now... Isn't the book almost finished? Can't you move on to pastures new?' I ask playfully, fluttering my eyelashes. But he laughs his booming laugh and says with a typically wicked twinkle in his eyes, 'a little more research is needed, Ruby, my dear, there are still a few angles I'm unsure of...'

As I pack my bags for the trip, I choose clothes, costumes, and masks with care.

I need all the help I can get.

I've been to see Miss Pauline. I'm toned and fit, exfoliated and waxed.

All my clothes are inscribed with other people's names.

Behind a barricade of Designers, I am invisible.

If anyone I once knew were to see me now, they would not recognise me.

Hugo

Peacocks can't fly, 'twas what I always thought. They're bred to look beautiful, proudly strutting over clipped green lawns. Birds of court, baroquely manicured civilizations. Happy with their lot. I kept her peacock feathers, her decorative plumage hanging on the bedroom wall, opposite the bed.

Even after our wildest, longest, nights when the peacock

mask had been shall I say delightfully put to service, I always took the greatest care to replace it, on its special hook, before we fell asleep. We kept the door open and the light on in the upstairs hallway, as Ruby is, charmingly, afraid of the dark...

In the gloom of our night boudoir, I can see the mask on the wall. Sometimes I glance up at it, reverently, just as I am going to sleep. I can still see her precious emerald eyes glittering all-powerfully through the eye-spaces and her voice echoes through time; through my mind. The Eleventh Commandment. 'What do you deserve, Sir Hugo, for being so bad? Tell me what you deserve. I can't hear you Sir, you'll have to speak up, Sir.' Thou shalt find pleasure on the whip-stroke edge of pain. And enter the kingdom of heaven.

In the cramped dark cloistered rooms at the back of chapel, the beatings grew fiercer as bells for morning-song rang out at 9:00 a.m. It was all highly secret, no one told then.

Under the carefully ministering hands of the Brothers, Father Montague and his paddle, many boys grew up gay. I grew up with a desire that has dominated my life, my inner realm. I close my eyes and hear lashes crack through time and space, slicing through the still air of my study. My secret place where She will always be my master.

We did not go to school, from the start, in England. We try to keep that to ourselves. Myself and the nursery chaps. Ticky, the donkey. Milo, the sausage dog. And Clariss—the bear. I was sent to St Ignatius, Catholic prep school, in a leafy suburb in Ottawa, age of five, when my late Father, the Earl of Ode was British Ambassador. As his eldest son, when Father and Mother travelled with his subsequent posting, I was left, joining them sometimes for hols; at least I finished my schooling at Railton. But, damningly, when I went there, I found myself feeling as much of an outsider as I felt in Ontario. Mother was a Catholic and it was apparently a condition of the parents' marriage that I board at St Ignatius. It was only after Grandmother, a tyrant in her mourning black lace and pince-nez, passed, that the parents dared change the brief.

Of course it's no actual secret that my early education was in Canada. The effect of not being part of the club from the start has always been with me, spurring me on, motivating my drive to succeed and pour scorn as I do so. Pour on scorn and in my private life receive it. Cop my just desserts and love it.

She was a golden eagle. Proudly, gracefully, soaring into the blue Australian sky when I was not looking. Didn't even see her go. I should have requested she wear her peacock mask, decorative plumage; not the golden eagle. Foolish. What could one expect heading for that wide-open distant land? Why did I not see it coming? How could I not have seen the danger, the warning signs? Her strange behaviour. Those feints, and panics. In one so assertive, strong. Peacocks. They are bred to look beautiful. Happy with their lot. Ticky says, if we'd packed her peacock feathers, maybe, just maybe she would still be here with me now. I was wrong. Peacocks can fly.

Ruby

It's the night before departure and Hugo is talking about his research topic. It's 'intellectual aspect.'

'Sad-masochism is the most highly evolved form of sexual expression, Ruby,' he lectures with relish. 'It involves a finely-tuned awareness and delightful erotic exploitation of hierarchical power inherent in every relationship. That's what

I argue in my chapter. If both parties enjoy the—'

My face is impervious. I am staring into the flames dancing in the white marble fireplace in our drawing room, a large book-lined room that Hugo calls the Hall. After-dinner ports are balanced in our hands. Silence tosses between us, through our words, like the shadows of the roaring trees shaking their branches outside on Primrose Hill.

'It's the biggest test of trust,' he booms enthusiastically. 'Trusting someone enough to let them hurt you, trusting they will stop at request. Trusting that it is your pleasure, need that motivates their love-as-violence, violence-as-love. That's the biggest test, the greatest game…'

I can no longer hear his voice droning in my ears.
I am swinging.
High and wide on the beach swing, beneath our apartment in Brighton. I see myself as I imagine you, staring down from the third-floor window, high above the street, the beach, the pier, the pub, the bait and tackle shop. My red circular-skirted gypsy dress is blowing like a parachute in the wind, the dress I wore busking with Margarita. Leaning back, hair flying. Sea and sky collide, in a prism of light penetrating eyes, my mind, my heart, my guts, my love—for you….

And I wish that Nietzsche were right and time really would come again; and the return would be eternal.

And I think of you, standing there, watching me from that window.

And I want you
    Again and
        again
    and

again

After-words

    After the fact

A ray-glow still lingers in my brain. Before my eyes, hovering in the teeming muted mutant air, the humming dark of eyes-closed, mind-open before I go to sleep. An after-image projected onto my inner body, injected into my inner-mind, a secret lover, my obsession.

He walks within me. Sleeps inside me. At night as I glide into sleep, he is the one I rush to meet.

Who put him there? Why is he there? Driving me mad with impossible desire, a crazy yearning that cannot be satisfied. A memory of a longing, or a longing for a memory, it's so confused, crazy, I don't know what to think. But it's always then, when I'm not thinking, that he comes striding in again, cackling that infamous challenge, go on, strike me down for irreverence, for hubris; defying death, reason, common sense and getting away with it again.

But aren't I forgetting something?

I don't know, I can't remember.

Anxieties, uncertainties, buzz in my brain, and for days I've had the feeling I've forgotten something; missed an appointment, haven't done something important I was supposed to. I think and I think. But I can't think what it is.

The last thing I'd do is see an analyst. Once a doctor had even a vague idea of what's seething away inside my mind, I wouldn't like to rate my chances. They'd lock me up or have me on heavy duty psych drugs straight away.

After the 'procedure,' my doctor suggested I see a counsellor. 'I must tell you, though, that the counsellor who comes to this medical centre is eight months pregnant.' That had a certain black appeal. I laughed darkly, aware of the wary eyes of the assertive down-to-earth Scottish doctor, in a leather jacket and her hair cropped. I knew what she was thinking—is she cracking? I declined to see anyone about my pain, which I endure every month. PMS. Pre-Menstrual Syndrome. What's the point in telling anyone? What difference would it make? It's my pain. I have to deal with it myself.

If good old Dr Mael's face contorts with barely concealed disgust every time I tell her about my displaced, minor pains— and I've had enough hypochondriac twinges and hiccups to pack a fairly hefty volume: Career Woman as Paranoid Neurotic: A Case Study; if she prescribes diazepam when I confide my fear of opening doors, in case I freeze when I walk through the doorway, which is one of the first signs of Parkinson's Disease, it's true I read about it in Oliver Sach's deeply disturbing book; then what would she, or the shrink she'd no doubt refer me to, do—if I blurted out what really troubles me?

Keep it hidden,
that secret wound.

Can't tell anyone, not a soul, about the desire that plagues and torments me. For lost love. Ghosts from the past, a phantom that haunts my waking dreams; almost drives me mad in days of living half-in, half-out, of the present-very-tense, not-here not-now; stumbling shuffling, hands outstretched, sleep-walker through shadow-zone of memory, dream, desire which I only manage to escape, push down, through a rule-governed timetable of workworkwork. Work, it gets thing done. Work, it's my salvation.

When I started philosophy at the prestigious London college I became excited by the possibilities. Now at last I was where I belonged! In the realm of pure thought. Intellectual life.

The longer I lived with Hugo, the more I found out, about the complex social codes and conventions that structured his life. It was a hierarchical realm of tradition, of old school-tie. Old blood. Old money… I am a dealer in contemporary art. But the age and tradition Hugo literally stands for made me feel secure—when I could not remember a thing about who I was. Losing all memory of myself and my past life made me feel as if I had been ravaged by a tempest, tossed around in the night so fast and so remorselessly by the winds of change that the dizziness blanked out everything in my mind. But finding Hugo, or letting him find me, made me feel safe. I felt as if I had been blown by a fierce gale onto the ledge of an upper floor window in one of his family's stately homes. Pushed against the glass I was at least temporarily protected from being blown away into the night.

'Hugo,' I say, breaking out of my reverie, staring at the flames. 'I've been thinking…According to Brentano's theory of intentionality—'

'Hmm…' he says.

'Everything we can think of exists as an object of thought in our minds, right, and it's that inexistent object, idea of that thing, to which our thoughts, feelings, desires and so on for it are, intentionally, directed…'

'Hmm…'

'So that if I say, I am thinking of Paris, it is not the real city denoted by the word 'Paris' that I am thinking about, it's my idea of 'Paris,' which is comprised of the conglomerate of my knowledge and impressions of Paris, an inexistent object of thought, which I'm thinking about.'

'Hmmm…'

'So that if I say, for example, I'm in love with someone, I desire someone, it's not a real person I'm thinking of and desiring, it's my idea of that person, which I desire.'

He is watching me with an amused expression on his large, flushed face.

'So, doesn't it logically follow from this that we can never really connect with our object of desire, we can only relate to ideas, and fantasies, of or about that person?'

'Ruby, you've just proved the danger of applying logical principles outside the realm of logical possibility; that is to real life. You can't define real life, other people, and love, with neat logical formulae, you've been listening to our friend Professor Bear, the logician! Logic comes from the world of non-sense, it's a world constrained by logical deduction and is created by language, although language dissolves into abstraction within it. Come here! Before you turn into a rational, or irrational, number…'

He pulls me onto his lap.

'The Marquis de Sade had a theory about women philosophers,' he says in a playful tone.

'Tell me if you think the aristocratic French reprobate might have had a point!' He roars with drunken laughter, but doesn't continue.

'Yes?' I say, breaking the silence.

'Well, Ruby, I'll tell you this because I know you're intelligent enough to understand what de Sade was really getting at, hmmm…' he fixes me with a wicked, piercing, beam from his blue eyes. 'In *120 Days of Sodom* a woman philosopher was considered an oxymoron, with the emphasis on 'moron'!'

He roars with laughter again. 'And d'you know what the libertines in *120 Days of Sodom* did to women who attempted to be philosophers, Ruby?' He pauses dramatically, staring with narrowed eyes into the flickering flames.

'They gave them a jolly good rogering! And then they tortured and executed them!' Again he roars heartily, against my silence.

'I see,' I say curtly, curling my lip. 'How charming.'

'However,' he trumpets, mopping his brow, smiling apologetically at me. 'They spared art dealers and gallery directors!' He pushes himself up with difficulty from the red hollow of his favourite armchair and advances towards me with his big soft hand outstretched.

'To the bedroom, for Philosophy, Ruby, my dear!' he bellows. 'Come let us go now, you and I, for a touch of Philosophy in the Boudoir!'

'Hugo, have you forgotten?' I reply. 'We need to get some rest. Tomorrow we're going to Australia. Tonight I will sleep—alone—in the mistress bedroom.'

With those words I stand up, turn on my heel and start to walk across the large airy space of the Hall.

Day Zero

Ruby

BOEING 747, LONDON-SYDNEY, 32,000 FEET

WE'RE FINALLY GOING. ON OUR WAY. In the plane. Hugo beside me, sunken and snuffling in sleep like a big beached creature, a whale or walrus, for whom I suddenly feel a strong rush of affection. All he's done for me, it's true…

When I compare the life I have in London, to what I had before I met Hugo, which was, in the eyes of the world, nothing, it all seems hard to believe. Believe it, Ruby; it's your life, your fate, destiny… It's real baby…

In the subdued pool of overhead light, my little cocoon of illumination in the sleeping plane, my stockings glow with a metallic sheen, that makes me want to slide on top of Hugo and wake him up with a surprise…

There's just something about the moneyed hush and swish of a First Class cabin, flying at 32,000 feet at night, cutting through the sky like a knife through silk. I can't resist. I look around the sleeping cabin. *On the night before Christmas, there was quiet in the house/not a creature was stirring, not even a mouse* [7]… No lights on, no cabin crew in sight..

I glance at my watch. 4:37 p.m., whatever that means now, flying through hemispheres, crossing time zones, the ultimate transgression of natural rhythm…

Up here time means nothing, normality is subverted, at any moment we could fall spinning and burning through the sky, terrorists could wrench us from comfort zones into terrifying media nightmares…and we are hidden in velvet darkness. I push the skirt of my travel suit up around my waist; slither upwards and slide onto Hugo. He moans slightly but doesn't wake up. I reach down to his pants, find the zip and, with a little difficulty, slowly pull it down.

Visions of terrorists in my head. Tough, muscled, in black balaclavas bursting into the cabin, brandishing weapons; hot-cold electric shock, fear, scissoring the air, cutting the certain world to bits…There's no time to lose…Quick, let's make love before we die…He's waking up with a growl…

'Welcome to Australia, Hugo,' I say as he realises where we are. I watch his astonishment, then a smile lifts his face and we explode together in laughter, in our cabin of illicit smuggler's dreams.

Hugo

Naughty brave Ruby. My Venus, my vixen.
Straddling me at night in business class.
Despite royal blue curtains that were draped around our seats, I suspected from the knowing looks of the tall lissome Australian, blonde-and-tanned hostess—at breakfast as she served matching trays of grapefruit, bacon, eggs and toast, cereal and coffee, a hearty repast after crossing half the world— that our airborne high-jinx had not gone entirely unnoticed.

My suspicions were soon to be confirmed. The same smiling hostess, dressed, I noticed appreciatively in scarlet stilettos, slid along the aisle to present us—just as the plane tumbled through a burst of sudden turbulence—with a gold-and-blue logo certificate emblazoned with the airline's REPUBLICAN logo, bearing the legend: Transports of Rapture, and underneath, in ceremonial copperplate script:

> *Let it be known:*
> *On 15 December 2001*
> *The Earl and Countess Rivers*
> *Gained entry into the elevated realm of erotic delights, at a height of 15,000 feet, thus automatically conferring membership (constituting initiation) into the select and privileged circle of REPUBLICAN sensual connoisseurs known as The Transports of Rapture Club.*
> *CONGRATULATIONS!*
> *MAY YOUR DREAMS FLY HIGH WITH REPUBLICAN!*

The blonde flight attendant opened her red-lipped mouth and began to speak with an assertive twang:

'Professor Lord Hugo and Mrs Ruby Rivers. Lord Sir Hugo and Countess Ruby. I hereby present you with membership of the Transports of Rapture Club. Congratulations!! It is indeed a pleasure to have fearless, adventurous and libidinous, that is, sexy (hee hee!) souls such as yourselves on board! We like the life force to flow freely on our airline. Health, fitness, the body beautiful and lots of hot hearty gym-pumping physical Congress is what we're all about! Please feel free to enjoy the rest of your flight with Republican—however you feel fit!!

The cabin crew, who had assembled silently, I now noticed, down the aisle, and the passengers whose heads were craning with smiles of congratulation, broke into uproarious applause, cheers, catcalls and wolf whistles. I shuddered at the appalling lack of personal privacy and decorum this club entailed. But I could not let Ruby down, my darling who had got us into, indeed initiated this scrape, so I let it all pass just hoping that there were no media on board to broadcast, or podcast, the scintillating news. No doubt our new, elevated, status would make a tasty morsel for the British, Australian, or even world press.

They clapped as the smiling blonde flight attendant, whom it occurred to me, with her flat-featured gleaming expressionlessly smiling face atop a broad flat body, bore an increasing resemblance to nothing more or less than a surfboard, thrust the certificate insistently towards me with handfuls of assorted leaflets.

After the applause and merriment had died down and the attendant who turned into a surfboard had left us, I looked through the leaflets which all seemed to pertain to our new club 'membership.'

I opened one entitled: 'Duties of membership,' and read:

> *Members shall fornicate in public places as frequently and imaginatively as they desire.*

> *Each successful act of public fornication (documented by reliable witness) earns 50 Frequent Fornicator points. These can be saved and traded in for consumer goods at approved Republican stores, or put towards further flights on Republican—The Way To Go...*

'Hugo, wake up— we're landing. We're coming into Hong Kong. We have to fasten seat belts.'

Ruby's sweet treble voice penetrates my dreams. I open my eyes. We're still in business class. Nobody is looking. There are no pamphlets, not a certificate to be seen.

Ruby

Flying into Hong Kong is like flying into a dream I have had before. The forest of high-rise so close to the airport.

A towering ragged fringe of poverty or imperialism or both.

I remembered from somewhere that the 'old' runway at Hong Kong airport was infamous amongst the jet set as being amongst the most risky airstrips in the world. A vein running down a finger protruding into the harbour. Because the residential towers were so close pilots had to bank at a nerve-racking right angles to descend to and rise up from the runway. Famously, passengers could see what was on residents' TV screens as the planes landed and took off. But that was the old runway. It changed years ago. I don't know where it's coming from but I have such a strong image of what it was like to be a passenger in one of those planes ascending and descending into Hong Kong airport in the dangerous colonial days. Too strong to be visualisation of facts I read somewhere. I am sure that my image of flying into Hong Kong, as the plane banked hair-raisingly close is—a memory.

The intimate hands of tropical heat pressing upon us as we disembark to stroll the airport lounge, duty-free parade, the humid heat, it all feels strangely familiar. Like a pleasurable dream one struggles to remember when one awakes; like the name of something of unknown significance on the tip of one's tongue.

We drink bottles of water, coffee at five pounds a cup at a jazz bar-restaurant. Hugo buys me a dress with a five-pound discount in one of the many duty free boutiques. Spend the rest of the time in a First Class Global Traveller Lounge where Hugo has a shower and a massage. After two hours stopover, we re-board the plane.

The closer it gets, more unreal it seems. There's no turning back, no running away. My path of flight is taking me straight into what I most desire and fear. If it was dark, maybe I could 'relieve my anxiety' again with Hugo—his teasing nod to psychoanalytic theory. But it's broad daylight up here in the heavens, and all I can do is hyperventilate into an airline sick bag as Dr Mael instructed me to do, in a moment of mortal terror such as this. Hugo pats my shoulder, absently but sympathetically, poring over Wittgenstein.

Sydney:

Wheels touch ground. The dream connects
The plan proceeds according to plan
The wheels roll, the brakes pull back
Jet engines decompress
The passengers'
Stale crumbs of fear and crumpled dreams
On successful completion
Another passage in their lives, turning to the
New Land
The Old World, the Cold World
Crowds of pushing hungry bodies
Far behind
Greyness of low skies
Film noir seep of black city rain
Away
Brilliant blue mid-morning sky
Sydney in mid-December

Metal glitter
Spears along the edges of buildings, windows,
Lines of heat
Wheels spin on fire
—Violet violent dazzle
Walls of airport glass erupt into a golden blaze
The alchemy of Renaissance dreams
17th century Italian painters
Gained
Lost
Perspective
In the blink of an
eye

Antipodean Space

Hugo

WELL, YES. I DON'T THINK ANY thinking person could dispute that. I put down my somewhat dog-eared copy of Wittgenstein, at Ruby's behest, and look around me.

'Isn't the view wonderful, Hugo?'

Yes, the view is magnificent. Framed by the windows of the Southern Spiral Hotel, on the edge of Circular Quay, nine floors high. An afternoon fiesta of Southern colour and light delights the eye, with the overwhelming perfection of a tourist brochure photograph. All one can see is harbour and sky. The savage glitter of sunlight on water, the darting tug and glide of ferries, yachts with colourful spinnakers, red, blue, purple, and yellow sails; white frothy wake of speedboats, pleasure craft of all descriptions. So much healthy activity. Makes one exhausted to look at it. And over there beyond the stately white sails of the Opera House, isn't that the ominous-grey periscope of a submarine?

O yes, hmm, I have to agree it beats the Thames. And Ruby seems to want to turn the landscape into a competition, now we're here. The imperious glittering excited edge to her voice impels me to wisely keep my thoughts to myself and simply make myself agreeable.

Coughing, I light another cigarette, watching her, agreeably.

Yes, Sydney Harbour is bigger and far bluer than the ancient waterway that runs through my blighted city. Yes, it really is a most energetic outdoors city, blasted by laser-light and high-rise to the skies, like this hotel. Yes, a very beautiful city. Yes, a wonderful modern city, what's that, post-modern city, sugar. You're right. Remarkably there's not an old building in sight… The developers must have been working overtime…

Yes, yes, yes. I agree again with my darling who is pacing around the room like a mad thing. My fearless Aussie Amazon in a perplexing tizzy, hunting down sunscreen, silk shirts and trousers, just like an English rose, my perfect lady. I shuffle away from the window with its energetic views, smoke pluming comfortably above me, and lie down on the bed, glancing surreptitiously, in between pages of *Remarks on the Philosophy of Psychology*.

I read Wittgenstein, Ruby and Sydney Harbour glittering and slipping between the words. I watch Ruby and try to read her moods, thoughts, what's going on behind that rather hyper-active flurry of unpacking, of clothes hanging, of briefcase searching, diary scribbling. I watch her through a veil I have no desire to pull away. I love her mystery, her masks. It's true attention is slipping from Ludwig's words. But if Ruby said 'Pay Attention!' I would be at her mercy.

Ruby, Ruby Love. It's hot, too hot for furs here.

But there are still feathers, proud, tantalising, and teasing.

Golden eagle feathers; her sky-hunter mask.

There are feathers, and there are frocks. A tea dress. Floral, chaste and alluring, in the just-right boldness of its simplicity. And another dress, long, full skirted, fragile with age.

The gifts I have to surprise her with, nestled in a cocoon of softest palest shell-pink tissue paper, awaiting the startled rapture of her gaze, exclamation of delight, pleasure, at the slip-slither of materials, concealed in my leather portmanteau.

Gorgeous translucent stuff cascades through my fumbling hands, sweaty grasp, like water. Like air. Like it always does.

As if there's nothing there.

Ruby

So we're finally here. We're in Australia but we're not in 'Australia' as I imagine it, I'm sure I must know it, deeply and intimately inside me, as part of me, the most essential, secret part of me. Not yet, anyway. The hotel room is impersonal luxury. Like the rest of my life. It's someone else's dream. An ad tycoon. A mall chick. Bored housewife in suburbia. I don't know. Fuck it, like the Princess; I think no one would want my life if they really knew what it was like. If they knew what was going to happen to it. But let us not anticipate events. Even when the darkness of the shadow of death falls across our path we must not second-guess the future. Put away that crystal ball!! And there's nothing more pathetic, no one more politically spurned and derided, on all counts, in all eyes, more incorrect than the poor little rich girl (unless of course you happen to be a real live renegade princess. Wanted, dead or alive). Don't even have the good tough backing of poverty to hold my credibility together now. God, I don't know what

I'm thinking...

I retrieved the files from the briefcase. There, that's better. Sanity. Order. Organisation. Control. Good Hard Work. A diary and briefcase. A mobile phone and calculator. And a very good fountain pen. Think: art. Think Art. That's why I'm here. No other reason at all. Art is my agenda, my whole agenda.

There's nothing hidden in my life.

Hugo is asleep now. Stretched out like a large beached sea mammal on the duvet. Hefty philosophical tome beside him, as usual. Breathing heavily. Snuffling like a rootling pig.

Hugo, have you found the sweet truffle of your dreams? I hope so, baby, if so: Enjoy...

His sleep apnoea terrifies me. I find myself listening intently despite myself, holding my breath that he's going to hold his, the silence will go on like it did one night in Primrose Hill so I went into a panic and was about to start mouth-to-mouth resuscitation, heart massage. All those last minute measures to try to seduce someone back to life, the land of the living. Bodies, warm blood, hot breath, yes it's worth it, I'm here...! But he pre-empted me with a deep shuddering inhalation that rocked the bed.

It's late afternoon. Still looks very hot outside beyond the privileged realm of air-conditioning. The harbour glistens in a way I've not seen before. Or not. Perfectly framed in a picture window. I'm buzzing from the flight but feel strangely empty. With a Do To list as long as a hangover.

Have to, have to... ring my mother and brother in Newcastle. Ha! I joke with Hugo. Leave some flowers on my father's grave!! The words tumble unbidden from my mouth, like a voice in my head. He looks at me oddly for a moment then smiles absently and turns back to his book.

Have to, have to...go through my notes, the information. Aboriginal; Asian/Australian; Abstraction; who's representing the new landscape of the 21st century? And so forth. Have to get my head together. We've got a day to recover tomorrow. In the evening, it's the opening we came for. New Millennium, New Republic at David Orricks Gallery.

And it could not be occurring at a more synchronistic time as regards the monthly cycle.

Already I feel the weight of sadness long repressed, the tug of hands unborn, the touch of death upon my brow. And anger. Anger rising, spreading like red ink across a blotter.

Deep inside of me, is you.

A big event is anticipated, Springer from DOG informed me. 'Hollywood movie moguls, fashionistas, photographers, rock'n'roll musicians, the Arts and Culture minister, the Ambassador, even the Prime Minister has been invited.'

'Quite an eclectic gathering,' I murmured into my mobile, tickling Hugo's tummy with the shapely, perfectly pedicured, toes of my bare left foot. My husband was lying on the tan shag-pile carpet beneath me, wearing nothing but a pair of royal blue boxers with large crimson spots, which I had given him for his birthday, two months before.

When our engagement was announced some media professed to find it outrageous that he was years older than me, I thought there was a pleasing symmetry to it.

I admired puce-painted curves of my toenails against the chalky-white mottled-pink flesh-fields of his large hairy belly.

'Ret Felix and Diana Shaw both showing in the millennial group show, NEW MILLENNIUM, NEW REPUBLIC—'

I read the invitation I was sent in London.

The fierce hunting instinct, which has propelled my career, rises up. The Art Dealer in me stands up, hungry, with a glint in the eye.

I put down the blurb on the glass-topped hotel coffee table. It's calling me. The lure of the quarry, the thrill of the chase.

I want to find something rare that no one will believe can exist...

What is that? I say to Hugo.

What?

Did you say something?

No.

I thought I heard a voice?

No I heard nothing. He replies.

I stroll the expanse of imperial blue carpet. Blue as the empire sunken into the sea. The empire under the sea. Illusions of power make me feel better.

A bluegold haze—late afternoon summer light—is settling over the harbour vista in a swoon of impossible smoggy beauty, inciting me onto the balcony, into its gilded embrace. Out here, the air feels close...stifling...heavy...warm...like an abandoned, long-lost mother I can no longer refuse or deny.

Something is calling. My ears are straining to catch every sound, every note, harmony, and discord of the evening's music, its magic...

Traffic in the distance moans, the mournful blast of a ferry horn, trains swish on mono-rails... whirring, clanking, pulsating, breezy... The city, the evening, the harbour is calling me.

Sydney, the glittering.

My city.

I have returned.

Margarita

Raymond said.

Raymond said Come. Come and see. Come to the show. Get out of the penthouse death house! It'll do you good! Or have you become too high and mighty now? Don't you want to go out with me again, now you've moved up in the world? Would you rather be with Georgie-Porgie apartment friends?? George of George Street, by the way, how is George? Got tired of slumming it? You need to watch out, Mars, you'll get so straight you'll end up really twisted. I mean bent. Look at you, in that suit. You've really become an orchestra player, haven't you Mars?'

Raymond can cut from invitation to insult quicker than a playground bully sticks out a leg. He's sharp, too sharp, and I'm trying not to trip but I can't stop myself starting to fall into his trap. Falling in a humiliating heap at his feet. Giving in to his emotional blackmail. His neediness: he wants me there...I'll be there for him, no matter how rude he is, being rude, a bad artist, an enfant terrible, breaking all the rules of normal behaviour, is what he's all about... And, anyway, I have to stay with him because of what happened. Because of what I did. Because of Ruby.

At least, that's how I always used to think. But I'm evolving beyond that now. Struggling to break away, I will break away from him, for my survival I must leave him behind. After years of living as his support system/victim; his nurse-maid and girlfriend; paying his bills and debts; carrying him home from hopeless nights; washing the vomit from his face and body; cleaning him up; washing his clothes; earning the income which paid for everything: rent, food, his drugs no doubt at the worst of times; helping him organise his shows before he totally lost it; helping him get through rehab; helping him get off heroin, that's it, I've had it.

I've got my own life to lead now. I'm getting back onto my feet again and I don't need him hanging around my neck like a millstone, albatross, dragging me down just so he can walk all over me again.

I'm a survivor of an unfortunate relationship I tell myself. (I don't like the word 'abusive'). A survivor. And I will keep on surviving. In my apartment. Or rather the apartment George has so kindly lent me, whilst he's on sabbatical for a year. Yes, he is called George, he works with me in admin. At the university, and he does live on George Street. What's so extraordinary about that?

I don't need Raymond now. Shouldn't have agreed to meet him at the Museum of Contemporary Art café after work for a coffee; but he sounded down, pitiful on the phone, so repentant, I went along thinking I could cheer him up with tales of the cicada.

'Well, you heard a cicada. In George's George-on-George 'let's have a cappuccino' apartment. On George Street. Yeah, that'd be right. Mars you're cracking girl. But what d'you expect with all that violin playing?'

He cackled, stirring four spoons of sugar into his cup, slopping froth into his saucer and onto the table.

'Cheers big ears!' he took a sip.

The fact he was drinking a cappuccino didn't seem to strike him as hypocritically ironic. And he wasn't looking very helpless in his beaten-up leather jacket, paint-splattered jeans, big boots. In fact he looked quite cute and cocky, with his cropped red hair; typical extreme pallor; the delicate cutting angles of his cheekbones, nose, jaw, brow; razor-sharp mouth and pale blue eyes behind glasses held together with masking tape.

I looked away from him, quickly. I had made a conscious decision to ignore veiled pleas; his emotional need, the hurt I saw in his eyes, heard in his voice; his dependency, which had kept me running around in circles for him, doing everything for him, for years.

I watched a ferry chug into the quay, watched a little girl in a pink dress chasing pigeons. I listened to the roar of the city, laughter from a nearby table, a mother's voice calling kindly to her daughter, *Lindy, let's get an ice-cream,* and I said:

'No, Ray, I'm not going with you, I don't care who's there, I've got other things to do.'

And with that, I got up and walked away. Leaving him to pay.

Raymond

ALCHEMY STUDIOS, MATRAVILLE

—Could have hurled it against a wall, on the back, broken its bloody neck——through rehab, she did a lot, yeah. But she wanted to be there, and I had a lot of crap to—
—had enough of her—'looking after me'—
—I went off drinking—
—when I've been broke, now that Mars's left me—
—reaction to psychiatric medication he'd prescribed, which sent me off the loop—fair dinkum—
—After Mars when she jumped ship... All I could do—
—there after all, it was on offer. I never did quite—

—number. He's said I can ring him, go and see him, any
time I like. He's a decent bloke a—
—But I restrained myself, every time. Instead I went out,
picked fights with drunk-fucks—
—Bitch who does she think she is…I was never interested in
her in the first—
—with my old painting mates—
—After all, it wasn't love. I never told her that I loved her—
—as she so insultingly put it. It's true she helped me—
—reached the Wealth Bank, when the officers stopped me.
Two of them. 'Hey son'—
— He even got me off the charges the cops were pressing.
They wanted me in—
—million pieces—   —that violin playing—
—up in hospital unconscious. Mars had to come to take me
home—
—get it that I was supposed to treat Mars as if she were—
—I am searching for something —
—Sometimes I see him five times a week. Keeps me on the
rails. He's even lent me money—
— rare—
—I walked down George Street, Sydney, kicking in all the
shop windows—
—no one will be—
—jail. But old Jeffrey Bellow stood up in court and said that
I was having an allergic—
—some kind of Love Goddess—
—can exist—

Ruby

Hugo and I spend our first full day in Sydney, in our hotel room. Early morning, he awakens me with a gift, a pink cardboard box. Beneath unruly black curls, streaked with grey, his face— handsome, despite a rubescent tinge of good living, the fleshiness around his jaw— radiating an expression of sweetly wicked anticipation. I smile graciously in return, even though all I want to do is go back to sleep. I lift the lid, and through layers of tissue paper, pull out the dress.

'Oh Hugo. It's beautiful!' I exclaim, dutifully, feeling as I always do when he gives me a present, often, that I have to make my voice, smile, and the delight in my eyes, seem as authentic as possible. Put on a convincing show of pleasure and surprise. Exude! Darling. Exude!! (It's never enough to simply be myself with Hugo. To him, the dramatic statement, the theatrical gesture, is all).

'What a lovely dress!' I hold it up against me. Stroke the pale silk and antique lace. Hugo is always trying to get me out of my 'Mrs P.M. business suits' as he puts it.

'I thought you'd like it, darling,' he says, 'I thought you could wear it while we're in Sydney. Get you out of your power shoulders.'

His blue eyes twinkle at me. He gives me the second part of my costume. And now I understand what he wants.

'Your head-dress, darling,' he says shyly, insistently, handing me the extraordinary gold and turquoise Egyptian helmet.

For a long time he has mentioned his Cleopatra fantasy.

In a past life he was a slave on the Nile. One day he was spotted by the stately queen who took time off from her royal duties, surveying river work to trample on his back as he lay prostrate on a river bank; her strong bare feet with long henna-red toenails pushing deeper and deeper into the squelching black mud of the delta....

When we left the hotel, in mid-afternoon, to 'take the air' as Hugo put it, I wore my new dress. I would have preferred to wear something more concealing to protect my skin against the sun's ultra-violet rays. The fragile material was almost see through. I wore a cream silk slip underneath it. Whatever the circumstances I do not like to look transparent. This situation was unusual. For reasons I couldn't attempt to psychoanalyse I was feeling extremely attached to Hugo, almost dependent on him, as I leaned on his arm in that o-so-feminine dress and we strolled around the rocks like any happily married tourist couple doing a spot of window shopping.

Hugo

That day now remains etched in my memory in a black frame of grief, grief that does not so much dissolve, but maybe fades to hardest steely grey; as the ocean of Time washes me away from that static point in time, hardness of submerged rocks, that treacherous Australian reef, that sank our ship, my unsuspecting boat of ruby love. Ruby Love, delightful, sweet, hard-hearted Venus im pelz.

The day itself had been more than pleasant. I awoke Ruby with her gift, the antique dress I bought for her at Sotheby's. 'It belonged to Princess Eugenie of Russia, my darling,' I tell her. 'So surely it will fit a Countess.' (I know her size, it was not a guess). I nibble her shoulder and bury my head in the perfumed cleft between her adorable breasts. Ticky watches on. The taste and smell of her skin transforms me into a beast, a hungry bear. A bear with wild appetites who needs to be tamed by his clever mistress with the whip, before he turns dangerous and eats her up.

So I say, I say to my flint-eyed darling, I say, 'the whip is in the suitcase Ruby, the bear needs to be beaten, he is a wicked bear.' She doesn't look at me. Thrilling contempt emanates in waves from her slight feminine frame as she slides out of bed in her oyster silk negligee and stalks haughtily, divinely to my gentleman's portmanteau.

I stare at an invisible spot on the ceiling. I do not allow myself to watch.

'Ruby, can you see the Egyptian head-dress?'

'Yes,' she replies.

'Put it on.' I close my eyes. From the blood-red cave of my blindness every tiny sound is amplified, it's as if the field of my auditory nerve has extended to cover my entire body and all my nerve endings are straining in an exquisite, excruciating ecstasy of anticipation at the slightest sound she makes as she busies herself with her preparations to discipline me, the way she is a master at. My mistress. The way that has me writhing helplessly in an agony of erotic bliss that transcends the conjugal counterpoint of pleasure-pain; takes me to a state where I no longer exist, where the boundaries of self and world are blurred, I become animal and then become nothing, no more than a throbbing point of intensity, razed and set free to drift, lose myself deeper and deeper, again and again; at the complete and utter mercy of my fickle and capricious mistress. She who terrifies me with her power to such an extent that I have to beg her to beat me over and over, to beat the fear out of me; beat the fear into pleasure that is unspeakable in its quivering pitch, its magnitude! Yes! Yes!!

'Open your eyes,' her voice is curt, commanding.

Obediently I do as I'm told.

She is standing at the end of the bed on which I'm lying fully clothed.

She is wearing the collar and the band. The fishnet tights.

The black PVC corset with silver zipper, the black mini skirt with silver zipper and even the black leather eye-mask, which I willed would not be unearthed by uniformed officers at Customs— who waved us through unstripped, unsearched, un-manhandled, with deferential politesse.

To top off this outfit, she has attached a head-dress, buckling the leather strap beneath her chin, and now my darling is the Egyptian queen herself. Her red-blonde hair is scraped back from her face in a severe ponytail. She is holding the riding crop in her left hand, tapping it lightly, reflectively, against her naked thigh. Yes!

I tremble as she advances towards the bed. In her right hand are the leather straps.

She stops. Looks down at me for an agonisingly long moment.

'Take your clothes off,' she commands, watching as I clumsily fumble with buttons, zips and laces. She doesn't move a muscle to help me.

'Hurry up—can't you see you're making me impatient. I'm getting angry,' her harsh tone slaps against the still warm air. 'Yes! That's it! Good!' I encourage her.

'I'm getting angry Hugo, I think you're going slowly on purpose, I think you must want to be beaten.'

I look at her. Oh dear, she hasn't quite got it right. 'Relax your mouth' I tell her. 'Yes, that's better.'

She advances towards me, teetering on her red stiletto heels with a convincing look of menace. Yes!

'Turn over.' I do as she says, one sock still dangling pitifully from a foot. 'You've been naughty, Hugo. Tell me what you deserve.'

I look at her.

'What do you deserve?'

'I deserve to be punished.'

'Tell me what I should do Hugo.'

'Er—you should beat me, Ruby.'

'Ask me nicely.'

'Please...'

'Please, what?'

'Please... beat me.'

—Slash—

Oh, good God. 'Not so high up, Ruby.'

'Say it again.'

'Beat me.'

'What do you say?'

'Please, beat me please.'

'Say it again.'

'I beg you please...Countess Ruby, please.'

—Slash—

'Lower, lower, remember what I told you, you can do serious damage you know...'

The riding crop descends with a stinging crack that lashes my buttocks with the burn of redemption, of rightful justice, of necessity ...

'Turn over, Hugo. You know what I'm going to do.'

'Tell me.'

'Ask me nicely.'

'Tell me. Please, I beg you, tell me.'

'I'm going to tie you to the bed because you've been bad, Hugo, I'm going to have to tie you down. What do you say?'

My tongue is tied, I cannot speak, overawed by her power.

(We've been through this scenario a good two dozen times so far but I find, to my delight, that it excites me, uncontrollably. And to think I always thought leather was just some tacky Soho cliché! Of interest only to the vulgar classes!).

'Yes, what?' She commands.

'Yes...Please...!'

'Yes please, what?'

'Yes, please, I'd like you tie me up.'

'Tell me why you need to be tied up?'

'Because I've been bad.'

'What did you say?' Images of Frobisher, feared Latin teacher of Junior Prep bolt into my consciousness. Frobisher wielding the cane like it's a baton and he's a mad genius conductor ruling the world. Whacking us into a bent line. I'm quivering with fear which I need like an enema. Fear, which keeps me honest. Fear which keeps me clean. Fear which I need like the air I breathe. Like cigarettes. Alcohol. Like Ticky. I need it now, need it hard, need it hot, fast and furious…

'Make sure you avoid the kidney area. Remember? Okay. Let's go…

I've been bad.'

—Slash—

'What have you been?'

'Bad.'

—Slash—

'Are there marks, Ruby?'

'Yes, there're marks. Of course there're marks!'

She sounds annoyed. Very good!

She ties me to the hotel bedpost with the four leather straps from the portmanteau. She ties me and then she stands quite still and surveys me for a moment as I lie beneath her, in my shame. I look at her. 'Yes!!'

'Now I'm going to leave you here Hugo, while I go and get dressed. And when I come back' (her tone taunting, a ferocious feral cat playing with a pitiful kangaroo mouse) 'you're going to get ready too, and we're going to go out and look at the sights of Sydney, Hugo. My city; my beautiful, glittering, hot-hearted city.'

And that was when, looking back, I realised that it happened. When she mentioned getting ready. Sydney. Her city. I stared at her in shock, disappointment. This was not the way it worked. We'd been through the Prelude, the appetiser, and the teaser—there were three acts to come! It could take hours in London, sometimes all day! I was flabbergasted, hurt. She wasn't doing it. Wasn't playing the game. I wasn't going to lose myself. She wasn't going to let me. After a few measly marks, we'd gone as far as we were going. I watched her as she walked into the bathroom.

Her curves delightfully framed by the costume.

The spiky heels of red stilettos lined with silver diamanté sparkles.

The golden helmet, and turquoise paste jewels of the headdress glinting.

I held out a vain hope that she might return to play, stride out again. I turned to Ticky who was sitting on the bedside table. He winked, smiled quizzically. Cleopatra? Boadicea? Or even appear dressed. My Countess. An interesting thought.

But when she walked out it was looking so sweet and utterly guileless in her new tea dress, with such a soft smile playing on her lips. I melted instantly; and the bear went home.

'Hello, Ruby,' said Ticky.

'Let me untie you,' she smiled at me kindly as she walked over to rescue me, kiss me affectionately, chastely, on the lips.

'Thank you.' I said as my bonds fell beneath her quick deft fingers.

My selfish disappointment evaporated at the sight of her, of course she should enjoy the day. We would enjoy the day, together!

The pleasures of Sydney, her Sydney, lay in waiting....

Ruby

I had my itinerary planned to a tee. I didn't want any free time, any spaces, in my timetable. Gaps are dangerous, you can fall through gaps. And there was so much I had to do if I was to capture the antipodean butterflies in my collector's net! Ret Felix. Diana Shaw. Jack Spade. Brolga. I repeated names like a mantra. I reckoned, with my usual business acumen, that if I aimed for all four with absolute confidence, we would get at least two.

I sat on the black leather lounge with my organiser, my mobile, and my briefcase. Susan had finally compiled the material I'd asked her to sort for me, giving it to me with one of her ambiguously half-defiant, half-acquiescent, half smiles, and I had half a mind to—but no, slow down, hold on there, let's curb those aggressive urges, baby! Sweet, stay sweet. I'd brought the Sugar file, looking at it on the flight in between meals; conversations with Hugo about Wittgenstein.

Hugo is obsessed with contradicting an idea that we cannot know what a person is thinking. We talked about 'the famous' Private Language argument; Beetle in a box argument, and he tells me: 'Ruby, Language! Communication! The fact that we do talk like this! And understand each other! In our dramas playing a language game that we understand! Once we understand the rules of the agreement, nothing more needs to be said!' That was kind of Wittgensteinian.

But the assertion nothing more needs to be said has never stopped Hugo. He talked on and on, as the clouds hundreds of feet beneath the window which I was staring at fascinated, lulled, blaze pink-and-gold, illuminated by heavenly light, like a fresco by Bernini; in the sunset over planet Earth.

As Hugo's persuasive passionate voice had boomed in my ear, I remembered that long ago when Margarita and I were only about fourteen, Margy, precocious, argumentative, provocative was full of the same kinds of questions which later I read in Wittgenstein, star of the Vienna Circle and the analytic Oxford school of philosophy. 'How can you know that what I see is red, is what you see as red?' she asked brightly. And I had no answer, secretly miffed by the prescience and originality of her question.

There was always a hidden undercurrent of competition between us. My art. Her music. Our intelligence and understanding of the world; our perceptiveness. We were both so determined to be on top of everything, of life, to get ahead, to know. Continually vying with each other to sharpen the blades of perception faster, more acutely. To gain knowledge, the key to power. Knowledge will set you free. That's what we both believed. And beneath friendly concerns, we were both struggling neck and neck to get it. And then, as we grew older and our golden carefree friendship headed unknown to me and probably to her, towards the rocks, the object of inquiry, our search for knowledge, shifted to Number One: Boys.

The nature of that knowledge, in the biblical sense…

The thoughts swim lazily through my mind, slow fish in a sun-drenched, shadow-dappled creek…

It was Margy who said: 'I would never commit suicide. If my life got so bad that I hated it, and wanted to end it, I'd move somewhere, start living a completely new life, do what I'd always wanted, become the person I most wanted to be…'

But instead it was me who'd left. Me who must have somehow believed it on a deep level. Me, who took on a new persona, the new life. And I could honestly say, reply, Margy: those were great sentiments baby, but life is not quite so easy, not so simple as that; not so accommodating and clean as you might imagine at sweet fourteen and never been kissed.

But I am digressing, allowing my thoughts to dart off all over the place.

Daydreaming.

I pick up my leather-bound artists file, and turn to the job in hand.

Tonight's opening at DOG. I must ring Orricks and let him know that we've arrived.

It is late afternoon when we leave the hotel. Hugo is so insistent, so demanding, so full of entreaties, begging me over and over: 'Beat me again, Ruby!' until I feel as if I will go mad. But I get dressed with my good manners on, my gracious civilised self on, real feelings, as usual, kept down-down-DOWN girl!!! like a bad dog, a dark dog, a hound, a whelp, a mongrel of wild snarling aggro—DESIRE! my real desire. What, or rather, whom, I really want.

Can't think about it. Won't think about it. Push it all aside. The whirling void. Black hole. Madnesses tearing behind my eyes like harpies, weird spirits from the Highlands of Papua New Guinea. Confusion.

The city is glowing with an unearthly sinister golden light. On the hotel radio we heard about bushfires outside the city, too far away for their effects to be felt. But now as we walk out of The Spiral the air crackles with a strange static.

'My goodness, look at that sky,' exclaims Hugo.

Looking up, I follow his gaze into the fiery-red blood-black clouds stretching over the skyline from south to north like a stain.

Ruby-Rose

On the way to a Northern NSW rainforest, years ago

I arrived in the middle of the night. I'd taken the northbound train up the coast from Sydney, the hippie train, as it was known. Never having been there, I was confident I would somehow find my way to your cousin's place. I had the address; from the wonderful compulsive twenty-page letters you'd been sending me.

As the train neared Grafton we passed through mile after mile of flying fruit bats. The evening sky was seething, stippled, with a scattering mesh of shrieking winged bodies, a fruit-bat-cloud. I leaned from the open window of the train carriage with the warm tropical wind pulling at my hair, staring out into billions of bombarding black silhouettes, Dracula's friends, screaming like a thousand infants being slaughtered.

I was astonished and thrilled by the exotic strangeness of it. The adventure and the power of taking my destiny into my hands, after our strained and tense encounter in Mum's house in Sydney. Going all the way we had originally planned. But going with my arrival unannounced. On my own.

I'd left Margarita with her violin, at Aphrodite's (booked in to do a Psychic Healing Workshop together in my absence). I had a change of clothes, army surplus-store trousers, shorts, tee shirts, a towel and sleeping bag in my backpack. My Gurudu Airlines bag was filled with writing and painting things. Decaffeinated coffee and apples; Rimbaud.

I was prepared to stay for as long as it felt right.

The train pulled into the station at nightfall. I stepped onto the platform, carrying my backpack. I stopped and looked around me. Only a couple of people had disembarked from the train. A tall thin man with a neatly trimmed brown beard was talking to the stationmaster, a large man in blue uniform whose cheerful voice boomed through the thickening dusk.

I pulled out the scrap of paper with Ray's cousin's address from the front pocket of my shorts, well; I guessed I would have to set off to… wherever it was.

I walked out of the station and stopped again.

In front of me was an almost empty car park, sloping up to a road. Beyond the road was a ragged fringe of dark tall trees. A few wooden houses on stilts. Sub-tropical outer suburbia.

There were no shops. No people to be seen. The cloudy sky was almost dark, purple-black; hot and close with humidity. Electrical screeching of fruit bats ripped through the stillness.

I turned back towards the lights, movement, of the station.

The bearded man, who'd been talking to the stationmaster, was now walking purposefully towards the only vehicle in the car park, a white four-wheel drive.

Clutching my piece of paper, I strode quickly towards him.

'Excuse me, d'you know how to get to—' I glanced down, 'Styx Creek?' smiling with a full-wattage of determined charm.

He paused, his hand on the car door.

'Styx Creek?' he repeated slowly.

'Yeah,' I said quickly. I'm going to a friend's place. But I've never been there before and I don't know how to get there. Do you know where I could get a bus?'

He looked doubtful.

'You won't get a bus out there. Buses don't go out there. It's right out in the forest.'

'In the forest?' I tried not to think of Little Red Riding Hood.

'You're going to a friend's place?'

He was looking at me appraisingly.

'Yeah, that's right. I've just come up from Sydney.'

His face tightened in sudden resolution.

'Well, I can take you there, if you want. I'm driving out in that direction. Some of the way, anyhow.'

He unlocked the vehicle. Quickly I pulled myself up into the front seat. Taking a lift from a stranger (almost) didn't cost me a thought. I'd been hitching alone since I was thirteen, after we moved to Sydney from Beijing. You develop an instinct for who's okay, and who's not I told myself with a rush of uncertainty. But this was all part of the adventure. There was no other way I could have got out there.

'I'm Tony, by the way,' he said as we left the town behind us.

'Ruby,' I replied firmly, turning to look at him. 'Pleased to meet you.'

Tony was keen to know the details of my journey, and me.

Where was my accent from? Who was I going to see?

He seemed to want to talk but I was used to the hitch-hiker's bargain. Talk, but with a willed psychic strength, which is your protection, so that (you pray) even a serial killer couldn't think dangerous thoughts about you. And all this done with a kind of risky inner thrill. After all, you never know when your lucky charm could break, when your guardian angel might be off-duty.

It was further from Grafton than I'd imagined. A few miles out of town, when we were still on the sealed road, we passed an intersection. 'That's my turn-off,' Tony said. 'I'll drive you a bit further out, though,' he added.

We hit the dirt track.

The road wound deeper into the rainforest. After we'd been driving for about an hour, Tony was becoming upset. Several rocks had flown up from the track and hit the underside of his vehicle.

'My petrol tank will get punctured,' he'd said, several times. 'Where is it?' he repeated. 'We must have reached it by now...'

'Well, it says here, it's just after Styx Creek, there should be a gate on the left side of the road,' I said, helpfully, squinting at the directions Ray had given me, a month before in Sydney. Tony was clearly a decent kind of guy. Not the sort to leave a girl in the middle of a forest, in the middle of nowhere, in the night. At least that's what I very much hoped. The tension was growing sharper, and 'tsk'ing louder, rocks kept flying beneath the tires; eventually we crossed a splashing creek, to the left of which we could just make out a five-barred farm gate.

Through the gate, the four-wheel drive's headlights picked out a field, a dirt track, but there were no lights. There was no house to be seen.

'Well, thanks,' I said. 'That was great. I don't know what I would have done—' I started to open the car door.

'I'll take you there,' said Tony.

'It's okay, I'm sure I can find it from here.'

I was beginning to feel excited now about surprising Ray. I really didn't care what this bearded stranger, who seemed to be quite enthusiastic, did; didn't care if he came further.

'No, no, I'll take you there,' he insisted.

I got out of the four-wheel drive, opened the gate, which he drove through, then closed it again behind the vehicle and climbed back in. We drove down a steep dip in the field and up, a roller coaster in the dark, over a hillock, and there was a light shining in a black shaped mass ahead. I remembered that Ray said his cousin and cousin's wife were living in the barn they'd built. One day they would build a house.

As we approached, doors opened and a wild bearded figure ran out in front of us, shrieking and screaming and waving a rifle.

'What the fuck do you want? Stop right there!! Fuck off you bastards, go on fuck off or I'll kill ya!!! I'll fucken kill ya!!!'

He was pointing the rifle at the four-wheel drive.

'Christ,' said Tony. I heard his sharp intake of breath. But I stared through the windscreen with interest. Ray had said that his cousin was wild.

'It's okay,' I said. 'That must be Jim, my friend's cousin.'

'Your friend's cousin—who is your friend anyway?' Tony did not sound reassured.

I opened the car door and climbed out, calling loudly as I did so.

'Hello! Jim! Jim? Are you Jim? I'm Ruby—a friend of Ray's—is Ray here?'

'What?' The wild bearded man put down his gun, staring at me, looking stunned and bewildered. 'Ruby? You're Ruby? You're looking for Ray?'

'Yes,' I said, walking over to him.

'I'm sorry I didn't get in touch before I got here. I know it's a bit unexpected. Is Ray here?'

'Netta! Netta!' Jim called into the door of the barn.

'Ruby's here! It's Ruby!!' (I was surprised that he seemed to know who I was). 'Ruby's here! Come in! Come in then! Ray's not here, he's down at the lean-to, the shack, that's where he's staying, down the track. We'll go down and get him in a few minutes…'

It was when we were all standing in the barn that he asked, 'and who's this?'

'Tony,' said Tony, the neat clean bearded guy, smiling and stepping forward with his hand outstretched.

'Fuck off,' said Jim, stepping back with a sneer.

I was surprised that Tony stayed around after that but he did. He stayed, eagerly sharing the huge joint of homegrown, which I declined, and he even accompanied us as we all walked down a hill to find Ray.

Netta, Tony and I stumbling through the darkness, following the lantern swinging in Jim's hand as we traversed slippery leaf-strewn ground through forest trees. After a while we could see a glimmering light.

We followed Jim in single file, crossing a creek on stepping stones, walked across a track.

And there he was.

Ray, emerging out of a shack, wearing a pair of blue shorts, looking puzzled, blinking in the lantern light Jim was holding aloft—like a forest creature disturbed in its hibernation.

Jim and Netta were smiling broadly, sharing a private joke.

'Ray!'

'Hey-Ray!'

'Ray-you-old-bastard, you've got a visitor!'

'Look who's here...!'

'What are you doing here?'

Ray was staring at me as if he literally could not believe his eyes. As if I were some kind of apparition.

'I just happened to be in the area and I thought I'd drop in for a visit,' I said, airily, just managing to keep a straight face.

Later he told me he'd believed me, he really thought that I had 'just happened' to be driving through the rainforest outside Grafton, in the middle of the night, in the middle of the week, in the middle of nowhere, and had decided to call in on him. He said he thought Tony was my latest boyfriend.

And nothing I could say or do to try to convince him otherwise had any real effect.

Early morning. Not quite sure of day or date. Decide to go down to river for swim. Nearby is a half-built house on stilts, perched in tall sub-tropical trees above the river. Ray has told me that it belongs to an architect who comes down every few months to work on it. There's a water tap outside the house, and we fill our bottles there—it's closer than Jim and Netta's barn.

Very sensual swim—feeling like a cross between Lady Godiva, Ophelia and the Lady of Shallot—abandon oneself to pure sensation, eyes shut, drifting on the surface of the water, green light, gold light, warm air, mermaid girl. On either side the river lay deep rustling rainforest. Slither onto riverbank, dripping, sunlight. Walk along track past the architect's house, which I have to pass, walking through the shady forest, no clothes between air and skin. I spy Ray at the tap, filling a water bottle. He looks at me rather blankly. We haven't slept together the last couple of nights, but instead have both lain snugly zipped in our separate sleeping bags, on opposite sides of the small shack, which has one side open to the rainforest. Developing a new concept of single sleeping bag as full-body chastity belt.

Ray has been working late every night in his studio—a tiny room, which might have once been used to store tools, with a table and shelves, in the back of the shack. We've both been waking early, as the first rays of dawnlight slide into the open side. Up and out of full-body chastity belts, into clothes, more refined version of the same, as it has turned out. Somehow we are tuned to different wavelengths. For breakfast I have been drinking decaffeinated coffee and eating my way through the large bag of golden delicious apples I brought with me in my backpack. Trying to get healthy and detox in the country.

Ray's diet consists mainly of over-proof rum, dark chocolate, his cousin's homegrown and the occasional magic mushroom. Every now and then, he wanders out from his studio to consult one of the few books he has brought with him, which he keeps on an old vinyl car seat sofa next to the small fire in a ring of stones on the ground. *Food of the Gods*, a hardcover tome, details a history and geography of humanity's divinely inspired relationship with intoxicants; with full colour illustrations.

He's been obsessed with his work, buried in his drawings. He rarely leaves his studio where I hear him, sometimes, muttering to himself. *Trying to find something rare that no one will believe can exist…* I have been sketching and reading quietly.

I haven't felt like drinking with Ray. I just want to connect with the landscape, my feelings, the forest, naturally, with no stimulants, intoxicants, depressants. Nothing to intercept sensations of my experience.

He's been faintly contemptuous of my attitude, which has irritated me and made me withdraw from him. But I am happy to see him, more than happy. Right here, right now.

'Hi,' I say.

'Yep,' he replies.

'Do you want to go up into the house?'

I follow him up the steep flight of skeleton steps into the large half-built room that has a completed floor and the frames of walls, with window spaces looking out over the river. The air is warm and close against my skin. Golden rays filter through the canopy of ferns. The sounds of bird-song, fragrances of leaves, rich, sensual—morning's light and nature-rush—what could be more natural than love in the middle of a rainforest? All the whispering magic of morning around us...He lies on the floorboards. Desire like golden light slides through my veins slowly, warmly, sweet as honey—

His body freezes. He turns his head away.

I sit up, and so does he. 'What's wrong?' I ask. 'Don't you feel like 'making love,' darling?'

'No, I don't. And I'm not going to.'

'What?'

He's pulling on his tee shirt, face pale. Looking very serious.

'You don't mean it?'

'Yes I do. It's not right.'

'What are you talking about: not right?'

'I'm waiting for the right woman.'

He's pulling on his shorts now.

I look at him in disbelief. He could not be for real. What did he mean? What about the letter he sent me, and everything that's happened between us. And then it clicks. Tony, or whatever he was called.

'God, you don't still think I was really going out with that guy do you? How many times do I have to tell you—'

But he is bending down and picking up the water bottle.

'I'm going back to the hut.'

I watch him disappearing down the stairwell, as if descending through a trap door on a stage, first his feet are swallowed up, then his legs, torso, shoulders, his head is last to go topped by those wicked flame red locks.

Bye-bye baby.

Sitting in the unfinished room. Skeletal, bones of hope. The architect he? she? will one day have a whole house. Sounds of morning drift, river plashes. Gazing at the raw joists, naked frames, plasterboards piled in stacks. Out here in nature's paradise, walls are going up everywhere.

Get up, off the floor, dust the sawdust from your skin, walk down the steps, you've given him enough time to get back, you're not following him. Walk slowly, calmly, back along the forest track, Little Red riding girl without her 'hood, without fake 'grandma' in a bed, scheming to pounce. Licking wolfish lips. *All the better to taste you with my dear!* He's not worth it anyway. Whatever did you see in the creep.

There was only one thing to do now.

Not much to pack. A couple of books. *Rimbaud—a selection.* Borges, *Gold of the Tigers.* My diary, decaffeinated coffee and the water bottle that I'd filled at the architect's house. I'd eaten the apples I'd brought with me.

When it's done, I sit on the car seat on the ground in the lean-to, and open Rimbaud at random.

> They leave, forgetting that their flesh prickles
> Where the Priest of Christ laid his forceful claws.
> The Priest is provided with the shaded roof of a bower [8]

...Well, I would leave, leave Raymond working away beneath the shaded roof of his arbour, and I would go once more out into the sun, to travel across the land by rule of thumb, shouldering my backpack of dreams, hitching my luck to the endless afternoon, and just hope I'll get a lift.

Ray was just for a change working at the back of the shack. I walked to his doorway and looked in at him, bent over the immensely elaborately detailed sketch he'd been immersed in. Ray Furness, long-distance swimmer of Art, scarcely able to raise his head from the creative briny to accept food and drink from a support boat (not that I was offering him sustenance). He was making studies for a work that, he said, would open a crack in optical illusion, reveal the truth of infinity beyond...

He'd explained to me what he was doing. Trying to find or capture that elusive something that would transport the viewer into new states of mind perception. But the search seemed to require amounts of mind-altering substances. Until now I had accepted this as part of the artistic process. Beware, stand back, genius at work... Attempting orbit of the sun... Prepare for blast-off, etcetera.

Now for the first time, I wondered, what was he doing? I didn't see much evidence of his heroic metaphysical quest. All there really was to show for his time here were a few geometric drawings, and some bits of rubbish he'd found in the bush. A couple of coke cans, a chip packet, faded wrappers, which he'd nailed onto the makeshift walls. A rural counterpart to the collages of leaves he'd pinned onto the wall of his parent's garage in suburban Adelaide, which I'd been so taken by, millions of years ago.

'I'm going to go.'

I stand in the doorway, staring at his back. Naked torso, pink-white skin, blue shorts, the gold of his hair flaming in the light filtering in through the tiny dirty windows, cracks in the walls… 'I said, I'm GOING TO GO.'

'Wha—' he spins around, looking dazed and bemused.

'Go? Where?'

'Sydney.' I gaze past his head, through the window. Psychedelic lime-green grass. Irradiated in the dazzling fluorescence of morning, glowing as if lit from within. Who needs drugs out here? I shift my line of sight; turn upon my ex-boyfriend a controlled hard glare.

'You're going? When?'

'Today. Now. No time like the present. The train leaves at six this evening. I'll walk through the forest and hitch a lift to Grafton on the main road. It could take a few hours.'

He's looking at me as if he can't believe it.

I stand in the doorway prolonging my base satisfaction at seeing his shock. But what did he expect I would do? What else could a girl do, after this morning?

He walked me almost all the way to the road to Grafton, seven miles down the winding dirt track through the forest. We didn't talk much. The air seemed thin and insubstantial against my striding body. As if it had lost some of its heavy hypnotic humidity, its hold over me. I was glad of the chance to stretch my legs, to walk somewhere. The dirt track turned into a sealed road before it reached the highway. We stopped as we reached the tarmac.

'Well, I'll leave you here, skipper,' Ray said. 'Hope you get a lift alright.'

'I will,' I said. 'Bye.'

And that was that.

I turned abruptly and walked on by myself. Trying to tell myself I felt better the further away from him I walked. Why was everything so confusing, difficult? I was acting as if I believed uncertainty and chaos could be resolved by making a firm decision, taking definite action one way or another. I was walking away from Ray now, and all I felt was flat. Dull and flat, empty— *An instant of Nothingness expands to soul-consuming proportions...*

It's not so bad I told myself.

You've only lost the love of your life.

Light of your days and nights.

Ha! I forced myself to gaze resolutely across the paddocks I was passing through, having reached a clearing in the rainforest preceding the main road. I stopped walking at the main road. I didn't have a watch. After what seemed like a very long while, a white car appeared around the corner. I stuck out my thumb, smiled, willing it to stop. It sped by obliviously.

An undefined period of time expanded into itself as I sat on the grass at the side of the road.

The steady rumble of an engine approached from the west.

A truck appeared around the bend, heading towards me. I jumped up; stuck out my thumb. It swerved to a stop. I ran to meet it.

Two young blonde guys sitting high up in the cabin. The long-haired guy in the passenger seat opened the door, calling down: 'where are ya goin?'

'I'm going to Grafton,' I called back.

'You can get a lift in the back, if you want, there's no room in here.'

'Okay, thanks,' I said, picking up my backpack.

'You sure you want to go in there?' he added, smiling. They were both looking at me.

I glanced around me at the small truck.

'Yeah,' I replied, why wouldn't I?

He jumped down onto the road and I walked to the back of the truck. It was a removal van, I thought. The door lifted up. He pulled it open. The interior was empty and dark. 'You sure you'll be alright in there?' he asked again, looking at me quizzically.

I gazed into the space before me. It wasn't going to be comfortable, but so? It was only forty k's, I calculated, and I had to get there, soon, or I'd miss the train—and that was a possibility that just couldn't happen.

'If you're not okay, just give us a yell and we'll stop,' he said as I scrambled into the container, about one and half meters off the ground.

'Okay,' I said, brightly.

The door slammed shut with a great clang that shook my whole body. When it closed, I discovered what it carried. Fish. The stench was overpowering.

We drove off. I could feel every bump. There seemed to be almost continuous bumps and craters in the road, which rattled and shook my body, jarring every cell. It was dark, stifling hot, the fish smell was nauseating. It wasn't long before I felt dizzy, faint; I was panting, gasping for air.

I realised it must be a sealed container. There was limited

oxygen. I thought of kids who suffocated in dumped fridges. I crawled to the driver's cabin, banged fists on the metal.

'Hello!' 'Hello!' 'Please stop the truck!' I called with all my strength, weakly.

Nothing happened. They couldn't have a chance of hearing me in the front, above the thundering roar of the engine.

Surely they must have known that, just as they must have known there was no air in the back.

I feebly pulled myself, on my stomach, back to the door.

I would die in here when all the oxygen ran out. How long would that take? fifteen minutes, maybe, at the most... So this was it, this was how my life would end...In a sealed fish truck.

Then I saw, miraculously, that there was what looked like a crack in the seal around the edge of the door. Through a miniscule crack in the frayed rubber, a faint glimmer of light. Digging my fingernails into the rubber, I pushed and poked and pulled, until I'd made a bigger pinhole. I put my mouth right onto it, breathing in deeply. That's how I remained for the rest of the journey, which seemed to take forever. Crouched in the stifling rattling darkness, swooning in the stench of dead fish, lips sucking greedily on the rubber of the seal, thanking God for small mercies, tiny cracks and gaps, my chance to keep on breathing.

Eventually the truck ground and shuddered to a halt.

The door was pulled opened and I reeled with the impact of light, fresh air, the world. Life! I was alive. The blonde guy was standing before me, watching me, he was laughing as if at some big private joke— had he really tried to kill me?

'Okay?' he asked, peering at me darkly.

'Yes,' I said, staggering down onto terra firma.

'Thanks for the lift.' I added with as much cheerfulness as

I could muster, calling his bluff. I'd got here, that was all that mattered now. I wasn't going to give them the satisfaction of knowing that I had almost expired in their stinking truck.

The truck had stopped opposite the railway station. Next to a car park. Almost exactly the same spot I'd set off from in Tony's four-wheel drive, to go to find Ray, six days ago.

As I walked down the hill to the station, every step I took felt like a trampoline. The stench of fish remained in my nostrils for several hours, even after I was comfortably ensconced on the southward train, a small bottle of State Rail burgundy before me, trying to forget everything that had just happened. My Grafton trip. My dream lover. My cynicism deepened and took hold, like a lie you come to believe, all the way back to Sydney. To Margy waiting for me at Aphrodite's house, an all too eager recipient of bad news on the relationship front.

Now that I have returned Margy will hardly say a word to me, let alone look at me. It's only when I assure and reassure her, that Ray and I have split up, it was all a disaster, we hadn't got on, that she begins to relent just a fraction.

'I find him physically repulsive,' I tell her as we sit on Aphrodite's terrace. An image of his back turned to me flashes into my thoughts. 'He has soft arms.'

She gives me a weird look—Hello?

But I can see she's beginning to relax.

Now when she spends hours practicing piano and violin, I feel there's not so much a wall between us as a thin gauzy veil, which I could easily push aside. If I wanted to.

A few nights after my return I ask her to move to Adelaide with me.

'Okay,' she says seriously.

'But you'd better not change your mind.'

'No, of course I won't,' I say. 'I told you. There's no way I'm ever having anything to do with him again.'

Every morning I brew strong coffee and sit at the table in the kitchenette, legs jammed against the asbestos fibro wall, staring through hazy window panes into the limp lime-green heat exhausted leaves of the linden tree below. Outside is the tangled undergrowth, intensely blue sky. But I can't focus on the scenery. In my mind all I see is he. Ever since I left him in the rainforest I haven't been able to stop thinking about him. I keep it secret, don't tell Margarita. By keeping it secret it is assuming the quality of addiction, and with all the power of its repression. I want him. I miss him. Already my thoughts of him that started in an intermittent trickle have grown into a torrent. I'm longing for him. Dreaming him into my days and nights. I am beginning to think this must be reciprocal. Am I dreaming him or is he dreaming me? Surely I must be picking up on the psychic rays of his desire. Or will I never see him again? Is it possible that it is over, when I feel this way? I do not think so.

It was one of the first days of the season. A brilliant blue skied early autumn. Margy and I went for a long walk on the beach from Glenelg to Brighton. It was when we reached the esplanade we saw him. A familiar figure dressed in black, sloping past the bottle shop.

'Furness!' Margy shouted. I was surprised that she wanted to attract his attention, after all the negative things she'd said about him, and how much she didn't want me to have anything more to do with him.

We approached each other. Margy and I walking up from

the sand. Ray walking down towards us from the street. The three of us meeting in a triangle of hope, despair and lust. Excitement and danger crackled in the air, like the smell of sulphur mingled with salt. I looked into his pale blue eyes and felt myself starting to fall.

That night I woke at some indeterminate hour. The light thick and grey. A strange body was lying next to me, breathing. I stumbled out of bed. I tried to find the kitchen, the fridge. It seemed to have disappeared. When I stumbled back to bed there were two bodies there, both were breathing. I fell asleep. In my dreams I was inside the fridge with two bodies, all connected by fine skeins of red cotton. Instead of breathing we pulled in time on the cotton threads. If anyone forgot the others' systems would stop. We'd turn into blocks of cheese, cold cuts. In the morning she got out of bed first, then Ray.

Ruby

Circular Quay, Sydney, December 2001

'My, my, look at that sky,' says Hugo. Already the sharpness, edge, the exhilaration of arrival, has passed into something altogether ominous. Darkly angry, dangerous, elemental. Fire-clouds are above us, encircling the city.

Hugo hails a cab. He is wearing a white three-piece suit, rose pink shirt with white collar and darker silk bow tie. White leather shoes. Very spiff and dapper. I am, at his request, still wearing the dress he gave me, covered by a gauzy black wrap, not because the temperature's fallen, but because it makes me feel less vulnerable and self-conscious, to have a little more protection. We walked now, hands held, fingers entwined, to stand on the curb. The white cab does a quick U-turn. Hugo opens the door, I climb in placing my black leather briefcase gently on the floor beside me. Only as we were stepping into the gallery did I realise that I'd forgotten my briefcase. Turning to Hugo with an exclamation of dismay, but by that time the taxi had disappeared into the evening traffic, which was grid-locking the streets of Surry Hills. I didn't even have my mobile to call the cab company because it was in my briefcase. What an inauspicious start, to put it mildly, to my arrival into the Sydney art world! And things from there were, of course, only to get dramatically worse in terms of public appearances. Although in terms of my private life, my inner secret hidden world, what was to happen next was nothing short of a miracle. Or a curse. A hollow joke, spinning out, at thirty-two feet per second, the speed at which bodies fall.

Hugo

I was preparing to meet the Australian Prime Minister. I was more than up to it, used as I am to meeting with heads of state. Although my position of authority has sadly dwindled somewhat since our chaps were ousted by the New Labour rabble-rousers in the last election, of course. A parallel state of affairs existing here since last year bringing the loonies in for another term. But, just as at home, it is my duty to meet and greet, as civilly as only an Englishman abroad knows how. I'd always play the game for Ruby, with the greatest of pleasure.

Ruby

I went into the gallery and met David Orricks and asked to use his phone to ring the taxi company. I was told the taxi company would ring back when the cab had been traced, but when they did ring it was only to say there was no trace of my briefcase. By then I'd met the Prime Minister, and perused, between eager wine-swilling heads, the works of Ret Felix and Diana Shaw. Ret Felix's abstract landscapes of dislocation, vast canvases segmented into labelled pieces of loss and discovery drew the eye into them like the needle of a compass seeking north, seeking Home, but never finding it and, instead, wavering, torn, caught in a continuum of missing and desiring, the tension created constituting a new self... Already the blurb for the catalogue was forming in my mind, as my eyes swam searching and found a lot I liked, a lot I may say Yes to, agree to, with a small internal curl of pleasure, recognition as the millennial themes of identity struggles, dislocation, fractured longing resonated through my body—or was it just the wine, the heat, jet lag coursing through my veins on bubbles of high excitement?

'Zhou Li Yun let me introduce you to Countess Rivers from London.'

David Orricks was waving his arms expansively.

'Oh yes, I love your use of the colour red, what a wonderful shade,' I exclaimed taking a deep sip of purple Shiraz.

'In China, red is very symbolic. It stands for the family, for life, it's considered good luck in houses, everyone puts up red things in their houses, that's why it was taken over by the communists...'

His words were threading in and out of my hearing. My eyes were vaguely swinging away from the paintings, dimly searching the crowd, the sea of bodies and heads as I moved on, doing my soft-shoe opening shuffle, weaving in between the groups of drinkers, vaguely aware of Sir Hugo on the pe-

riphery of my vision, locked in head-bent chat with the P.M.
when I turned towards the wall of Diana Shaw's at the end of
the gallery and it happened.

I saw him.

I looked up and my eyes met his. Falling at a million feet
per second.

He was walking from a back room into the main gallery.
Glass of wine in his hand. Dressed in lime green pants, yellow
shirt, red sandals; long red hair sticking out around his head
making him look like a crazy inventor who's just been electrocuted by his own mad genius. But it's in retrospect I see him
in such bit-by-bit, piece-by-piece, detail, so that I can closely
scrutinise and analyse at my leisure, the individual idiosyn-
cratic details that made up the sum of his appearance. Which
I registered then in a frozen-moment-in-time, heart-stopping,
gut-wrenching, soul-pumping, shock—

Ray?

It can't be.

Ray, O my god it is.

His eyes the same sky-blue— mouth curving in a smile of
disbelieving recognition.

'Excuse me,' I place my hand on the arm of the artist, smiling with what I imagine —or hope— to be a kind of delirious
charm, but which probably just looks like what it is, intoxicat-
ed grappling for the moment, the disappearing social world.
'I've just seen someone I have to catch!' I head away, make my
way, ducking and weaving through the throng.

I move towards Raymond like a sleepwalker.

Like I'm hypnotised.

He's looking at me as if he can't believe his eyes either.

Raymond

I am searching for something
                              rare
        that no one
                   will believe
              can

Ruby

I was looking at a parchment map. As I gazed into the wiggling coastline all of a sudden I was there in that world; sailing towards the coast in a great big clipper ship.

The sea was high and blue; a fresh wind tossed my hair, big white sails cracked above me.

We sped towards a coast; the port came rushing up, opened to greet us in the mouth of a canal.

And now sailing in a much smaller boat, a gondola, down that canal lined with tall stonewalls over which tumble bright coloured masses of flowers.

And you are beside me, my love, as we speed onwards and inwards, glorious, festive, and perfect as a king and a queen in a fairy tale, taking the angles of the ancient oriental city in the golden light of day.

And then the gondola is stopping. I am climbing up some narrow steps onto a street crowded with curious smiling locals wearing traditional dress, smocks, long black pigtails; smiling faces, chattering voices.

Led, alone, by courteous citizens into a traditional wooden inn. The building is big, the first rooms I enter are large. I am accompanied up flights of wooden stairs, hurried through one room after another.

Each room I enter swiftly as a gliding ghost, is smaller and darker than the one before.

I enter the last room at the top. Tiny, dark, tucked in like a womb. Doubled over to fit, with no room to move, I crouch down and curl up.

Knowing I will never return.

Hugo

I was telling the Prime Minister about what happened in London in the Sixties when we had our first wave of what was called third world immigration, when I realised I couldn't see Ruby. Over the hour or so we'd been in the gallery, when we weren't actually together, I had kept her more or less in sight. My eyes restlessly swept the sea of heads, the sea of strangers. I had a terrible sinking feeling in my stomach, a dull panic. Extraordinary. A real fear overtook me. As if I knew something terrible had befallen, or was about to befall, my love.

Margarita

No. 16, The Mayfair, Sydney, December 2001

WHEN DOES IT START, THE DARK wordless urge to smash, to destroy; when does it start, the decay in the heart of love?

I loved him and I thought that he loved me. Maybe I made the naïve mistake of confusing sex with love. As if an orgasm had a spiritual corollary and true love overflowed. But it was more than only a physical relationship for him. I know it was. His dependence on me. The way he kept on and on coming back. The way he still keeps coming back. Despite the fact we are supposed to have split up.

He won't leave me alone. He's tied to me with many ropes, but amongst the ties are problems he creates for himself. That I would always solve when we were together. Bail him out, pay his bills. Lend him money. Before he gets cut off, or done in.

Ties which he wraps around me, until I feel I can't breathe; and he's going to cut me to pieces with his ropes and chains, his multitude of burdens, shackles of pain, uncertainties.

We arrived in Sydney from Adelaide almost five years ago. We'd been together five years then. It seems impossible now looking back on it that it could ever have felt good, thrilling, and fun. But it did.

When it first started.

Illicitly, deliciously, like a feather whispering over the most delicate tantalising planes and dips of your skin in the depths of night.

A masked intruder whose rough caresses you long for, you silently, urgently invite.

Like a thief.

Willing his dangerous advances upon you.

The most treacherous thing you could do! When Ruby was still in Australia. When Ruby was with Ray. Two girls, best-friends, and Ray. Margarita was ever persistent and practical, in the flat they shared in that house, the Haunted Castle, they called it, she would try it on…We moved to Newtown because Adelaide had become too small. Everywhere we went we encountered people Ray had offended or upset. Ringed in by small-minded small town hypocrisy and boredom as I saw it, I was on Ray's side. Admired his guts, his 'battle against the bourgeoisie', although I didn't join in. I smiled as he heckled in The Playhouse, with his artist mates, walked out laughing with them as they were forcefully evicted for their improvised performance.

I helped pick him up, nursed his head in taxis bringing him home from debauched parties, or if he was immovable, I swept the broken glass from around his comatose body. I covered him with my coat, remembering the story of the entire Russian army dying one snow-swept night because the vodka they drank to keep out the cold fatally lowered their body temperatures. I lay next to him, put my arm around him and fell asleep.

In many ways being with Ray then reminded me of how it was with me and Ruby, when we were growing up, teenagers at Sterner school together in Sydney. She'd moved from Beijing where her father had been working for the government.

But despite our vastly different backgrounds Ruby and I hit it off immediately. We were both different. We both felt like Outsiders in a school for Outsiders; and we recognised each other as if we were related. It wasn't so much that Ruby expressed what I felt, she didn't. It wasn't so much that I wanted to be like her, no way. But I liked to watch her, to be there with her in her crazy battles and emotional dramas. I guess it made me feel strong to help her up when she fell, to hold her together when she was spinning out, bring her back to earth when she was losing it over something or other, and there was always something, or someone, driving her crazy with rage or desire. Some mad theory or idea she was arguing about as if her life depended on it.

Ruby was always on an emotional roller coaster of conviction, more than half-crazy, but it was never boring being with her, she had an element of conviction, as if she might possibly be brilliant, a misunderstood artist in the making. 'One day you'll be famous, or infamous, and then they'll be sorry,' I said to her loyally, imagining a future in which I continued to play a major supporting role, as she became renowned for brilliant daring acts, boldly forging a radical creative path, against the odds, in a glare of publicity and outrage. It made me feel good to be her alibi, her best friend.

Ruby had spent years in far-flung places, the Andes, Papua New Guinea, Beijing. I was lucky to get as far as the Central Coast for a weekend. But despite her international ways, her strangely unaccented voice, she was feral. She just couldn't settle in Sydney. Branded (unfairly) as a rebel, people seemed to misunderstand, or distrust her, and she was always getting in trouble, questioning shop-keepers, ticket collectors, authority figures but most of all her parents, with whom she seemed to be involved in a never-ending argument—from when she got up to when she went to bed at night, that is if she went to bed. Instead, more likely, sneaking out the window and hitting the streets, and music clubs. And I knew all about that, I stayed at her house often enough.

Yeah, it's funny, in the rebellion and the intimacy, the sense of being different, Art Criminals; being with Ray in Adelaide was a lot like being with Ruby.

There was a major difference between us though. Ruby had bought the marketing myth that having a Good Relationship with the 'right' kind of guy was the pinnacle of achievement that brought happiness and joy to a girl's life—the prized ideal—check the girls' mags, it's still the same. Airbrushed boy-stars are God. Sure, I would try to pump my interest to match hers. To keep up with her. I had to or I could not have been her friend.

Ruby was so restless she just couldn't stay in. She seemed to have a limitless supply of energy. Not to mention oestrogen, or whichever hormone it is which is supposed to fuel the female libido… She found it hard to sleep at night; unlike me she wasn't troubled by migraines or health problems. By the time we were sixteen 'going out,' or sneaking out, to meet guys, most of our nocturnal escapades were carried out under an elaborate cloak of secrecy and subterfuge—which to me was the whole adventure—had become a main aim of Ruby's existence. Along with her parallel objective—or obsession— to become an artist.

Somehow, in a twist of Ruby-logic I couldn't quite follow,

she seemed to think the sex drive and the art-urge were inextricably related, she even had a theory about it which she used to delight in relaying to anyone who cared to listen. Sex and art were respectively the physical and mental manifestations of the Creative Process. Ergo (in her words) the great artist needed to do one to fuel the other, each fulfilled the other, was a creative well from which works of genius were drawn, it went something like that. She'd reel off a list of celebrated artist lovers, Picasso, Renoir, Caravaggio, Frida Kahlo and Anna Akhmatova to back up her cause.

As a consequence when we were sixteen or so and together all the time, she spent her time and energy, preparing herself for the pursuit of love. Anticipating love, dreaming of love, of that perfect guy who would whisk her away from the troubles and boredom of the ordinary world, which so far as I could see she didn't inhabit anyway. We spent hours in her bedroom, plucking each other's eyebrows, applying make-up (until she gave up make-up), parading clothing choices in front of each other, dancing around to the radio, laughing hysterically...

After turning off lights and slipping into bed—we always slept beside each other in her bed—we'd wait a respectable length of time, then creep up, choking down laughter, stuff the towels previously hidden under the bed, under the sheets and, our fait accompli, 'leave by the window,' as Ruby put it, an idea and a line translated from the poet Rimbaud.

With a sneer I answered my satanic doctor, and left by the window...[9] She quoted, snorting on suppressed giggles, as she jumped from the sash window. Scrambling through the arboreal embrace of a big flower-filled hibiscus bush, we hit the street and started to run. Transformed by make-up and girly-gear, plucking stray twigs and petals from each other's hair, we'd catch a bus or cab to Newtown.

The houses Ruby and I lived in were quite close in terms of physical distance, about half a kilometre, but socially and economically we inhabited different sides of the planet. Ruby's family home was a huge luxurious terrace on a leafy street. After Aphrodite had finished the renovations, Ruby always made a big deal out of saying how much she disliked the Palace of Versailles, as she referred to it. She could, she had the option. The house where grandfather and I lived was a small dark never-to-be renovated terrace in a poor backstreet. Every night as a child I was kept awake by the drunken monologues of the neighbours and local wanderers who congregated under the street light behind our tiny back yard.

The music of lost nights remains in my mind. At the most unexpected times it plays through my dreams, my thoughts, a hidden undercurrent I'd like to celebrate but I can't; it hurt too much. Huddled fearfully under my grubby sheet, too cold in winter, hot in summer; wishing that my mother were still alive, a vision of light to come in and comfort me, read me a fairy-story from the big picture book I can still remember her reading to me from, even though I must have been only three years old.

Instead I heard swooping unintelligible threats and howls.

'Geroutof there, you bitch—'

The scary staccato shouts—'Hey, Princess!!'

—the berating of sodden bitterness and grief.

'You bastard, why did you do it, why did you fucken do it?'

Bellows of frustration, screeching insane laughter.

A woman's voice. Rising and falling terrifying out-of-control, swooping and slurring and sliding and falling—

Deep dark music.

Swirling on an undercurrent through my head. Swirling indelibly, forever, through my body. A music I know far more deeply, more closely, than I knew, or ever could know, Bach, or any of the classical masters whom grandpa played over and over, endlessly, as if spinning a web, a sonic cocoon, to block out the real world outside the door.

Beethoven, Chopin, Shostakovich. Rachmaninoff. Bach. Always Bach.

'Listen to this Margarita. Bach is the master of the fugue form. Listen. Now! The subject line: inverted, distorted, repeated, and embellished; the voices chasing each other. Listen to the circularity, the building chaos, the confusion, the sense of loss and in the centre of it again—here it comes, now! The subject finds itself in another version, transformed.'

In the daytime I heard sonatas and preludes and symphonies and grandfather's favourite, Bach's *Art of Fugue*. At night I heard the sounds of people being wounded, damaged, hurt. Jagged fragments—breaking glass, shouts—cutting and shattering the night.

Sometimes sounds of happiness—laughter—warm voices talking—woven through the nightnoise. But, mostly, voices of sadness, desolation and despair; voices of hopelessness, voices of people who have taken to drink and drugs to ease untold agony, and which then as they are unable to stop the pain, twist in bitterness, uncontrollable forms, spill out, overflow in abusive monologues, in fights that made me sweat with fear.

One night I heard running—A man's rough shout, a woman's frightened squeal—A struggle, a fight—Her voice grew shrill, hysterical—His voice—Bitch—kiss me, go on kiss me, why won't you kiss me, go on you there you like it don't—Thumping—cracking—a fence breaking—A woman sobbing, sobbing—hard running—broken footsteps trailing away...

I cried myself to sleep terrified of what had happened outside, what might happen to me if I found myself caught out alone at night.

That was how it was when I was a child. Before I grew up. Grew tough. Learned how to put on make-up, swear, hold my own. Met Ruby.

If I heard the sad backstreet nocturnes when I was a teenager, the dark night music, I swore at it, put a pillow over my head, told myself that they were stupid, those losers out there. It was their problem if they abused themselves like that, let themselves get in such a state. Why didn't they do something constructive with their lives. Life was a gift; if you wasted it like that you deserved to be unhappy. I was never going to be like that.

We hit the music clubs. Ruby leading the way, but needing me beside her to give her moral support. I was her sidekick; I found that out pretty quick. But, deep down, secretly, I wasn't going to let her get away with treating me like her emotional crutch, her valet, without getting my own back. And I did. It used to give me a secret kick to test her, tease her (which I never let her know). Some nights I'd say 'I'm tired, why don't you go out on your own tonight, Ruby?' Or, even crueller, I'd suggest leaving her on her own halfway through the night. 'I'm thinking of going, Ruby, this is boring.' Her reaction was always worth the lie: dripping love and affection underscored by panic: she put her arm around me, stroked my hair. 'What?!' 'Surely you jest!!' Becoming anxious. 'You can't go now, Margy, you must stay, you have to stay— It's no fun when you're not here...' Then, 'Please stay Margs PLEASE! I beg you, don't leave me this way! You can't leave me here on my own.' Sulking and pouting, becoming desperate, about to do anything for me (I think). 'Go on, Margo, please! Pretty please… I'll let you wear my purple flares, my white platforms and my red dress! I'll bring you breakfast in bed!' That usually did the trick. After letting her grovel for a bit I always gave in. Her wheedling-coaxing-pleading voice, her spoilt-little-rich-girl voice, begging, was irresistible to me…

Ruby was looking to meet some good-looking musician or artist or other, to fall in love with and bore me stupid about. In that way her only 'rebellion' was to make sure she crossed the great divide into womanhood before it was a legalised journey, when she was still fifteen (as I recall, she might have finally achieved her goal a few days before her sixteenth birthday though I'm not sure). Three years before me. A fact she practically inscribed upon a badge and wore, she made me so aware of it with her suddenly knowing ways, her secretive self-satisfied smile, the distance that was suddenly there, like a chasm, a silent gulf war, a boyfriend, between us.

Yes, the years in Adelaide with Ray were fun. More than fun. Triumphant, dripping with sweat, musky with the smell of his patchouli and our love, salty with sea-water and outrage. I felt vindicated. Exultant. I studied at the Conservatorium. I was in love with my violin. I had no regrets, no bad feelings about the relationship. Why should I have? Ray was on a fairly even keel. 'All's fair in love and war'—wasn't that one of La Love's own expressions—delivered, always, with a laugh and a toss of her long hair? Now, at last, I was the one getting the chance to say it, and say it I did to Raymond, often, in the early days in the flat in Brighten overlooking The Bay, the flat in the old rundown weatherboard apartment house above a bait and fishing tackle shop; the cheap flat which Ruby had found for herself and Ray, which she used to rave on and on about as if it were supposed to be some kind of *auto da fe*.

I could never see what all the fuss she made was about. I couldn't wait till Ray and I got out of there. It was much too small.

One by one all Ray's friends, his 'partners in art and crime,' shifted to Sydney. Then we were making the trek ourselves. Packing up a few bags and hitching a ride in a truck. It took under three days before we were banging on John-Boy's door in Newtown, out of breath, laughing, high on the adventure. It took under a couple of months before Ray began to go off the rails, big time, in a trajectory of negation and destruction, which I couldn't, wouldn't, begin to follow him on. For me, moving to Sydney was returning home. For Ray it was like a chance to play lead roles in Hieronymus Bosch's *Garden of Earthly Delights*. Doing heroin with John-Boy. Hanging out at The Cross, with whom? I used to wonder, unable to sleep for fear of intruders in the house in Matraville, alone at night, waiting for him to come home— sometimes two days later, spinning out, spattered in blood or vomit, track marks big as eyes in his arms, eyes big as black holes in his head, lipstick smeared all over his body.

The Cross attracted him immediately to its rotten heart, like a putrid corpse to a crazy child that doesn't know to avoid the smell of death. He was fascinated by decomposition, decay. The shapes that humans make as they fall. The flash of steel as it slides through skin, the dizzy rush of toxic blood as it hits the brain.

His art-works reflected his sick obsessions. The 'Dissection Suite.' Shots of a rabbit pinned open, exposing its red raw insides, its meat, superimposed onto the prostrate back of a naked woman. He so tried the lesbian-feminist art lecturers at university where he was attempting his degree again, after its being withheld due to the nature of his final project—self mutilation—a series; that a new term of leave was coined 'Raymond-leave.' Just one on the endless list of controversial Ray facts, everyday horrors from the X-Ray Files, which I found out by chance on running into one of his ex-lecturers, Cherie, in Elyssianne's after Ray and I split up, and—finally seeing sense, after all those wasted years—I took to hanging out there.

When I told Cherie I used to go out with Ray, she almost fell off her barstool with shock. I had to buy her another drink to help her recover, as she recounted tale after tale of his depravities, which were not, unfortunately, news to me.

Prostitutes, pimps, junkies I imagined Ray fell in love with the Cross underworld, like Peter Pan in Never-Never land, at first returning to be bandaged up by his Wendy. And then later, as the decline kicked in, to abuse and attempt to destroy her too. To drag her down with him, to his particular niche in Dante's vision of Hell.

It's strange that I still find it easier to talk about his abuse in the third person, to describe it in metaphor, in terms of other people's visions. I still find it hard to believe that an abusive relationship—that sordid, uncool, unhip, unfeminist thing—could have happened to me. Although whether or not he, the real Raymond—and I still believe that somewhere beneath the bubbling cauldron of toxins that's polluting his mind there is such a thing to be found—was responsible, or whether it was the drugs or alcohol or combination of the two that turned him into such a monster, the Ray-from-Hell, Hell-Raiser, or indeed, Hell's Razor—slashing through the skin of my affection; and whether that makes any difference, whether I should feel sorry for him, which somehow I can't help, is a matter I haven't yet worked out.

Which is probably why he still keeps leaning on my buzzer, at the strangest hours, pleading with me through the intercom to be let in, to be looked after, to be sheltered from the storm raging uncontrollably. And why, even if I have someone else in bed beside me, I always do let him in to crawl onto my couch. Which has caused some problems with my new girlfriends. But the last thing I want is to feel guilty if he jumps off the Harbour Bridge because I won't open the door. Ruby's disappearance was bad enough.

I don't want to have Ray's death on my hands.

I go to visit grandfather. He is very old, very sick now.

He brings out the records. Puts one on the creaking turntable of his radiogram. Burst of static. Fluff on the needle. He picks up the arm of the record player, blows off the fluff, and replaces the spike in the worn groove.

The first slow haunting bars of Bach's *Art of Fugue* drift, quivering majestically through the musty air, the searing clean profound beauty of a violin solo.

'Ah,' he says, leaning his head against the tapestry antimacassar on the back of his favourite armchair; a hart in a dark wood, sewn by my mother as a young girl, long ago in another country. His eyes close.

Desert Ruby-Ray

Ruby

David Orricks Gallery, Sydney, December 2001

'RUBY.' HIS VOICE WAS THE SAME, a breathy mid-tone.

'Raymond,' I replied, staring as he was at me, in bemusement.

'What are you doing here?' as if the last time I'd seen him was two weeks ago.

"Here to see Art. What about you?'

I laughed. 'Likewise!'

Behind him the open door, the Australian night.

'I can't hear you, too noisy, let's go outside,' he said.

It happened so fast. I followed him out the door of the gallery and, bang, I told myself, and we were back there again, where we'd left off...as if years hadn't happened. At least I tried to tell myself that. But the Ray I was with was bigger, more filled out, no longer a boy. His face which I remembered as dead pale, was reddened, the skin coarsened, dried out by the life I'd never know, thousands of unknown days in the sun; thousands of nights doing who knows what. His eyes, which I remembered as visionary looked distant and washed out behind his glasses, hip frames: no longer held together by tape.

His red hair, which had been short cropped and spiky, was

much longer, standing out in tufty clumps.

We walked for about ten minutes through dark backstreets; through air that felt soft and warm. We didn't say much. Years, the past, was behind us like an ocean I wasn't sure I'd finished crossing. Didn't know if I'd landed on a beach or if I was still out in a flimsy rocking boat, on my own. He stopped next to a beaten-up old beetle.

'I parked here to try and avoid the junkies!' he said with a cackle like a cross between a sewing machine and a chainsaw.

I must have looked surprised.

'This car has been broken into seven times,' he assured me. 'They'd break into anything those junkies!'

I looked around apprehensively, pulling my wrap tightly around me. I'd made mistakes, done some pretty silly things. But at least I'd never gone near smack. Never had anything to do with junkies.

I'd become used to Sir Hugo holding the door of the sports car open for me, when we went driving together. Ray was a lot more casual; he just jumped into the driver's seat, leaned over and unlocked the passenger door; which I opened for myself. Then I climbed in. A lot more natural, I told myself. None of that hierarchical stuff. That formal power-play which was Sir Hugo's life blood.

'Off to Matraville,' he wound down his window.

Who really needs air conditioning? I asked myself.

But suddenly I felt faint, gasping, I was finding it hard to breathe, humidity and heat after the crisp cold London air. As we sped off through the evening traffic, I stared through the windscreen in shock, a kind of suspended disbelief. The inner city streets looked strangely familiar as if I had entered, in reality, a landscape that had existed previously only in dreams.

Discovering and entering a landscape one has imagined very intensely and finding that it's real. *Like waking from a dream and finding that one is holding objects from that dream...* A line from a letter he wrote so long ago, rippled unsteadily through my thoughts, weaving, flashing... But what was I thinking of? I knew this place, I'd been here before, I came from here!!! He was beside me! There was nothing imaginary about my knowledge of my hometown... nothing unreal about Ray. We were driving from Surry Hills to Newtown. I had spent much time as a teenager hanging out around here... We turned into King Street. The colours of the street lights, restaurants, shops, bars, night clubs and cinemas swirled and bled together in a flashing dazzling incandescence which hurt my eyes and made my brain tremble. My hands were shaking.

'How's Margy?' I forced myself to say.

'Ha! Mars? hardly ever see her,' he said. 'We stopped living together a few months ago.'

'Are you living with anyone else?'

'Nope,' he said. 'I'm on my own, and that's how I like it.' He laughed.

I was trembling all over as he parked, with another cackle, and we got out and I followed him down a dark, narrow, uneven path overhung with scratchy bushes and creepers, towards a cottage.

The sign Alchemy Studios hung on the porch, from chains. He unlocked the front door.

We walked into a cave-like room full of looming shapes.

'Home sweet home,' he announced, turning on the light with a flourish. A cluttered studio was dimly illuminated. Bits of electrical equipment, broken dolls and mannequins were strewn about the place. Dissecting bottles filled with dead and dismembered things I did not want to see lined wall-to-ceiling shelves next to a repurposed fireplace displaying a large snow dome surrounded by an assortment of plastic toys. It looked practically identical to studios he'd worked in when we were living together, I thought looking around, taking it in silently. As if the whole room was an exhibit of itself: In Remembrance of Things Past. A set in which we were clumsy fumbling amateur actors.

I was glad when he brought out an escape route. The further away I could get from reality at that moment, the better. We sat on old car seats in front of rows of dead pickled things (was there no escape from the contemporary obsession with death? I wondered. I'd come to Australia to try to find something wonderful and new and here I was looking at the same morbid stuff I'd left behind me.) On the ninth bottle of beer, and his wacky-backy he staggered over and kissed me. I kissed him back through the blurriness. I felt, disconcertingly, as if my back was breaking up into sections like sheets of Arctic ice disintegrating and floating off into vast oceans of Time.

'Come and lie down,' he said, after a while. 'My sleeping quarters are up here.' He took my hand and I followed him to a ladder in the corner of the room, which led up to a small mezzanine, just big enough for a double mattress. 'This is the cubby,' he said. 'I built it myself.'

It felt good to just relax, go with the flow. Not to have to bark commands, and attempt to verbalise every nuance of desire into an elaborate codified artifice of ritual and theatre. Not to have to put on a costume drama, play the old-world roles in infinite variations. Cleopatra, Boadicea, Venus in Furs. The Countess. To just be natural, be myself…Ruby Love.

Afterwards, neither of us could sleep.

'What are you doing in your art?' I asked, dragging on a cigarette.

'Just pushing buttons trying to find something marvellous, I'm going on a trip to the desert tomorrow. Leaving at eleven thirty. I'm flying to Coober Pedy. It's this opal mining town in the middle of the desert where people go, barbecuing their brains mining for opals. Some of these blokes leave their families, sink their entire savings into their opal mines, and stay out there for twenty years hoping to make a fortune. They all live in caves they dig below ground because it's too hot above ground.'

'I know Coober Pedy. I went there once with Wolfie on the bike, before I met you. Did you say you were flying there?'

'Yeah, with this mate of mine, Bob. He's got his instructor's license. I'm learning how to fly. I've almost got my pilot's license. Just need to do another twenty hours flying time. I'm going to stay five days, painting, while Bob goes on to Perth, he's doing some courier work.... then he's returning to Coober Pedy and I'm going to fly the biplane back to Sydney. Should be a blast, baby, a real blast.'

I turned my head and looked at him with narrowed eyes.

'Can I come with you?'

'You want to come?' He laughed. 'What about what's-his-face?'

'Sir Hugo?' I reached over for his cigarette.

I took a long drag and blew a steady plume of smoke above our faces.

'Hugo's history.'

Going down. I fall under, sucked into succulent juicy waving rolling clouds of bliss that funnel into cyclone dark suction clouds that fog my eyes and suck me down. I think it will be into him but then I find myself all alone on a dark plain, the cyclone man has disappeared sucked me in with sweet seduction lines a low tone spun me round with wild abandon, addictive as necessity then dumped me on a lonely plain and blasted off somewhere else.

I'm all alone in the middle of a dark desert. Wind is howling. Stunted bushes ripped flat against the dusty ground, uprooted flung against the night sky. Where am I? In the howling night, in the middle of the howling storm?

I wake up, and the walls and roof of the tin hut are rattling and shaking as if they're going to blow away. The wind is screeching outside like a banshee. Like a thousand demons, Aboriginal spirits furious that we are here in their country, Art Criminals, foreigners who do not even know their names, cannot recognise them. Suddenly terrified, I turn over, reach out for Ray. He's not beside me. My hand feels further and further over the narrow bed. My fingertips touch the shaking tin. He's not there.

I sit up, struggling to breathe. There's a torch beside the bed, somewhere. My hands fumble in the absolute darkness. I'm filled with horror, my head spins with thoughts of ghosts and spirits. What is going on?

My hand locates the metallic barrel of the torch, I push the switch and a thin beam of light extends before me, lighting up a stripe of the hut.

My God, what's that? Crouched against the far wall of the hut is... A hideously deformed shape, the colour of flesh and blood, wrenchingly familiar in shape, but there's something wrong, it's curled into itself like a stunted bud; it's grotesque, and impossibly sad. When I was pregnant I had a dream, a nightmare, of a baby with no head sitting on my bed. That's what's before my eyes now. A foetus with no head in the corner of the hut. O God. It's like one of those nightmares where you open your mouth but the scream freezes inside your head. I close my eyes. Panicking on swirling waves of fear. I'm the suspended silence, the terror, in the middle of a frozen scream. There's nothing for me to hold onto. No talisman, no rock of comfort. No other person. My fingernails gouge into the flesh of my hands, I bite my lip.

I open my eyes and force myself to look again. The image of the foetus disappears. Transforms benignly. Into the shape of Ray's canvas backpack, filled with his painting things, flung carelessly into a corner of the hut. But its after-image lingers in my mind. Foetus. Ray's baby. What was never talked about between the two of us. One of the many things that was never talked about between he and me. My baby. The baby that was deformed, that never existed, that was never viable. What was it doing in this hut, in my head?

The corrugated iron walls and roof are rattling and shaking, I think of a tin can bouncing down the street, kicked by a careless schoolgirl. Dorothy from Kansas. At least she had her little dog. I've never had a little dog. Where is Ray? I shine the torch around the hut. Don't see any more phantoms. One is enough. His coat is gone from the hook on the back of the door. I decide that I'd better get up and go and see if I can find him. There seems to be a strange relation developing between me and my thoughts, even between my thoughts and the thoughts themselves. As if there's me, a tiny shining lamp, a bulb of illumination, and then there's a long, long, jagged unravelling line, string of a balloon connecting my little glow of consciousness to the thought which flies high and almost free like a balloon on the end of a string above my head. A bunch of balloons in the hand of a Parisian balloon seller in a book from my childhood. A funfair balloon clutched in my tiny child's hand, but I'm the child, the child, there's been no other child in my life. Only me.

I get up unsteadily, and swing in a sweeping arc towards the door. I reach up like a princess, like a goddess in an arc of perfection to the leather jacket hanging on the hook crawling with ants.

Then I stroll, I bowl open the door into the gusting night. Opening the door is like opening your mouth to laugh, and the laughter is the wind ripping through the tin hut shanty town of the camp-site, like the life of the party.

Ray is nowhere in sight.
But then I look up.
And I see him.

Raymond and Margarita—and me…
Our images are huge, airbrushed, gorgeous like balloons floating in the sky, suspended in glorious technicolour on the screen of the drive-in movie theatre, which towers above the campsite like a message from god, or an alien visitation.

I lean against the shaking tin hut wall and turn my eyes to heaven, the images projected into the sky.

Oh no. Not another pornographic movie. The drive-in has been showing them at nights. I don't want to watch. And the images look disturbingly familiar, Raymond, Margy and me, in bed wearing nightclothes in states of disarray. I'm up there in the sky, reduced transformed, a play of lights, a trick of the light, flickering, ghost in the sky. Margarita is leaning on top of Ray's back clinging onto him like a marsupial baby a crazy spirit that won't let go, three ghosts tangling in the sky, falling through time-space, bound in skeins of memory, a loose skin of dreams...Whirling swirling like motes of dust in the wind.

Going down, down, falling down into unconsciousness.

Next morning, I sip mineral water and brush dust from my hair, Ray laughs.

'But I thought that you would have liked drugs, Ruby,' he says. 'It was a surprise, a gift, straight from John's home lab. LSD to make Mr Leary's eyes pop.'

'I only like drugs when I know I'm doing them Ray, and often not then.' I say, weakly, glancing up at the huge white screen of the drive-in movie theatre hovering above us. 'I never want to take another drug in my life.'

'Ooh-Ooh,' Ray makes goo-goo baby eyes.

The headless foetus flashes into my mind again. Last night is not exactly a night I want to remember. It turned out that Ray had gone for a walk in the desert, in the windstorm. He had found me on his return slumped on the ground outside the hut, carried me in to bed. I turn and look away from the town. Away from the tin hut camp-site. Into the distance. The endless horizon surrounds the desert settlement with a sense of enclosure more profound than fences.

Does the future have any less reality than the past or does it hold more because it's going to happen, it's heavy and full with immanence, whereas the past is over, it's gone; it remains in shadows, memories, causes rather than effects? What has more reality, the possible cause or effect? and if it's effect, is it a future effect or the tiny beam of the present moment slicing like a scythe, the grim reaper's sickle, through the great seething mass of Time—time and action, corporeal events, matter, space—which we call 'reality'?

And if we take this model of reality, of Time to be true, how do we account for the fact that so many worlds are sealed off, separated from us, by Time; they exist in a different time to us. A different time and a different space. The farther away in space, the farther away in time; but we can travel through Time, through Space now, in our thoughts, in our dreams, in our space probe missions; watch images beamed down from Mars and the moon, images beamed from five thousand years 'past' that I am watching now, that are happening now. What *is* happening? What is going on? Photographing, filming, 'recording' the past as it happens, but from a vantage point here in the present.

I am not there, but here on earth, a billion miles away. We can see the images but they are so removed as to be objects of curiosity, wonder, dream only.

I have the strangest sense that I am in my present but that I am also in another world, observing and recording images of another time dimension of existence. The Past. Planet Mars. Planet Raymond. In a spacecart on a space mission to Planet Raymond. I'm filming everything around me as it happens. But it's a million light years away, another life away, a thousand years away from my present life.

That's what I think. And then I realise, I remember that I'm not at home now with Sir Hugo comfortably curled up in front of the TV screen watching images from the red planet with the green sky. Watching the space cart lumber over to investigate a Martian rock. I am in the space cart, I'm driving the vehicle, and I'm operating the controls, the camera. This is my reality, my present. I am here.

Stepping out from the space vehicle, stepping out onto the red earth.

I look up and above me is the green sky.

I exist beyond boundaries, beyond limits, in the mirage shimmer, illusory ripples of water riding and tightening and shaking the still hot air in the desert like waves on the body of a long-distant ocean. All that exists now of the ancient inland sea is this massive sand pan, the rock pan which stretches all around like the surface of the planet Mars beamed down from Pathfinder onto camp-site TV screens at night. In this morning's paper I read an article by an Australian astrophysicist who said that we do not need to go to Mars to find out what time does. Right here in Australia we have the oldest land forms, most ancient life forms. Right here in this landscape of eerie endlessness, waste, parched, famished, dried-out rock forms, we have the scenario to test why oceans dry up and disappear. In central Australia, as on Mars, baby, it's already happened, a very long time ago.

The catastrophe of nature struck and what exists now is the parched future of an ancient inland sea.

Find out from the landscape, find out from the art. I lie on my back on the red earth and I screw up my eyes against the sky. Tears like rivers rush down the sides of my face.

How many perished trying to find that sea? To find water, teeming with life. And arrived here, in the desert, the illusory wilderness, a million years or two, too late.

I wake up with grit in my eyes and my hair stiff with red bull dust. Corrugated iron wall-rattle shakes down my bones like a wake-up call from a dream of death from the splintering noisy past I'm trying to box up and present as an okay sweet gift for this morning, a feeling of everything's alright that Sir Hugo might be proud of. Lasting out so long on this endless highway—Raymond's tousled hair pasty white face sleeping on the thin pillow beside me, twisted almost grotesquely and in my mind's eye I can see Margarita. See her bigger than the movie screen looming over this camping site like eyes of society, corrupt god, spying, even here. I can see my friend, my old best friend, laughing coiled caught forever in a headlight of doom and brilliance notoriety scandal in a dark deep corner. Margarita playing her violin through the granulated gloom, laughing so sweetly in the shadows of Ronny's Green Room, playing pool, playing madam, playing the girl we all want to have, to be become devour consume eat eradicate my sweetest delicious plump sweet- fleshed Margarita.

But what am I thinking of, I am past thinking of what am I thinking of, just doing it doing it doing it living in the present moment of pure psychic derangement blowing past the window like screeching billiohs of grains of bull-dust red thick sticky dust matting in my hair, maddening as bees in full swarm; heat, shimmers, melts, coalesces white-slide white-hide white-blast white UV-radiation-blaze white-fear shimmy ripple black white black white caught in the crack of the devil's fork..

I get up, risen proud free—I say—I turn, and say to Ray— wake up we're here—in the middle of the desert baby you and me—and the words stick in my throat like the shape of the stranded travellers I have heard of who lie down in the middle of the highway and get run over by road-train trucks. A kind of crescent like a kind of smile, curled up, the grin-grim reality of foetal attraction...thirsty...

I shake Ray and try to wake him sticking my tongue between his inert sticky sleeper's lips, salt taste of slug-like necrophilia the numbness of no-response sliding my hot dry urgent tongue over hard enamel of his teeth distant from his life his soul as rocks from the spring that bubbles up from deep within them, I explore the outside husk of Ray like another planet, the non-responsive dead exterior of his sleeping skin where are you? Where are you? WHEN I NEED YOU??? Shake him awake baby wake up wake up we're in the desert and it's ten years later and I want you, I want you to make me feel real, feel like a woman again deep inside of me is you, put your hand inside my heart and make a fist pumping pumping...

But I cannot stir him. It's as if he really is dead in there. Dead within his skin. I'd like to catch his REM with the whisper of my tongue across the endless plain of his sleeping eyelid but I know it's hopeless. I shall have to get up alone.

Go it alone

So alone

Need water

Dizzy

When I push open the tin door of the hut, the glare hits me in the eyes like the onslaught of a full-on migraine—flashing lights, ringing bells—trembling, blurry, flicker—mirage-whirl like how I imagine an epileptic fit might start—

I see Margy playing violin in an empty room—shadows—disconcerting—distorting—shimmering—head—reality—daze-e-rays like water—it all looks like water out there...

I rub my eyes and the colours run and run and run—like tears—blurring, merging, refracting, rainbow-resonance-sad as children lost forever in the endless desert—that stretches all around us—like a mother who has forgotten how to nurture

—nature disaffected barren illusory playing games rippling ripping into dust—

All we can do now is look after each other...

But we've forgotten how to do that...

I think of the opal miners out there in their stony heat blasted plots turning their brains to dust in the heat of hope crazed desire and shudder deep on the inside and in my heart I hear her, Margy calling from a long way off. The trembling high-pitched note of her pure violin solos soaring through the glistening shiny skies on fire with light and heat and water—dripping on a slippery-slide into my eyes, mouth, vessel being-boat of my soul. Physical. Bodily. Generative. Re-generative.

Reflection of my origins—Shimmering ripple wave— Unfolding—fold (unfold) all around me—Deep inside of me is you—

I stare one more time around me at the endless shimmering vista of the vast sun-blasted Aboriginal interior of my country and I walk, away from the campsite towards the town, hoping to find Coffee, hoping to touch base, civilisation.

Cappuccino, latte, espresso, short black, long black, Vienna—would do.

Although trying to ignore it, forget it, the vista of rippling illusions and mirages is not one which can be easily dismissed. Keep my head turned to the unsealed road. Red sun-blasted surface beneath which there could be, there are, opals to be found, mined, polished and sold in shops like the opal shops in the Rocks where Sir Hugo and I browsed absorbed as any tourists in the expensive trivia, the glittering baubles of the tourist economy.

The supermarket windows are pasted with press clippings detailing Wild West Shoot Outs in Cooper Pedy Main Street. I walk past. I reach a sign to Tilly's Treasure Trove, an underground cave-café, Coober Pedy-stylie.

In Cooper Pedy like all of outback Oz it's BYO psychedelia, and the land helps out as always. Even here in this cavern with no windows I feel almost as hip and happening as I did in inner city London jazz basements, just, mainly, because it all feels so surreal.

So surreal I've almost forgotten Ray lying in our corrugated hut, almost forgotten—although the blur is washing through me like an eradicating sponge—the drug hangover from last night (what drugs? what night?)—I'm living in the moment in this cave-café, and the past is another country, it can take care of itself. I drink two jugs of water.

A waitress approaches. She is tall, past the flush of youth, dressed in pink and white overall, smiling scarily beneath died dishwater blonde hair, who could tint their hair such a colour as 'dishwater' ('I'll have the dirty blonde rinse thanks'), her nose is large bulbous, eyes blue and bloodshot. I expect her to hand me a menu carved on steak, bad-taste joke for my hangover mouth but no its the usual acceptable plastic laminate of focaccia and bagels and Coffee.

'A flat white, please,' I say.

'Sugar?' she asks.

'Sugar, uh no thanks.'

When I was studying—
when I first met Sir Hugo—
I loved the Pre-Socratic philosophers the most, whose ideas

are passed on to us as fragments only, like the poetry of Sappho, of the ancient world...

Raw voices, first voices, freshness of ancient voices speaking down the centuries, through time and space, from an ancient sun-drenched world of light, the first 'glimmerings of reason,' as Sir Hugo put it, although I did not read their words as such, rather as a strange and brilliant poetry which made a sense beyond sense, described a world beyond, beneath our world, which spoke to me deeply in some ancient place some purer place in the forgotten essential me, my origin....

All humans are composed from atoms that once were stars... you're a star, baby...

Lying in this tin hut in the middle of the desert, in the middle of opal fields, in the middle of nowhere, lying on my back on a narrow camp bed on a sheet red with throat-catching dust, tin door propped open. The furnace-hot watercolours of the world outside the hut shimmer like a dream. I see: a slice of wooden camp-site fence, above it the looming white screen of the drive-in flanked by the ochre red of the land, the impossible blue of the sky, a blue so impossible it's white, rippling and shaking like it's painted onto water, impossible not to smile at the unreality of it all, like lying in the middle of a hallucination, but, no it's like lying in the middle of a landscape as it's being painted; a world in formation, a gaseous, watery unstable world still in the shimmering ancient phase before it sets into material form, fluid, intangible, untouchable—before the colours dry.

I want to merge with those waves and tremors, I want to lose myself in that haze of unreality, disappear in the illusion of water in the heat, give up: dissolve my spirit in the spirit

of this ancient land this country that is not my country that
is no-body's country which is neither a state of being nor of
nothingness, a state of non-being, like water vapour changing
its shape and form but never disappearing, metamorphosing
into Dreamtime spirit and living forever in the mind of an
ancient race...

Open the Pre-Socratics book...43...52...63...71...82...
My eyes slide down the numbered sections and take a hold...

Words, letters, run together dance off the page before my
eyes...

Outside the world sways and shimmies, crackling in the
desert-dance of heat/haze—heat/raze the purifying joy of
burning in a burning world where the intensity of heat pro-
duces the illusion, the mockery, of water. Gives birth to the
buzz of a billion flies, a swarm of black madnesses approaching and descending in random patterns of distraction onto
my hyper-sensitive skin. I swat again and again flick the hand-
made newspaper fan, in front of my face, between myself and
the dry and dusty text book...

Turn my eyes to the door to the shimmering veil waving
moistly, seductively, before me...

Once again the landscape is doing its dance of the seven
veils, stripping off certainties, securities, layer by layer... first
to go is the perception of solidity, the solid tangible substance

of matter, the idea that it holds its shape that goes in a sweet-ly joyous ripple; next is the perception of distance, the comforting security of a horizon to put a boundary, a limit, on your view of the world–that goes with an ecstatic roll of the belly of infinite space; the buzz of flies, the stench of rotten flesh decomposing by the side of a single road that stretches like a ribbon, a life-line, or impartial death-line, across a desert of ancient subtle tracks invisible to the western eye; earth is blown away, rock exposed, reduced to sand, to dust and blown away layer by layer, the surface shifts and slides blown away by the wind.

I imagine a city street being blown away in the night, city parks eroded to dust and blown away, towerblocks rippling in a haze and disappearing, Gallery, our house in Primrose Hill, shaking, sliding into a puddle of heat, they were never really there at all...

I think of Hugo secure, beaming in his olive-green three piece corduroy suit, glass of good burgundy in hand, beaming at me with that cheeky twinkle in his eye that only I see; and then Hugo is rippling and shimmering, Hugo is sliding and slipping, growing enormously long and thin, then hugely fat and squat, Hugo is doing the dance of the seven veils, Hugo is blowing me a kiss, Hugo is holding out his arms entreatingly seductively towards me, Hugo is disappearing fast, and now I can see that all along Sir Hugo was nothing but a mirage in a desert—which I couldn't even see.

Now I can see it, and he's not there. Vanished. Gone. Along with all the other secure comfortable trappings of my life with him. England, London, our house and gallery, the good food and wine, measured regulated lifestyle, his impeccable sense of order and his peculiar internal corruption of it. The luxury and fine clothes, the car and our racehorse. My position in the social register of his life, the Establishment.

It's all been blown away like sand by the wind at night. It's all been revealed as illusory-insubstantial-nothing, a film of watery colours floating across a void.

And I'm here. In the desert. The real desert. The real Ruby. With the heat and the flies. With mirages, illusions. And Ray. Brilliance and light. Infinite space and distance. In the wild red heart of Australia. At last. I am where I belong. Where I have always belonged.

I can hear and feel an approach now. Feel footsteps reverberating through the dry ground. The tin walls are rattling.

He is standing in the doorway, his slight, but wiry frame made bigger by smallness of the hut, his tee-shirt and shorts covered in a layer of dust reddening his hair which sticks out around his head as if he's been electrocuted, his eyes pale-blue as sky and as distant behind his glasses. I catch all this in half a second, like a drowner, going down, desperately recognises, in one final splashing upsurge, the once-familiar longed-for shore.

'What're you up to?'

'Oh—I'm just reading some of this Pre-Socratic stuff. It seems strangely appropriate out here.'

'Hmmm.' He swings his backpack off his shoulder, onto the floor. The crash resounds through my brain like a pick-axe swinging through my skull. But let us not get too carried away.

'Did you do any painting?' I ask tenderly, encouraging. Nurturing. As was my wont.

'Nah. I went to that cafe on main street next to the supermarket, the one with all that Wild West shoot-out shit on the walls. I wrote a letter to Mars.'

'What?' I cannot help myself. My shock blurts out. Uncool as the day, which is admittedly—in true Australian extremis style—way beyond any such categories. What-the-fuck is he talking about? I find myself gabbling trying to cover up yet still express my horror. I am confused, beginning to whirl.

'Margy?' I didn't know you were still in touch, I mean I didn't know you were still communicating, you told me that you hadn't seen her for ages—You said you weren't together any more.'

He looks at me, eyes bemused behind this season's hip Sydney frames. Or do I just want to see that I've affected him. I'm furious. Suddenly freezing cold despite the ridiculous temperature in the tin hut.

'Why were you writing to Margy, then?' My voice sounds very English, very London, in my ears.

He's sitting down, easing onto the ground, the iron-hard earth that is the floor of the hut. No floor boards for Coober Pedy.

He leans his back against the tin wall and springs forward again immediately. 'Whoa! Hold on there! That's hot!'

'Well?' I ask again, staring at his glasses, trying to see his soul. For I shall know your secrets and I shall understand. And I shall stop at nothing till I know.

'We haven't lived together for months but we still see each other, Ruby.' His tone is casual. 'Mars is my best friend. She's done a lot for me, mate.'

The casual 'normal' Raymond, the social Ray of relation-ship-speak, Ray and 'Mars', is not one I know. The incongruity momentarily winds me.

Best friend. He called her his best friend.

Flies whine through the weight of the silent heat that has suddenly fallen between us, dividing us, splitting us into our separate parts.

All of a sudden, after so many years of imagining this time, through all my intense hidden feelings, it is not 'us' any more in a future dreamland, a vision of golden light in my mind. It is the two of us here in this tin hut. In the here and now. And it is He and Me. Separate. Autonomous. Individual. Alone.

I hold up my left hand, spread my fingers slowly and stare at my hand and arm stretched out above my head.

Hand of Ruby against tin roof.

Ray seen through outstretched fingers of Ruby's left hand.
Margy always was my best friend. Ray was my lover.
I slowly pull my fingers tight
twist into a fist I know is pretty.

Ray's head is in his hands. He looks up suddenly.

My eyes connect, lock with his. Go on; ignore me if you dare —This has to stop. What am I thinking of? My security blanket, Hugo sugar daddy encouraging me to release his tension, in stylised ritual. Every girl should have a—But did I love Hugo, love Sir Hugo? Dependent on him; I was tied to my English gentleman, Old World Establishment heavy, with a pedigree.

Now I'm home I've broken free, at last—to be myself, to

discover and enjoy my own true identity follow my authentic desires. Govern my own life. O my God. It's the heat getting to me.

The heat pressing like hands of the devil squeezing each of my temples in a vice grip, the devil, but I don't believe in the devil, I've never believed in the devil, not since I was a little kid, at Sunday school in Port Hagen, secretly terrified of the stories of sinners, men and women burning in hell, terrified I'd stumble off the path when I grew up and lose the grace of childhood innocence that meant all God's little children went to Heaven. Made me want to stay childlike, innocent, pure, blessed and beloved forever. I haven't believed in the devil since I stopped believing in God. So what's going on now, some primal fear, like a spirit, an Aboriginal rai, stirring in my bones? a furious fear that fills me with energy.

'Let's get out of this place, come on let's go out—into the furnace. I'll buy you a coffee. And I want to see that underground house that's open to the public. Let's see the sights of Coober Pedy!' He stands up. 'Come on: Tourist-ville!!'

Meekly I murmur, 'Uh-huh.' There's a sound like beating wings in my ears. Fruit bats passing in the night. Long dark shadowy shapes flitting through black skies. Screeching and wailing. Jump up, and dust falls out of my clothes. Thick red clouds of finely textured particles rise making me cough, fall, covering my kitten heeled pumps. I put on my sun-hat. An old white canvas thing I found. And follow Ray like a sleepwalker, out into the dissolving world.

We are sitting in the hut. Night-time. Margarita is my best friend. His words are looping through my brain. Flies, mate, buzzing around a corpse. Millions of flies seething black blanket festering over road-kill that litters the edges of the desert highways with stench of rotting death.

Margarita is my best friend, my best friend, best friend...

'So where's Margy living now that she's not living with you, Ray?' I ask casually, looking over to the bunk where he's lying on his back, smoking a joint.

'Ha!' he cackles. 'She's living in a penthouse on George Street. Penthouse death-house...'

He tried to laugh but from the look of sudden blankness that crossed his face I thought he sounded hurt.

'Do you have her address, phone number?'

Margarita

No. 16, The Mayfair, George Street, December 2001

I am developing a routine, a rhythm, living here alone.

It's been four months now; since I left Ray in that cluttered run-down Matraville cottage I shared with him for so many turbulent years. And I can feel myself starting to slip into the solitary self-determined life of a single person with the same 'ah' of satisfaction I feel when I slide into the welcome waters of a warm fragrant bath. Feels like letting go. It feels good.

I hear the cicada sometimes. But it's not bothering me so much. I am developing strategies for dealing with my anxieties.

Like now, as I write this, I am lying on the Sir Hugo velvet couch propped up on silk cushions as the slow haunting first bars of Bach's *Die Kunst der Fuge* drift through the still hot air which presses all around me, all over me, close as a caress against my skin.

As soon as I close the door, I take off my glasses. I strip out of my work clothes, as I do most days now when I get in from the office. Kick off my black sandals. Wriggle out of the black silky skirt, sky blue satin blouse. Then I roll down black sheer tights; first one leg and then the other, pleasing no one but myself. The plump white skin of legs hairless-smooth (recently waxed by Cynthia at Poppets). I run my hands over my calves admiring my slim ankles, the delicate iron-blue swirls of an anklet tattoo on my left ankle. I leave the tights on the polished floorboards, turning towards the wash of bright light pouring through windows which open onto the tiny balcony balanced precariously above the thundering traffic of George Street.

Outside, at eye-level, there is nothing, only buildings on the far side of the street. I am five storeys high. It always gives me a thrill these afternoons, to unhook my bra, twirl it around my head and hurl it to land, draped over the back of the sofa. Free of under-wiring and elastic it's as is my breasts breathe a sigh of relief. As no one can see, I don't need to dim lights or hide behind flattering lingerie. Now I step out of my slip, leave it with my tights, already forgotten on the floor...

I am walking around almost naked, on my own, in someone else's luxury apartment. The delightful sensation of bare feet cool on the clean polished boards, is deliciously shocking as paddling through warm water at the beach after months of socks-and-shoes confinement. It feels so good, it's catching. I want to feel this relaxation more and more; as if the air, close moist humid, stroking and touching my skin is inciting me to passion, I cannot fulfil. I lie on the couch and look up at the walls of photographs covering the walls to the ceiling. My photographs. Black and white shots of the great disappearing trick. Clothed and unclothed (whether she wore clothes or not she always seemed very naked to me). Photos I took in the summer before she left. I have arranged the prints in a circle around a central starting image. Ray's colour study. The image he gave me on an afternoon he came to visit me, long ago.

That had been such a surprise.

I opened the door to see him standing there, bottle of wine in one hand and colour study in the other.

'Came to visit ya sport. Thought you must get lonely here all on your own. Thought I'd come and cheer you up.'

I was holding my violin. I'd been practicing. He sat on the bed and I played him one of the fugues I was working on, my audition piece for the Conservatorium.

He opened the wine, we drank the bottle. I can't remember all we talked about. Just chatted, I guess, about art and music. And Ruby. He said she was difficult to live with. She didn't eat, let alone cook. She was always working, painting or writing. Ignoring him. I sympathised with him. Surprised he was confiding in me, and that they were both confiding in me. I wasn't too happy with Ruby then, not after she let me down the way she did, it was great to have a visitor, someone to talk to, who cared about me, in the Haunted Castle. And that's all we did on that first visit talk.

I was aware of his unexpected new interest in me, which I found exciting and flattering.

I walk into the bathroom. The airy white room is cool and smells of jasmine. I look at my reflection in the mirror, which covers an entire wall. An attractive long-haired woman in her early-thirties stares back. For years, all the time I was with Ruby, I used to think that I was plain, ugly. It's taken a long time for me to be able to see myself as perhaps attractive. Long black hair frames a heart-shaped face, curling over my shoulders to cover breasts. I'm plump, yes, but so what. I've grown to like my thighs and round belly, the softness of my chin. It's only when viewed with a critical eye, that I still sometimes become self-conscious. Ray didn't mind my body at first. 'I like a bit of tummy,' he said. 'I don't like anorexic women.' But in the last few years, for my weight as much as my violin. For anything in the end, before I moved out.

With my right hand I sweep my long black curly hair away from my face; stare into my blue eyes, which I inherited from mother. 'Irish eyes,' she used to say. It's ridiculous. I can't even look at myself in a mirror without thinking of Ray and Ruby: how they saw me. It's as if they're hiding forever within me, as if they've become so deeply a part of 'me,' my sense of self, the image and meaning I have of myself, that I'll never escape their gaze. The subtle imprint of their words. The combined pressures of their touch.

I can hear the cicada starting up again. That all too familiar shriek powering up in my ears, drilling into my brain. Maybe it is a drill, a worker's drill outside in the city street?

They're digging up pavements again in the eternal reconstruction of the face of Sydney's Central Business District, as if everything that is done to tart up this most worked over post-modern of cities is not enough. Sydney's a neurotic glamour queen addicted to cosmetic surgery; the more surgery she has, the more interesting old character is removed, the more superficially blank and 'perfected' she looks, the quicker she has the next operation.

To drown out the drilling I walk to the CD player. Put on Bach's *Art of Fugue*, once more.

As the first haunting bars drift through the hot air I throw myself onto the sofa. I stare up at photographs of bony white limbs spread out on the jagged branches of a fallen ghost gum. The white span of hands flung up to the sky; the sharp angelic arcs of her hipbones.

The humidity is overwhelming, pressing ever more heavily, insistently against my unbearably sensitive skin. I am feverish in the afternoon, alone...where is she? What happened to her?

Images from last night flash through my thoughts. I went to the women's club on my own. It was late-ish around eleven. Too hot, I couldn't sleep. After pacing around the apartment I realised I had to get out into the fresh air. I walked to the club on King Street, through the construction sites on the streets. I feel the exquisitely tender skin of my plump thighs, my calves, my hips, touching the velvet sofa, which holds me like a lover. In the crowded hot shadowy cave of the club I saw a familiar face. It's not long since I've been going to women's bars and clubs, but I have a feeling I could become part of the scene....

Forgotten images flutter and fall through my mind sweet as drifts of rose petals in a summer garden, long ago, at dusk... Muted colours, grape juice mauve, purple wine stains around her lips, wine-black tongue, in the secret garden, as the warm air gives way to the soft velvety enveloping touch of approaching night, the rising full moon casting beams of silvery light. Splashing water sings from a fountain beyond a rose bower, the arbour, and a bench where she sits as I approach down a pebbled path... She's waiting for me, pretending she can't see me.

But I know better and I have ways...

I have means...

I have a bottle of wine to convince her in our secret garden game...

She looks up now and rises swiftly to her feet, she vanishes,

in and out of sight, as she flits down the darkening paths I follow her fleeting form the tantalizing glimpse of ivory-pale skin
floating on the edges of darkness as she disappears into the arbour. The glow of candlelight appears, I walk in, heart-racing
trembling with anxiety. And there she is. A sight that makes it
all worthwhile. The chase, the longing, the fear.

She is stretched out on the cushions of the chaise longue,
Looking at me feigning indifference.

In the light of candles glittering in the candelabra on the
low table, her skin, which was shining silver in the moonlight
now glows golden as honey...

I walk in after her. Put down offerings, wine and armful of
flowers, and a script that I wrote and give to her.

M

She glances at me, looks away. Something else is needed in
this perfect scenario. To bring it alive, make my baby mine...I
find the corkscrew under the chaise longue. Open the wine.
Pour two goblets. I hand one to her and raising our hands in a
solemn toast we drink deeply. I am transfixed by the darkness
of her full lips so near to me.

I lean towards her, touch her cheek with my hand, slide my
hands behind her neck and pull her face, her mouth, and her
lips towards mine. I kiss her gently at first, and then—

—Outside a bell rings and suddenly she jumps up, a strick-
en look on her face. She rushes into the dark garden through
which, I find as I hastily attempt to follow, a wild savage hot
wind is blowing, straight from the deserts of central Australia
hundreds of miles inland to the west. A burning wind, whip-
ping my hair, pushing me backwards until I cannot see where
I am going, where she has gone. And she has gone.

Lost in Newcastle

Hugo

Sydney-Newcastle train, December 2001

I TRAVELLED UP TO NEWCASTLE ON the train. Caught the express at Central at 7:35 a.m. By the time I left the hotel it was already very hot. Maybe it was the humid Sydney climate, or the anxiety, but the skin on my hands and lower arms was itchy and red and already blistering into the lizard scales of the eczema I suffered as a boy, which had not afflicted me since then until now. It was particularly uncomfortable with my arm in a sling. My skin felt as if it were crawling with insects and every movement made me want to scratch but all I could think about was Ruby, and the phone conversations I'd had the previous afternoon, firstly with the Police detectives and then the boy, Alex Robinson, from Newcastle, who may or may not be Ruby's brother, and whom I was now travelling north to meet.

I didn't stop the cab at a chemist to purchase anti-itching unguent; I might have been held up and missed the train. I didn't risk looking for a pharmacy or general store at Central Station to try and find a source of relief, but instead board-ed the waiting train, scratching surreptitiously at the already bloody back of my hand, peeling scaly shreds in-between my fingers. Along with Wittgenstein and Kant, I had brought a few bottles of beer with me, and three or four packets of the Voyager cigarettes which I'd purchased in a couple of duty-free cartons at Sydney airport, to cover our stay in Sydney.

But the moment I lit up with a grateful sigh, even before the train had left, I was accosted by a shrieking wild woman with long dark hair, in a kaftan dress, who shot up out of the row of seats in front of me like a furious puppet-show Judy, demanding to know if I could read.

'Yes, my dear,' I replied evenly. 'I can read and I can also write.'

'Well what does that say?' she demanded stabbing the forefinger of her left hand with what I thought was commendable authority at a small sign that, now I peered through my reading pince-nez, I did notice, thanks to her attentions, attached to the wall at the far end of the carriage, just below the ceiling.

'Oh yes, I see. No Smoking.' I laughed weakly as much as I was capable of laughing under the circumstances. If she hadn't been so energetic and domineering I would not have been able to raise so much as a smile.

But how could I think such things? An image of Ruby, my Ruby, resplendent in her peacock feather mask, whipped my conscience into an instant agony of remorse. I stabbed out my cigarette on the heel of my bespoke brogue, and, itching and scratching, set off to find the smoking carriage.

Every carriage I walked through displayed a No Smoking sign, the ubiquitous icon of our puritanical times. The Health Fascists have wasted no time here I thought grimly as the train took off and I located a uniformed guard in the buffet car.

'I'm looking for the Smoker's carriage,' I said.

'Sorry sir, no smoking in Spirit of Progress.'

'What, not at all?'

'It's against health regulations. This is a non-smoking train.'

'What about drinking? Is one allowed to drink in the Spirit of Progress?'

'You can buy alcoholic and non-alcoholic beverages in the buffet car, along with light meals and refreshments. The buffet car opens in approximately ten minutes time.'

'Thank you.' I'd had enough of his monotonous singsong voice. An alcoholic carriage that's what I needed.

Not being able to smoke, all I could do was scratch. And read. And drink. Where is she? Ruby, what's happened, what's happening to you? Beer was not strong enough. I got through the ten minutes then headed for the buffet car to purchase the first scotch of the journey.

The keen interest I might otherwise have reserved for the passing scenery was submerged by my growing anxiety. As a consequence my thoughts and emotions were removed and detached from the wooded country beyond the window. Still, I gazed into it, blindly, as if hoping to find answers out there, in the strange landscape. What's happening to you, right now?

The train sped over a suspension bridge across the Hawkesbury River's wide estuary—I'd looked it up and remarked on its size to Ruby when I was consulting maps and guides. The train skirted an expanse of water; oyster banks were exposed. All around the inlet, densely forested hillsides sloped at steep angles against a dazzling blue sky.

I scratched my wrists and gazed up into that foreign blue and opened another ridiculously economical bottle of scotch, and for the first time since my gall bladder operation six years ago, almost wished that I believed in a God I could pray to.

Alex

It was me who saw the pictures first and recognised Ruby. For a couple of weeks her face was all over the TV and newspapers, but even so, I don't know if Aphrodite would have recognised her if I hadn't told her, and even then I had to insist that it was her. When I first heard her mentioned it was on the radio. 'London Art Dealer Disappears at Sydney Exhibition Opening,' something like that. I was in the kitchen working on my old mountain bike, getting ready for my next big race, The Cyclops Trials. I was changing the bearings and oiling the brake cables. I thought it sounded a bit weird for some reason, like that Dark Dart hoax a few years ago, when that blonde woman was found tied up on a bed at the side of the highway—claiming she'd been abducted. Police couldn't find any trace of a suspect and it slowly came out that it was a publicity stunt designed to boost the career of some obscure singer.

Anyway that's what came into my head when I first heard the story about the 'contemporary art gallery director,' in Australia on an art collecting trip with her husband, 'the leading English philosopher and peer.'

Then, I was up at the shops getting a coke and half a dozen coconut finger buns (for carbohydrate intake) and I saw the front pages of the evening papers. Big black headlines:

MISSING! BRITISH ART DEALER DISAPPEARS

They're only making such a big deal of it as it's an English aristocrat, I thought. They don't do that for ordinary people. They didn't have media reports when Ruby disappeared ten years ago. There wasn't even a police investigation. It happens all the time…People lose touch with their families, start lives elsewhere…We can put up Missing Person posters, but that's all at this stage… Aphrodite was so upset. A slight to our family, she said. She joined a support group for families of Missing Persons. But it didn't do any real good—nothing ever came of it. Although I used to think it was good for her, it stopped her flipping out altogether, going 'missing' herself, then Harry died in the crash, not that they'd been together for years, and that was that. She's been losing her short-term memory since then.

As I walked past the newsagents I decided to buy a two-dollar Scratch-it. A pile of *Daily Demands* was stacked up on the counter. I handed over my money and took the Scratch-it and as I did so I looked down at the front-page photo and recognised my sister, with the Prime Minister.

It was staggering to see her there. Almost everything about her appearance was different to the sister I remembered. She looked like a Sydney society type in a silk dress. Her face was made up. Hair was long and dark and wavy when it used to just be messy looking. She was standing in between the Prime Minister and a fat chap in a suit, holding a glass and laughing. And I knew it was her.

It was the way that she was laughing that convinced me.

Her head dipped forward slightly, one side of her mouth higher, lop-sided; index and middle finger clutching her ear lobe as if playing with an ear-ring, a habit she developed after a home ear piercing went wrong, leaving Ruby with a small chunk out of her left ear.

'I'll buy the paper too,' I said to Peter behind the counter.

Clutching it tightly in my hand I ran home.

Hugo

I took a taxi outside Broadmeadow Station. 'Rose Street, Adamstown, if you please,' I instructed the driver. No sooner had I fastened my seat belt than the interrogation began.

'You from England?'

'Yes I am,' I replied, scratching absently, gazing out at the wide quiet street. There seemed to be a remarkable amount of space between the buildings and houses, lots of concrete, dazzling in the mid-morning glare, and a few trees.

'Whatcha doin' over here, on holiday?' the driver, a sallow faced, heavily accented fellow seemed intent on establishing a rapport.

'Yes, I suppose you could say that,' I answered; what a holiday this was turning out to be.

'So, you like Astraea do you?'

'Hmm. Oh yes. Wonderful place.'

'So what do you think—the big question, should Astraea be a Republic?' he grinned at me in the mirror.

I stared at the back of his head in disbelief. Did I look as if I wanted to play 'Twenty Questions' with a cabbie? And why was he referring to the Goddess of Justice? He obviously didn't know who he was talking to, or he would not be so familiar. At least in England, cabbies generally recognise me, from my regular appearances on television and the photos above my columns in the *Daily Deliverer* and the *Accord*. I am treated accordingly (usually) with deferential respect. My position in situations like this one is clear and consistent. If the hoi polloi want my opinions on matters of state, they can read my weekly column in the *Accord*. And if that venerable organ is not available here, which would be a surprise as the country is indeed not yet a Republic, well that's hardly my problem.

Of course I thought Australia should be a Republic. If they didn't want us, well we certainly didn't want them either. But I wasn't going to divulge my views to this minion.

I looked out the window, pointedly ignoring his question. My privacy was being invaded. Who did the fellow think he was?

Each street we drove through seemed wider than the last. We drove through acres of brightly painted wooden houses, all perched a few feet above the ground on short wooden legs, and surrounded by extraordinarily stiff looking gardens, the whole expanse glittering in the brilliant sunlight. I had a sudden flash of my dear one in Cleopatra feathers and red stilettos, standing imperiously above me, one leg raised, her knee bent, the pointy heel of the stiletto about to grind down, agonisingly, deliciously, into my unprotected helpless stomach... suspense is terrifying, thrilling... oh my goodness, the thought of her, with someone else... no, no, not good, not at all good. The thought of her being damaged, in any way far worse. I fumbled in my pocket, pulled out the hip flask She gave me, I took a deep swig, sweating copiously, felt very uncomfortable.

Since I'd stopped talking to the driver, dismissed him with my silence, the cab had accelerated and was going unnecessarily fast, lurching recklessly around every corner and bend, so that I was jolted against the door. At least I'd had the foresight to replenish my supply on the train. I needed it now, much needed it. I took a draught and, irritatingly, as we swerved and screeched from one side of the wide empty road to the other for no reason, I bumped my head on the side window.

Soon we were ascending a hill, pulling up with an alarming jolt outside a pink wooden cottage, surrounded by trees.

I paid the driver and gave him a five-dollar tip and walked stiffly towards the pink cottage, which, like a thousand others we'd passed, was set almost on the street, behind a wooden verandah with a paling fence. Given what Ruby had told me about her father, I was more than a little surprised to see the family home. If indeed it was.

Aphrodite

Nothing could have prepared me for that day.

I heard a loud authoritative knock-knock-knocking on our front door and went and opened it and saw this very large, very, you could say, well-dressed man, with his arm in a sling, standing before me, taking up the entire doorway, in his white suit, sweating profusely beneath a Panama hat. Taking out a silk handkerchief to mop his red cheeks and hurriedly stuffing it into his pocket as I opened the door, extending his unslung left hand with flustered politeness.

'Mrs Love, I presume? Good afternoon Sir Hugo Sir Hugo.' His deep bass, very English, voice boomed through the heat of the sweltering afternoon, loud and long as the foghorns of the big container ships on the harbour at night.

'No, I'm not Mrs Love. And I'm not Sir Hugo Sir Hugo, either.' I stared at him in astonishment. 'Who are you?'

Then Alex appeared, took over and explained to Sir Hugo that I was Mrs Robinson, he was Alex, Ruby's brother; and to me that this was Sir Hugo, Ruby's English husband, remember he had told me about him, and to Sir Hugo to come in. He's such a dear boy. Alex. I don't know what I'd do without him. Especially since Ruby disappeared, the first time. (And the second time. Or do I mean the third time? I don't know. How many times did she disappear? I forget these things).

Of course I had always hoped that Ruby would turn up again one day. That's a hope that never dies, no matter how much time goes by. When a child goes missing you never lose hope. But what I certainly didn't ever expect was that a strange man claiming to be her husband would turn up instead. Especially a husband like Sir Hugo. So English and large.

Alex led the way down the hall followed by myself and the English gentleman (I couldn't see them together) whose huffing and puffing was quite audible.

'I don't quite get it,' Alex said over his shoulder. 'Where did you say you met Ruby?'

'Ruby was a student in my aesthetics class at Prince's College,' Sir Hugo boomed.

'Aesthetics. Ruby was studying philosophy?' Alex sounded surprised.

'Come and sit beside the fan, Hugo,' I said. 'I can see you're not used to the heat. You must be uncomfortable in that suit! And your arm!' (He was closer in age to me than Ruby).

'She certainly did,' said Hugo. 'She studied it very well. A most diligent and I might add, delightful, student. A pleasure to teach. Hrmphh!' he cleared his throat noisily. Alcoholic fumes swept through the room. A truly extraordinary match. He must have made a mistake, the missing Ruby he was married to could not be my Ruby.

'In London?' asked Alex.

'Yes, of course, in London. Where else. Prince's College, London.' Ruby's so-called husband said, sitting down heavily in one of my gold and pink brocade 'Sun King' chairs.

The fat alcoholic only just fitted into it.

'But how can we be sure that my daughter Ruby is your wife?' I said, this character wasn't going to get away with conning me in my own salon. The visitor was staring around the living room as if in some kind of a daze.

I watched his swivelling eyes, his sweaty face, surreptitiously, in my favourite mirror, a gilt-framed cherub encrusted oval above the fireplace. A scaled-down reproduction of a mirror in Louis XVI's own bedroom in the Palace of Versailles. From where I sat on the crimson, pink and white striped loveseat I had an excellent hidden view of his reflection.

'Here, we are. The family photo albums.' Alex had brought a stack of albums from the bookshelves. He opened one up.

'Look, Sir Hugo—here's Ruby, down at the Farm, that's her first horse she's riding, that's Pluto, isn't it, Mum? She would have been about sixteen here, and here she is with Margarita, swimming in the dam—we'd just had that dam dug out, up above the house, to water the trees in the orchard we planted. We were filling it up for the first time, it was like a mud-bath, Mum, remember, the sides were so steep it was the best mud slide, we pumped the water from the river...' The stranger was staring at the photos of Ruby at the Farm as if he couldn't believe his eyes. My daughter was obviously not his wife.

'That's her, that's Ruby, alright,' he said in a relatively quieter tone. 'The way she's riding that pony, that straight back, her perfect seat. So proud.'

'Here's my daughter in my garden in the house in Glebe, in the university holidays, she would have been, what, twenty-one, twenty-two—'

'That's her,' he said again, fumbling in his pocket.

'Look here,' he boomed bringing out a black leather wallet.

'I have a couple of photos of Ruby myself. Would you care to compare?' He flicked open his wallet, pulled out a couple of snaps and passed them to me.

'That's my sister,' said Alex excitedly.

'Her face looks similar, but Ruby never looked like that.' I remonstrated. Was he mad? The sophisticated young woman in the photo was wearing a slinky leopard skin gown and some kind of extraordinary *haute couture* feathered headwear. Her face was heavily made-up, painted or powdered gold, her eyes were ringed with thick black lines like Queen Nefertiti and she was holding a small oar. I laughed dryly.

'No I'm sorry, you're quite wrong. This is all a mistake. It's a case of mistaken identity. Ruby never dressed like that. She always wore those awful old army-surplus things. And she never went rowing.'

'Aphrodite,' Alex said again, giving me one of his warning looks. 'Aphrodite's losing her short term memory and she gets a bit confused—' he smiled at me reassuringly. Before I could say anything he added, 'I'll make some tea, you sit down Aphrodite.'

'Sure she wore grungy stuff in the last couple of years before she disappeared,' Alex continued, talking very loudly, as he walked into the open plan kitchen area and turned on the electric jug. 'When she was at Art School. But when she was younger she and Margarita always really dressed up, remember?'

'Margarita?' said Sir Hugo. 'Is there a sister, too?'

'Yes, there is, but it's not Margarita. Lily is my other daughter. Margarita is Ruby's friend,' I said. 'They're so close people used to think they were sisters. Or lesbians,' I laughed.

'Aphrodite!' Alex was glaring openly at me.

'Oh Alex, loosen up, where's your sense of humour?' I chided him, turning to look at Sir Hugo in the flesh. 'Do you have any children?'

'No,' he said slowly, scratching his wrists, unpleasant habit. 'Ruby wanted to wait a while until the Gallery was established as she put it. Poor girl she worked so hard. I couldn't get her to stop working.'

'That's it— you can't be married to my daughter.' I said. 'Ruby could never have worked in business, she was an artist. Let alone work hard. And she didn't like art dealers. She used to say they exploited artists, ripped them off and made profits while artists, the producers, starved. She was a Marxist, like her father. Didn't like yuppies, eh Alex? Ruby will have told you about her father, Harry.'

'Oh yes. He was a property developer,' Sir Hugo said.

'A property developer? What are you talking about? Harry was an economist and a diplomat. He worked for the Australian government. Harry was killed in a car crash three years ago.'

I dabbed at my eyes with the hanky I always carry tucked into the wrist of my long sleeved sun-protection shirt.

'I'm sorry,' said Sir Hugo, looking dazed, wiping his brow with a red and white spotted handkerchief, which he pulled out from the pocket of his voluminous white Oxford bags.

'There's been so much loss in the family. First Lily moved to Iceland. Then Ruby disappeared. Then my parents died, and Aunty Vera, then Harry, but he'd already left us anyway. Now Alex and I have only got each other.'

'But, now we'll have Ruby again,' Alex said coming in with the tray and setting it down on the coffee table Harry built for me himself, from recycled jarrah, when we were first married.

His hobby was carpentry, as mine was raku pottery. After he left I never threw another pot. 'We've found her, Aphrodite, remember, that's why Sir Hugo's here. He's Ruby's husband! She's alive and well after all!'

'Well let's hope so,' said Sir Hugo. 'Let's hope the dear girl is alive and well. That's why I'm here after all. To meet you of course, and to try and find some clues that might help us find her.'

'Dear girl,' I repeated his words slowly. 'Do you love my daughter, Sir Hugo?' I looked at him directly for the first time. In the eyes. They were small heavily-lidded eyes, it was impossible to tell the colour behind his glasses. He could have been seen as an attractive man although very ample in proportion, and he was extremely well dressed. Over-dressed.

'I'm devoted to her, Aphrodite, in ways I could not even begin to explain.'

'Hmmm. Well you certainly look different to the louts she used to get involved with,' I said, slowly. 'She used to go crazy over them, but I don't think they ever thought that much of her. Wouldn't have carried on the way they did, in public, if they had.'

'Harrumph,' Sir Hugo cleared his throat loudly. 'Does Margarita live in Newcastle?'

'No, she's still in Sydney. She was living with Raymond for a long time. But she finally managed to get rid of him. I think she's living on her own now.'

'Raymond?'

'Her boyfriend. Used to be Ruby's boyfriend too, a long time ago. One of Ruby's hopeless cases, although he settled down a lot with Margarita. Now there's a girl with a head on her shoulders.'

'Could I have her address?' Hugo asked loudly. 'I'll go and visit her. She might have something, some information, a clue maybe to help give us an idea of where Ruby might be.'

'Could you get me my handbags, please, Alex?'

It can take a while to find people's details when you have handbags, with address books dating back over many years. Alex brought me my red leather Louis Vesey, my gold quilted Channel, and my black patent leather Gutty.

While I searched for the right address book, Sir Hugo and Alex continued talking.

'Did you say Ruby went to Art School?' Sir Hugo asked.

'For a couple of years, then she dropped out. We've still got a stack of her paintings in the Red Room.'

'Her bedroom,' said Sir Hugo quietly.

'No. We call it the Red Room because of the curtains and the carpet. Ruby never lived here. Mum and I moved up here from Sydney after Dad died. Mum didn't want to stay in the old house in Glebe. This is where you grew up, isn't it Aphrodite? In Adamstown. When I started going to the University Aphrodite moved up here too.'

'Margarita Minski. She was related to Randolph Sterner, you know, the educationist. That's where she and Ruby met. At the Sterner School in Phoenix Street. Ruby and Lily and Alex started going there after we came back from Papua New Guinea. Her father was the sweetest man. A violinist. Well of course Margarita plays violin, but he had been a master. It was a tragedy. He was so poor. He'd been a solo violinist in the Berlin Philharmonic. But he never fully recovered from being in a concentration camp. He worked as a street cleaner and played his violin, busking on the streets, and he managed to put Margarita, his only child, through the Randolph Sterner

School. He had such nobility of spirit. Gus Minski.' I fumbled with my cuff but the hanky seemed to be stuck.

'Would you like to see Ruby's paintings, Hugo?' Alex said, too brightly. What was the boy so uptight about? 'Mum, it's because of Ruby, that Sir Hugo's here. Ruby, remember? We're trying to find Ruby.'

'Well that's nothing new. We've been trying to find Ruby for years,' I muttered, angry suddenly at disrespect, his disregard for the past. The stories that are so important. The stories of my life… Of our life, family, and of Margarita's life, and of her family… After all, she was practically my third daughter. Making up for Lily when she left for Iceland and then Ruby when she vanished. Not that Ruby and I had ever been close anyway, I always felt as if Margarita was the kind of daughter I was supposed to have. She was sensible, she had a practical intelligence. Ruby was Harry's daughter. She had that larrikin streak of his I used to love and came to regret deeply.

'Yes, I would much like to see Ruby's pictures, very much indeed,' boomed the usurper in the suit, pushing himself up out of the Sun King chair with difficulty, with one arm. Such a carrying bass voice. I never liked any of Ruby's boyfriends. Even though he looked and sounded different, I couldn't bring myself to like this man who claimed to be her husband, either.

When he left, at last, he took half a dozen or so of Ruby's old paintings with him. Alex said he could have them. I wasn't sure, but Alex said it was okay. It was all 'in the family.' They'd been cluttering up the spare room for years, anyway, I'd just never known what to do with them.

Margarita's Metronome

Ruby

'MANGURI STATION TO SYDNEY'LL TAKE YOU two to three days travelling on Spirit of Progress trains. You need to book three tickets 'cause you've got three legs—'

Got three legs, what was the woman talking about?

'You've got the Manguri to Adelaide Bedouin Express; then Adelaide to Melbourne; then Melbourne to Sydney Express. The trains have private sleeping compartments. First class or economy?'

Through a ticket window festooned with tinsel, the ticket seller's high-pitched voice sounded suddenly far away. Was it really almost Christmas?

I had a vague sense of unreality exacerbated by the intense heat. I had caught a coach from Coober Pedy to catch a train here. In all directions the desert stretched shimmering apricot and violet hues in the early evening light. There was nothing at Manguri Station but a railway station and train-line. I was lucky, the train passed through here twice a week. I had just caught the coach in Coober; pulling out, it stopped for me as I arrived, breathless and streaming with sweat from walking from the tin shed campsite.

It was a fifty kilometres drive across the Simpson.

'Credit card or cash?' I noticed she was suddenly looking at me more intently. That shocked me into the present tense,

'Cash,' I shook hair over my face as I reached for my purse. 'Could I have a look at that timetable so I can work out which tickets to book? I want to get to Sydney as soon as possible.'

The Bedouin to Adelaide was due in less than an hour so I didn't have much time to kill, mooching around in the empty waiting room, strolling the platform, sitting on a green painted bench, gazing out at the desert and a passing camel. When it rolled into the station I couldn't get into its air-conditioned comfort, its promise of escape, quickly enough.

Raymond had given me the address of the apartment on George Street where Margy was staying. I'd decided not to let him know. I left him sleeping. After he'd slipped me that drug I felt no moral compunction to let him know what I was doing. And I'd decided not to contact her before I arrived. I planned to go straight to her apartment and surprise her, as she'd surprised me once, long ago. I'd seen the newspaper headlines as I walked up the main street in Coober Pedy, toiling under the blazing sun. I was being searched for, hunted. I couldn't jeopardize my plan to meet my friend, by ringing her. Who knows? She might tell someone. After being lost for so long I was not ready to be found quite yet.

As things were I didn't think there was too much likelihood of being spotted. Appearance-wise I was surely unrecognisable now as being the same woman in the press shots. The photos I'd seen splashed all over the newsstands were of me at DOG. I am standing with the Prime Minister, laughing, glass of wine in hand. In the background, over the P.M.'s left shoulder, Raymond is visible, in the vanishing point, standing in a doorway at the top of a small flight of stairs. In the photo my hair is styled. I'm wearing the Edwardian frock, I look like a professional gallery director, a million miles from where I am now: sitting in the train carriage wearing Ray's old jeans (too big) and his tee-shirt (big, none-too-clean). I'd also borrowed his big black hat which I wore low on my forehead, the rim pulled down, concealing my face. I hadn't washed my hair it was still caked in thick dust from the campsite. I kept my hair pulled forward over half my face, stiff ochre curtains, and when anyone came near me I lowered my head.

When I looked at myself in the mirror above the wash-hand basin in the bathroom, I almost fainted. Who was that witch from the west? I'd decided not to wear make-up. As I usually wore a heavy mask of cosmetics, my natural face was hard enough to recognise at the best of times. But the face that stared back at me now from the mirror was the face of a wild woman. A feral. I looked a fright. My skin was burnt red from the desert sun. My lips were blistered. Nose peeling. My eyes were wide and blood shot as if I was still under the influence of Ray's drugs, which I certainly was not. I never wanted to take another drug again in my life. Not even head-ache pills. I was using the time on the train to come down, unwind, and try to get thoughts together after the desert, after Ray. But it wasn't really working too well. My mind felt like it had been sand-blasted out there, my mental scenery had been re-arranged, I was still trying to find my way around the new landscape; bumping into things, confused.

Hugo? Every now and then loose thoughts of my husband came to mind, but it seemed impossible to place him in this picture at the present.

All I could think about was Margy, seeing Margy, my old

best friend. I was speeding towards Margy with a steady sway-
ing forward motion, looking out of the train windows at the
desert, Australia my country to which I had for once and for
all returned. Had she changed? Did she still play the violin?
Was she as bossy and as funny? Did she still smell the same?
That musky fragrance, the natural perfume of her skin that I
used to love.

As I remember Margarita, the sound of her violin swirls
through the still air. I can hear her playing that old sweet song,
that beautiful long lost fugue she used to play. I close my eyes.

I'm awoken by the sound of chewing in my ear. A strange
woman has taken the empty seat next to me.

I glance over and notice that there is a tabloid newspaper
open on her knees but she is not reading, she is eating.

I notice with shock there is an image of myself on the
open page. I look away heart pounding, keep my head turned
down. She is eating chocolate. I can hear the twisting of crin-
kly foil breaking off squares.

I look out the window. The desert shimmers in the heat.
High in the steel-blue sky white clouds roll and twist, puff and
drift in formations that make Dali look like photo-realism.

In between breaking off her squares I can feel her turning
and I imagine smiling in my direction. Any minute now she
might offer me a piece of chocolate. She will look at the newspaper, and see my face. I have to move.

I prepare my getaway. I seize the straps of my backpack and
pull a swatch of hair over my face holding it in place.

'Excuse me,' I walk past her.

Find a window seat, take a deep breath. When the adrena-
lin has abated, I sleep.

I open my eyes to see a group of camels ambling next to

the train. The flat landscape is beginning to give way to small ripples; ochre ground tinged faintly with green. The railway track veers close to a road. I stare in wonder.

Against the skyline I can see half a house, on a truck, being driven through the desert.

Where's it going to, on the way to where? I wonder. Looking for its other half?

I drift back into sleep again.

The train arrives in Adelaide at 4:20 p.m.

I have two hours to wait for the Melbourne connection. I wander around the station remembering the last time I was here. The memory is ringed in my mind with an air of pointless inevitability, the silent drive from Brighton to the station, none of us with anything to say. Nothing we were able to say anyway. The long afternoon of anti-climax. Having little time. Raymond carrying my bags. Margy looking worried, hurrying along beside. Getting onto the train, for once I am unable to make light of it, unable to come up with a quip. Not knowing what's happened, or happening and yet knowing exactly what I am doing. Getting out of there, away from them. Leaving it all behind. What? Without consciously knowing it, it's as if I am trying to run away from the future, the future that is now. The image of the two of them standing next to each other on the platform as the train begins to pull out of the station, Ray wearing his white jeans, blue jumper, looking forlorn; Margy in her 40's vamp dress, tap-dancing shoes. The last thing that I saw I focused on. The fingers of his hand fluttering like petals of a rose blowing in the wind.

I walk past newsstands where my photograph is displayed and keep my head turned to the ground.

When the Melbourne train arrives I embark immediately, find my private sleeping compartment, put down my luggage, close the door. I feel completely exhausted. Although I slept for hours on the last train, all I want to do is sleep again now. I lie down, close my eyes and descend into oblivion.

I open my eyes. I have a strange sense of déjà vu. Through the window, see rolling wheat fields of the southern Hay Plains, shining incandescently, like a sea of gold, in the evening light.

How many times did I cross the plains with Wolfie on the bike? Once in the huge quiet dark of night when the wheat fields shone silver in the light of a high bright full moon; in the brilliant golden heat of a long afternoon, when the steady roar of the engine and the dazzling glare of the road fused together into what seemed like a never-ending line, the receding line of the endless road pulling us onwards, forever onwards, into an immense mysterious future. As if we would always be young and free like this, racing towards the horizon, the wind pulling against us, the smell of the land in our nostrils, intoxicating and exotic. As if it could never end.

My throat is parched, my veins feel dried out, and my skin is dry and itchy as if I've been burnt, my inner-body lasered. I need to drink. Feels like my body's filled with toxins, which I have an overpowering urge to flush out, be rid of. I get up and head for the buffet car where I join a queue waiting to be served at a snacks counter.

As I wait my turn, leaning against the wall of the compartment, a man comes up behind me.

'This is the buffet I take it,' his voice is soft, evenly pitched.

'Yes,' I turn towards him as I answer. He is probably about forty, an attractive man with piercing blue eyes. He is staring at me intently. I quickly look away, turning my back on him.

Of course he couldn't have recognised me, I tell myself. No one could. I look horrendous, and don't feel too much better.

'I'll have a bottle of orange juice and two bottles of mineral water, and a white coffee, thanks.'

I take my fluids and head back to my private space, walking speedily with my head down. After drinking the bottles of water and coffee I decide to save the juice for later. I take off my bra under the tee shirt, pulling it out through one of the armholes, as if I'm changing on the beach, take off Ray's jeans.

I pull the bed out of the wall, clamber onto its cushioned surface, turn out the light and fall immediately into another deep sleep.

The train pulls into the Spencer Street station, Melbourne, at 7:45 a.m. I get off well rested after a night's sleep in my private compartment. But I have to hurry. There are only fifteen minutes before the next train goes from platform four, at the far side of the station. As I am walking through the main concourse I pass several newsstands. I can't believe it. My photo is still stuck up on one of them. Isn't anything more important happening? I glance up and there is a man staring at me. It is the same man with blue eyes who had been staring at me on the train.

'Excuse me,' he says coming towards me holding a guitar case in his hand. All I can think of is flight. Run Ruby run. I grab the straps of my pack and take off through the hurrying milling people, run helter-skelter out onto the street, past the taxi ranks, down a slope onto the main street where I race into a bar. I hide out in the ladies long enough for my heart to stop pounding and then some more.

By the time I feel safe enough to leave the toilets and head back up the street to the station I've missed the train.

Raymond

She'd done it again. Left me.

Upped and disappeared, leaving me alone in a tin hut in the middle of the blazing hot desert, a tin can heating up to incendiary point.

So much for her claims to have become another person; some things might have changed for her but she was still the same old Ruby. I could never understand her, figure out her moves. She could at least have stayed another three days till Bob returned in the plane. Could have flown her back to Sydney in style.

I drank another jar of water, the fifth in as many minutes. Sweat was pouring, running down my face, covering my body in sticky itchy moisture. No matter how much I drank, water didn't quench thirst. I picked up my old backpack and pulled out my visual dairy. Flipped it open at the sketch I'd done of Rube as she was sleeping the night before.

I was pleased with the image of her body sprawled across the bunk bed, half wrapped in a sheet. Long hair half-covering her face, arm thrown up behind her head. The soft texture of the ochre and white pastels which I used as I drew her, the angular planes and concave-convex dips, so satisfying to draw. She looked no different to when I had first met her. But she was unrecognisable as the sophisticate I had locked eyes with at DOG. I captured the Rube I knew and loved as she slept.

After all these years I didn't want to lose her. I didn't want her to disappear, to leave me, like Mars. I couldn't let it happen. And what would happen to her out there, face plastered across every newsstand in the land? I would follow her, go after her. The way she turned up like that from out of nowhere.

I reckon that was destiny at work. Our destiny.

I packed my bags and walked to the pub where I made a phone call to Bob on his mobile in Perth, cancelling. The next train left at 7.30 in the evening.

I arrived from Adelaide with approximately ten and a half hours to kill in Melbourne. What the hell to do? One thing was for sure I wasn't hanging around in the station.

Margarita

I had finally taken the plunge and had my hair cut.

On my way home from work, instead of turning the usual way down Broadway after leaving the university I crossed over the road and kept walking straight down Glebe Point Road. I reached a salon of women with very short crops or buzz cuts. It seemed almost obligatory these days for female hair stylists, in salons to have shaved heads. I would go in there and get it done, now.

I sat in the chair staring at my reflection. The woman behind me, whose hands roughly smoothed my hair was wearing that season's inner-city dyke's uniform: a black short-sleeved tee shirt, sleeved tattoos, dark indigo jeans, studs through nostrils. A small chain dangled, jangling, from rings in her nose to rings in her ear. When she was drying my hair, she banged my head assertively with the blow dryer like it was cool. She picked up the scissors and made the first cut at the nape of my neck. A twelve-inch tress of thick black hair fell to the ground. Snip-snip-snip, all the way around the nape of my neck. No doubt they sell the hair for wigs, I thought. My hair will probably end up shaking down the street in Mardi Gras.

In just under an hour I emerged, blinking, into the street.

Gone were waist length curly locks, in their place was a sharp crop. I glanced at my reflection in shop windows as I walked back to the apartment. Who was that elegant stranger with the angular profile? Despite the plumpness of my body, my newly exposed jaw was surprisingly chiselled, matching the sharp straight lines of my nose and high forehead. I felt pleased with my new appearance. The warm evening breeze caressed the naked nape of my neck. My head felt deliciously light. It felt as if a huge weight had fallen from me, which it had. My hair had gone. My hair, which had held the past within it like a shroud. My hair, which had held his kisses and his rough angry hands. I felt light and free as if I'd escaped, as if—with a few clean cuts—I could leave the past, and Raymond, behind.

Two days later a feeling of light optimism, excitement remains.

Now when I come home from work, and look at myself in the mirror, I am looking at M. A different person. That sexy vulnerable female self trashed and abused by Ray has gone. If he saw me, I am convinced he would not be attracted to me, he might even be intimidated by me, now I've finally got the haircut to match my suit. Now I look so much like a dyke.

I put up my hand, run it over my scalp, through the short stiff bristles of my hair, over and over again.

Ruby

I left the station.

Turned left, as if following some old automatic imperative, letting my feet walk and find the way. Of course, this was the way I walked when I was staying with Margy. When she lived in that converted stable in the back of Brunswick, and I was studying in Adelaide. I would always walk to her place from the station, to get the exercise, after the long muscle-cramping overnight train (no sleeping compartments). I found myself walking through streets I remembered as if from a dream, following a once-familiar route without thinking. My feet remembered, they were taking me there. It was a very hot dry morning. I was covered in sweat in no time...

As I walked, breathing heavily, a visual track of long forgotten events swirled through my thoughts as if emerging from the mists of time; or, like a transfer, revealing shape and form, beneath a soft persistent rubbing; just the right amount of pressure will yield a perfect image...

That time Ray and I spent in Margy's stable in the heatwave summer. How I'd been going to go with him to the rainforest outside Grafton, and then didn't. If I'd gone with Ray, everything would have been different, our relationship would have had a chance to grow strong and healthy, without being destroyed by fatal confusion, passivity, of those swelteringly hot days...

I remember his departure. He caught the train back to Adelaide, alone. I said good-bye at the station with a confused mixture of longing and regret.

Why couldn't I just go with him? Why couldn't I tell him I'd go to his cousin's? Why couldn't I tell him what I really thought, and act on it?

Why did I feel so torn?

As I reached the turning to Margy's old street, as I walked past the traffic island where Ray and I lay on a summer's night long ago, the answers come to me, ten years too late, ricocheting through my body into my mind with the deadly force of absolute certainty.

It was because of Margy I was confused. It was because of her I wasn't with Ray, that I didn't spend the whole summer with him, living simply, as nature intended, frolicking like Rousseau's noble savages, eating fruit and making babies in the sub-tropical paradise. Margy made me feel too guilty to leave her and simply go off with Ray, which was what I always wanted to do. Margy was jealous. Margy was plotting. So that she could have Ray to herself.

By the time I reach the entrance to the stable-yard complex where she used to live, I am dripping with sweat. My back is aching from the weight of the pack; my shoulder screams with the pain of my bag. But none of that means anything to me.

When I thought Margy was my closest friend, she was secretly scheming to steal my boyfriend. No wonder everything went wrong between Ray and me. What was she saying to him? She was obviously putting him off, turning him against me. One night we went to see a movie together, *Les Enfants du Paradis,* afterwards when we drove her home, because of her helpless female act and talk of drunks in the doorways, he walked her back up to her apartment, leaving me in the car. Things would never have gone off the rails the way they did after that, if it wasn't for her. And her helpless female games. Doing all she could to make me look bad for 'abandoning' her for him, and making him feel sorry for her, so he felt he had to take care of her.

I take one look at the gate that led into the stable-apartments. How I used to visit her there, that time I spent there with Ray, both of us in her bed, me never suspecting a thing. I spit in disgust and turn and walk away.

I spend all day walking the streets, sweat pouring from my face and body like rivers pumped from an inner estuary of my being. My thoughts are confused, swollen. Colours seem too bright and the light is always dazzling.

Raymond

I can do it. Give up drugs. Give up drinking. Not even tea or coffee. Every day will run to fine order. I will create Art from purity, where excess has failed. Lose weight and gain health. Drive a cab, good money. Long walks. Maybe join a gym. With Ruby by my side, on matching treadmills, we can begin again, one step at a time.

Ruby

The train ride to Sydney seemed to pass in no time.

Again I'd booked a private sleeping compartment. I fell asleep after the train left Spencer Street station. But whereas my sleep on the train from Adelaide to Melbourne had been deep and peaceful, this was a night of fast exhausting dreams. In my dreams I was running, running, running away from a force, a dark stranger. I was terrified but I couldn't run straight, I kept running round and around in circles, kept finding myself back at the point I'd started from. I woke just before dawn with the same furious energy powering through my veins. I was buzzing with adrenaline, watching dawn lighting the sky.

The bush looked increasingly grubby and denuded and it wasn't long before the first straggling wooden houses of Sydney's outer sprawl came into view. An hour later I was getting off the train at Central Station. It was 6:45 a.m.

M

I am floating in the delicious shadow-lands between sleep and waking when the doorbell rings.

Go away, I tell it; I'm not going to answer.

But the ringing doesn't stop. It's so persistent. Worse than that cicada boring through my brain. Whoever it is wants to make contact. I rise reluctantly, head spinning with the effort and walk over to the intercom by the front door.

'Hello?' I run my fingers absently through my spiky hair.

'Margy?' The voice is strangely familiar. It can't be.

Suddenly my senses are on full alert.

'Yes?'

'It's Ruby. Can you let me in?'

Ruby

The intercom buzzed and the glass doors of the building unlocked. The Mayfair was a contemporary Nouveau apartment building. The entrance foyer was large and spacious with mirrored walls and a sparkling chandelier suspended from the high ceiling.

An image of the entrance to the Haunted Castle flashed into my mind as I waited for the lift. The downstairs hallway had stunk of stale cigarette smoke and mould, a public phone was bolted onto the wall. Sunken men in ragged clothes had drifted like ghosts up and down the stairs.

Margarita's come a long way, I thought looking at my ravaged reflection in the wall mirrors. Looking as I did, I could well have come straight from there, as if years had not passed. But I look a lot more dishevelled and feral now than I'm sure

I did then. The doors to the lift slide open, and I step into the suave interior. It's on the sixth floor, she'd said. Number 16.

As the lift begins its smooth ascent, an anecdote Margarita told me many years ago, flashes into my mind. It was when we were both living in the Haunted Castle, that brief frantic highly pressured short time we spent together. The only time we ever lived together. It was when things had started to go off the rails between us, although I didn't know that then. All I knew was that she in a very stroppy mood; she was treating me with coldness that bordered on cruelty, as if she was playing with me, which of course, with the benefit of hindsight, I know she was.

She'd been playing violin, as she always did. I had finally got her to talk to me. I'd asked her about what she was playing and for once she'd not ignored me or dismissed me with a brusque put-down disguised as a 'joke' about my musical ignorance.

She told me a story about a piece of music known as the Unfinished Fugue, the title still sticks in my mind—and its composer, Bach. She'd told me about Bach's supposed interest in the power of numbers.

She even showed me a numerology or gematria chart she had drawn:

```
A=1  E=5  I/J=9  N=13  R=17  W=21
B=2  F=6  K=10   O=14  S=18  X=22
C=3  G=7  L=11   P=15  T=19  Y=23
D=4  H=8  M=12   Q=16  U/V=20  Z=24
```

'The working title in the printed edition although not the autograph, was *Fuga a Tre Soggetti*, fugue from three subjects, in Italian.

Scholars are still trying to solve the puzzle it left. For a start they are not sure if it was meant to be for three or four themes, the fourth would have been the *Art of Fugue* theme,' she said.

She told me how Bach transcribed the letters of his name into a melody line of musical notes, his signature:

'B flat-A-C-H. H is B natural in German,' she said.

'He was introducing his name, as a countersubject into the fugue. He was coding his name into the music. In numerology the letters of his name are: B-2; A-1; C-3; H-8. Adding up to 41. And 4 + 1 = 5. He was writing his name on bar 239.

2 + 3 + 9 = 14. 4 + 1 = 5 his 'magical' number, of his name, his self-reflexive occult number.

He chose to do this, symbolically, in his fourteenth fugue in the *Art of Fugue* cycle. 1 + 4 = 5.

As he was writing his name into the fugue he had a stroke, went blind and died, that's why it is unfinished.

His son Carl Philipp Emanuel wrote on the score: while he was working on the fugue, where he introduced the name BACH as a countersubject, the author, or composer, died.'[10]

She knew the quote by heart. I was impressed.

'Must have been pretty dangerous music,' I said, trying to make her smile. 'You'd better be careful...'

But she hadn't smiled she'd just picked up her bow, tossed her black hair over her shoulders with a disdainful frown; and resumed her eternal practicing.

I am leaning against the steel handrail in the lift, gripping onto its cool surface to steady myself. My mind is sliding giddily; I have to stop myself from falling. I can hear music now; echoing and swirling crazily round my head. I have an idea that when she opens the door she'll be wearing that old black silk slip, that Aphrodite gave her, that she always wore.

Holding her violin.

The lift stops with a slight bumping motion and the doors slide open. I step out into the luxurious carpeted hallway of the sixth floor. Number six, what's that supposed to mean in classical musician numerology, I wonder. Six, six, think back, a long time ago, when I was about twelve years old, read about that kind of thing. Six, connected to Venus, supposed to be the planet of love...and what is the number of the apartment? Sixteen. One plus six equals... seven. Isn't that supposed to be a mystical number?

At the moment of attaining self reference in music, Bach died. Whoever knows what is going to happen.

I walk straight up to the door, emblazoned with the elegant black numerals 1 and 6. I knock, three times.

The door opens.

'Hi,' I say, doing a double take. Cropped spiky hair, plumper than I recall, wrapped in a pale pink satin robe, looking disconcertingly mature, Margarita is staring at me in bemusement.

'Ruby—what's happened to you? You look as if you've been dragged through a hedge backwards.'

I try to smile. 'I've been in the desert.'

'Which desert?' She was always particular. But she's standing there holding the door as if she might slam it shut in my face any minute. 'Where have you been? What are you doing? Where have you come from?'

'It's a long story, probably too long. Are you going to let me come in?'

We are sitting on the sofa. She has made coffee. I have told her I've been living in London. I've come back for a holiday. She doesn't need to know more than that.

'It's just as well it's Saturday, or I would have had to go to work,' she says, making conversation.

'Work? What do you do?'

'I work in admin. At City university,' she says.

I laugh politely.

'What about you,' she says defensively. 'Still painting?'

'Only in my head.' I gaze ahead of me to the large windows, which give onto a view of windows in the buildings on the other side of the street. I can just make out people in the opposite windows.

'Have you been following the news?' I ask casually.

'No, I've been trying to cut myself off from the world for a while. That's why I'm here. I'm in recovery,' she says.

I breathe a private sigh of relief.

'Recovery from what?' I ask, staring in slight surprise at the photos of myself, arranged in a large mandala shape around a central image, which I recognise as one of the colour studies Ray used to make.

'The relationship with Raymond,' she says. 'It just got so bad. He treated me so badly. He went right off the rails. I can understand why you were scared of him. You were wise to get out when you did.'

Wise to get out when you did... I don't say anything. No words can adequately compensate for the huge yawning gulf that exists between experience, understanding and perceptions now. The fact that my whole life since then has been predicated on that unbearable sense of loss—wisdom scarcely—

23 224 225 226 227 228 229 230 231 232 233 234 235 236 237 238 239 240 241 242 243 244 245 246 247 248 282 492????????????
???????????????????????????????????—

I notice that she is sitting very close to me. Uncomfortably close. I look around me at the huge airy room with its polished blonde boards, its contemporary chic furniture, and walls hung with Art. Yes, Margarita has done pretty well for herself in admin, I think. She's done well all round. Despite what she says about 'abuse'.

'Ruby, you look like you really need a shower, would you like one?'

'Yes, I'd love a shower,' I say. It's been days since I last had a shower. How many? The last shower I had was at the Hotel with Hugo, the day I met Raymond. It must be five or six days ago. It seems like an eternity, infinity separates me from then, a length of time, nebulous and definite as the boundary between two worlds.

'It's this way,' she says, standing up and leading me to the bathroom.

The hot water cascades over my head, the nape of my neck, my shoulders and my back. But I can't relax. The water washes away the dust, the sweat, the grime but it doesn't wash away the tension, which is increasing the longer I'm in her flat.

I step out and wrap myself in a fluffy white spotlessly clean towel she has left for me. The blue and white striped towels in the en-suite of the bedroom in our house in Primrose Hill flash into my mind. That life seemed unreal. This is my real life. This is I. This is the real Ruby, the scorned point in the triangle of Ruby-Raymond-Margy. What she's said about 'abuse' doesn't exactly tie in with what he told me about Margy being his 'best friend.' She's obviously lying to me, to try and make me feel better, appease me. A hot, focused, high-tensile anger is powering through my veins. I walk out into the living room.

'How do you feel?' she asks, looking at me very intently.

'I'm really tired actually.'

'Why don't you have a rest, you can sleep on my bed? It's through here.'

She gets up and walks past me, brushing against me. I follow her meekly past the downstairs bathroom up a flight of stairs. There is a huge gilt framed mirror on the small landing, I watch us ascend, first Margy then me, and then we're turning the corner up another small flight of stairs and she's taking me into her bedroom.

Her violin is sitting on a dressing table. There is a music stand next to it with sheet music propped open. On top of a tall painted Mexican wardrobe, next to a fold-down bed, is a heavy old-fashioned metronome. The room is clean, light and airy. Somehow I can't connect it with her, not the Margarita I used to know. Too conventional.

I lie down on the bed.

She lies down next to me.

'Ruby.' She says my name as if it's a statement. I can feel her looking at me.

'Margy?'

'Yes?'

'Do you still play that music you used to play when we were living together, in the Haunted Castle?'

'Bach's fugues, do you mean? I was practicing one for my audition piece.'

'The Unfinished Fugue?'

'Yes, you remembered,' she sounds surprised. 'Oh, I play

sometimes. Ray used to hate me playing violin. He wouldn't let me practice in the house you know. I had to go and practice in a church hall down the road from where we were living in Matraville.'

'Would you play it? I'd like to hear it now.'

'I've got my *Art of Fugue* on CD,' she says. 'I can put that on. I listen to it as I'm going to sleep. It's my bedtime music,' she adds suggestively. She leans over to the CD player beside her bed and pushes a button.

The first haunting bars of the fugue drift, quivering majestically, a violin searing through the still warm air.

She sits up, leans over. The top of her robe falls open, and I see her breasts. I don't want to see her breasts. She leans down, kisses me on the mouth. I don't want her to kiss me. Our bodies push and brace against each other. The last thing I want to feel is her body wrapped around me. I wanted Raymond. The only true love of my life. The love she stole away from me.

'Ruby, I've never stopped wanting you,' she murmurs in my ear, pulling on my hair, she puts her lips on mine and kisses me deeply, passionately; her hands are running all over my body, from my shoulders down my arms, down my sides, over my breasts, she is pushing against me, crushing me beneath her perfumed weight, I'm struggling beneath her, my legs are flailing kicking against the wall, the wardrobe next to the bed, trying to gain solid ground—

And then the doorbell starts ringing.

Ringing and ringing and ringing…

Boring into my brain, a nuclear alarm siren. Like it did on that Adelaide morning so long ago, that morning that marked the beginning of the end; her arrival into my relationship with Raymond, my love.

There is a thundering crashing noise in my head. And that's when I saw red. That's when everything went blood red, crimson rage, magenta poison, pink thrills, crashing cerise, red—

Spilling over hands, sheets, gushing and dripping onto the polished floorboards of the immaculate designer interior.

Raymond

I was standing on the street. Ringing the bell.

But Margarita didn't answer. I was just about to turn away, when the intercom crackled and a slurred voice said,

'Hello?'

'Who's that?' I asked.

'Raymond! It's Ruby, Ruby red, ruby love, ruby Monday—do you want to come up to my ruby world of ruby joy?'

'What are you are on?' I asked, uneasily, usually it was me slurring and I don't much like to see a woman in that state.

'Cloud nine darling, I don't know, come up and see me, Raymond, make me smile.' The buzzer buzzed and the door unlocked and I walked through the lobby and ascended to the level of the rich and successful at a smooth even speed.

I walked to number 16, knowing that something was amiss. Rube was out of it. But I didn't know how out of it she was.

I knocked on the door.

It opened immediately.

Rube must have been standing there, waiting for me. She was naked, covered in blood.

Holding Mars's metronome.

Hugo

'Well, doesn't that say it all,' Harrison passed the madeleines.

'I maintain she was acting under duress, under threat, she was brainwashed. Of course. He took her into the desert! He gave her drugs— filled her head with fears and demands and threats—who will ever know what really happened out there? It says on the police report when she was picked up she was confused, disoriented—she didn't know what she was doing!'

I delicately nibbled the little cake.

'I'm trying to get a re-trial. She is innocent. But the plebeian fools, that judge and jury, could not, or would not, see it. You'd think they'd recognise diminished responsibility—the crooks are acting under it themselves. It was so obvious it was he—that remorseless red-headed ruffian—who was to blame, not Ruby. Not my Ruby. She was set up to it.'

I was sitting up last night, over complimentary room service with Harrison, English owner of the Southern Spiral hotel group. Even though he's chosen to live in this god-forsaken colony, he went to Yarrow so I can trust him. And he's become a pillar of support in this extraordinary time, first of all with Ruby's disappearance, now this.

'It's obvious that she was intimidated and pressured to go into the desert,' said Harrison. 'That psychopath wanted Margarita Minski killed—and, using his undoubtedly skilful techniques of persuasion, which made it possible for him to abduct Ruby in the first place, no doubt persuaded her to do it.'

I didn't quite catch what he was saying.

'It's not as if there aren't precedents for abductions, the Stockholm syndrome, where the abducted think they have fallen in love with the abductor, as a form of psychological defence. Patti Hearst—the girl was kidnapped and brainwashed into becoming a terrorist. Then freed to return to the bosom of her family and become her self again.

My wife needs that chance equally, and I shall not let this matter drop.'

The Mistress Departs and Takes her Whip
The Wife Hangs up her Apron
Ruby Goes Troppo in Antipodes and kills Best Friend.
Professor Peer's Wife a Killer Condemned to Life in Jail
What does one say? What does one think?

When one's world, one's belief system has been turned upside down? An anecdote about belief in First Year Epistemology: Until the end of the nineteenth century it was believed all swans were white. Then the first British explorers came out to (where else?) Australia and black swans were discovered.

Ruby black swan, sailing gracefully down a river from my heart, on a journey I can never follow.

The last thing I said to her as they led her away: 'Keep up with your reading!'

Poor girl, I tried to be encouraging.

Those eyes, which I remembered as flashing, proud, imperious, looked like Coleridge's lamps burning in her face of waxen pallor. But that's not how I remember her (although, already, that image has seared itself into my thoughts). In my mind I always see the Ruby Love I knew, mysterious, distant and desirable, imperious yet biddable—wielding her whip like Boadicea, daughter of the British Empire. No matter what the mudslingers, the howling hoi-polloi have to say. What do they know, vicious plebeian Press-parasites, about love?

Ruby Love. My wife.

But not anymore—it seems now—my life.

And it's at times like this that you turn and wipe your eye discreetly as a gentleman can, like the Governor as he departed Hong Kong. You wipe your eye with dignity, not ashamed at an unintended show of feeling, as you turn, back straight, head high, and beat a graceful and noble retreat—thinking of Britain—showing the world how to do it—always thinking of Britain, never thinking of the footling foreign fellows, vicious and unprincipled, falling over themselves to take over the colony.

What I cannot, will not ever think about is the trial, her testimony. The poor hysterical gibberish she came out with, hallucinatory, unreal and deluded.

That undisciplined talk about that ruffian who abducted her. Even worse, the sad confused psychobabble about her 'best friend.' Not that I have anything against that kind of hi-jinx. In fact, I'd been about to suggest it to Ruby on our return—as part of my research for my book. But what she said made me sure that depraved criminal put quite clearly fabricated nonsense into her head.

That was not my Ruby speaking.

My Ruby belonged to me.

Only to me.

When I return home I shall hire a lawyer—with an education—a lawyer who knows what the word 'law' means—not like this bunch of bushrangers. I shall not rest until we have a re-trial. I need her back. Have to have her back.

The image of her above me will not leave me alone, teasing and tormenting me with its excruciatingly sweet hope of our reunion, more than a hope, it must be a promise. First there is the pain and then the pleasure that will follow.

RIVERS CHASE, OCTOBER 2002

Writing is a process in which, through scrupulous bracketing, the writer finds the essential truth.

I rest the file on the polished oak of the ladies writing desk in the mistress bedroom, Ruby's old retreat.

I pause for a moment, staring through the window at the early morning autumn mist swirling eerily over Primrose Hill. I suck back on my sixth post-breakfast Voyager fag and wonder if, indeed, phenomena of 'Repressed Memory Syndrome,' 'Satanic/Ritual Abuse,' 'Taken by Aliens' claims, the hysteria of the last decade and a half of the twentieth century, could in all truth be seen as 'less dramatic and more subtle signs of distress,' than the Victorian vapours, fugues and seizures which plagued our young ladies of one hundred years ago. All are attention seeking behaviours, all hysterical, not subtle...I pour another nip of scotch from my silver hip flask, a gift from my dear one which, since her departure, I have kept at close range at all times. I take a deep dram, gazing out into the fog.

Curious, that in the (first) re-trial the respected criminal psychologist I hired from the Restock Institute, Dr Ranulph Thimpson, brought up the term 'dissociation state' (admittedly in tandem with 'drug-induced') and applied it to my dear one, in her defence. Of course, I appreciated any points that could be made in my darling's favour. And I was prepared to pay as much as it took to have those points clearly and convincingly presented. Indeed, it was this line that 'reduced' her sentence from first-degree murder (I shudder in horror at the term applied to my Ruby) to manslaughter due to 'diminished responsibility.' Phuff. Not Ruby.

That my commanding queen be accused of 'diminished responsibility' is a ludicrous joke. Ruby was my mistress, my master. She was always superbly in control, so regal. But how can I think this? I must not speak of her; think of her, in the past tense. Two years, so far, is nothing, I am, after all, used to deserts of love. In difficult times, self-control is all. Her sense of responsibility, the imperious, cruel, almost savage, beauty of composure as she wielded the whip above me, controlling me; perfect fearsome images remain, for now and forever, undiminished in my mind...

It is obvious it was that scoundrel, Raymond Furness, who is responsible for the crime; and that is the line we are pursuing in our campaign for a (second) re-trial.

Evidence has come to light that Furness was in the George Street apartment at the same time as Ruby. And that he had, indeed, taken her there on that ill-fated morning. He was seen in the building by a cleaner, Joe Spiro, a middle-aged Italian single man. It's sufficient evidence for another re-trial.

Pity the law demands a reprobate such as he needs proven motives to dignify shameful action. It's obvious he was driven into a violent fit of jealous rage by the fact that Margarita, whom he loved (poor girl) had finally been re-united with Ruby, after he had abducted her. Clearly, he had taken Ruby to the apartment in George Street, thinking that they would be alone there. Ruby and Margarita had been friends for years as girls, until Furness came between them, forbidding Margarita from seeing a friend she adored. (And who wouldn't adore my Ruby?) Obviously he had regretted the consequences of his abduction when it brought the two women back together, and he flew into an uncontrollable frenzy of jealous violence to see them in each other's company.

Although her current circumstances are heinous, I consider it a miracle that it is my darling who is the one still alive; that it was her friend, not Ruby, who was coshed by that barbaric brute.

And we'll get him yet. I won't rest 'till we do.

Rosa

NEWCASTLE JAIL, AUGUST 2002

Repetition, distortion, inversion, embellishment mirroring...

Margy's words echo. Her voice comes back to me, at odd times throughout the day and night, as I go through the motions of my regular pre-determined routine. It's all laid out for me here. All that is required from me now in this life is for me to make of my being an entity akin to the reliable rhythmic hands of a pre-wound clock.

No requirement for bursts of sudden movement—changes in speed, tempo. I am required only to be an accurate uncomplaining cog in regulated prison machinery. My set hours—my programs—don't change.

Not like Margy's metronome.

Sometimes images flash into horror, thoughts of Margy's metronome, on the wardrobe. Swinging out of control, as our bodies lay on the bed below and the sickening crash of it— the dull thud—as the heavy triangular mass smashed down into her pale brow. She fell from the bed onto the floor. And I am beside her now as she is falling onto the floor and the metronome is crashing, still smashing, over and over, against her brow and my mind's eye is splashed again by the redness of her blood, spurting with astonishing force—suddenly—all over her face, her short black hair, my hair, spiky with blood, the metronome which—to my amazement and horror as I look down, as my eyes begin to focus, as I start to comprehend the scene—is in my shaking hands.

My hands, wet with blood. I am clasping the metronome covered in blood. And I swear, I didn't know what I was doing. As I told the judge, numb with disbelief.

What I meant to say, but the words came out wrong was: I don't know what I did.

Did the metronome fall from the wardrobe, dislodged by an unintentional kick, as they wrestled, violently, naked, on the bed? Hitting Ms Minski accidentally on the head? Or did the defendant reach for it, grasp it deliberately, maybe she had already positioned it within easy hand's reach in readiness to pick it up and in a fit of rage, or coldly pre-meditated calm, smash it into the dead girl's beautiful soft face? The wardrobe was too high for her to reach. Could he have reached it?

The questions and the arguments, the judicial discourse, droned on and on, circling her warm body, her slaughtered body, her dead body, her culpable body, Margy's body of evidence; circling and feasting like flies around a corpse.

It's a blur, a dizzy spinning rush of colour and heat and pain. I sob, scream in the cell, I can't remember, can't remember. I can't remember what happened. I don't know what happened the moment when Margarita exited disappeared. Can't remember what happened before that. All I know is that one minute she was with me, there was a crash, a loud sound, and then violent movement. Pain. The next moment she was on her way out, going, going gone, light fading rapidly from her china-blue eyes, body limp as a drowned kitten, flopping onto my legs, blood spurting everywhere like buckets of red paint, a monochrome palette, as my mind closed over in a fog.

Blood kept flowing over me. And then the doorbell rang.
It kept ringing and ringing.
I wrapped myself in a bloody sheet stumbled through the apartment to the front door.
'Yes?' I spoke into the intercom my voice sounded like the voice of someone a long distance away. The voice that couldn't be mine sounded calm and controlled.
I opened the door. Raymond on the doorstep. It was a day of surprises. He was gazing at me with an expression of horror on his face.
He led me away. The terrible smell.
He led me to the shower where I washed away the blood.

Calling Paintings into Being

NEWCASTLE JAIL, DECEMBER 2002

Young woman alone.
Playing violin.
Falling dusk.
A darkening room.

HER STRONG FIGURE DRESSED IN BLACK, is gilded by the dying sun. Her glowing face transfigured, quivering, with the understated passion of the haunting ethereal music. Her expression is yearning, agonized, ecstatic, as if on the brink of a divine revelation. Caught in a ray of light sliding through the old French doors, lit up against the darkness, illuminated by an other-worldly brilliance. Caravaggio didn't paint many female figures. If he'd painted one, it could have been her.

Margy. Playing violin, she's wearing a black slip. Standing in the warm musty gloom of the big room with no windows in our apartment in the house we called the Haunted Castle.

Long black dreadlocks twitching snakily, Medusa-like, she pauses in her playing, turning the sheet music with a quick impatient flick. Her head tilts at a sharp angle, anchoring the treasured instrument to her shoulder. The light changes from gold to white. Black and white. She's a phantom-beauty from an old horror movie. Her pale heart-shaped face. Crimson lips, kohl-lined eyes. Soft plump wraith-like arms. Those long strong flickering fingers compressing, releasing, vibrating the strings. The jerky geometry of her bowing arm.

Grave majestic notes soar and drift through the still warm air.

Outside, unseen—I know, I can feel it falling!— the blood-black dust of approaching night. Softly sigh, ferns and palms, our treacherous secret garden, growing in the dark.

I pick up brush and paints, slowly with little brush strokes, dabbing at silver, at grey, at blue. Sliding the paint onto the canvas, neat as kitten licks, letting the colours blur and merge into the out-lines of the girl I see deep in my mind, my memory's inner eye.

Her face trembles with that expression of sweet intense private pain, which she gives herself to when she plays alone, believing herself unseen. This is her serious musical side, an acute sense of aesthetic anguish inherited from her grandfather, Gus Minski, a brilliant solo violinist with the Berlin Philharmonic until the SS sent him on a cattle truck to Treblinka, where his knuckles were cruelly crushed. He survived and emigrated to Australia, a broken man.

I hover in the shadows of the balcony doors, trapped in the kitchenette on the boarded up balcony, like one of those dark-eyed oblique-looking little girls in a painting by her favourite artist. Those huge-eyed little girls, who always seem to be caught up in obscure projects, seem to strike a chord with her.

I hold my breath; she doesn't give any indication of having seen me. Soaring on high-pitched ribbons of sound. Intense baroque folds swirling violently through the gloom.

What is it that she's playing? Something by Bach, one of his fugues. When she wasn't playing, she couldn't stop talking about the music. Lecturing me with an air of superior authority, which always secretly amused me. But I never let my amusement show. I didn't want to hurt her.

'A fugue has several parts, or voices, and up to four melody lines...played by baroque instruments, viola da gamba, violin, cello, harpsichord... Each part enters in turn, like in a round. Creating a complex polyphonic counterpoint. It was a playful form of composition. An intellectual mind-game, baroque fugue composers were fascinated by labyrinthine effects, mazes, mirrors...Bach was attempting to find or create infinity in his 'mirror' fugues.'

'Surely, you mean an illusion of infinity?' I interject. She has paused in her playing and I have joined her in the warmth and light of a single last sunbeam slanting through the open French doors.

'That's all the knowledge we have of it anyway,' she retorts. I smile at her forthright domineering tone. We have been arguing about the illusory qualities of matter and non-matter, and immaterial objects of knowledge and thought, since we studied philosophy, and quantum mechanics, at Randolph Sterner School together.

'Certain number patterns, digital configurations, inexist in a state of infinite regression. A bit like a fractal snowflake—which never stops. Except these patterns remain fixed. Mirror fugues do a similar thing. Notes imprisoned within musical bars which infinitely regress. They never stop, stop staying the same. Is the idea of infinity an illusion, or do mathematical patterns recur, *ad infinitum,* forever, and what does 'forever' mean?'

'"To find infinity in a grain of sand,"' I say, teasingly.

'"Heaven in a wild flower,"'[11] she jumps in, unable to resist an easy one. Quoting poets, at each other, line by line, is an old favourite game of ours.

'"It is found again!"' I continue.

'What?' she says, obligingly, if unwittingly...

'"Eternity/It is the sea mixed/With the sun." Rimbaud.'[12]

I finish the quatrain, gazing at her, willing her to respond. Smile, Margy-baby! She looks at me; and returns to her obsession: 'In a fugue, a part plays the melody. There's an answer, as the first part plays a countersubject; all parts enter, mixing up the melodies: in variations, embellished augmented, inverted.'

'Well, all I know about the subject,' I say, 'is that a 'fugue' is a psychological condition, a kind of memory loss. There was an article about it in the *Mirror* last week. In a state of fugue a person forgets who they are, loses awareness of their identity and wanders off...maybe even starting another life somewhere else, without remembering who they were or where they came from. In the article, a lawyer went missing from a fishing trip. His wife and children were desperate. He turned up at a local police station two weeks later, saying he'd totally lost his memory, couldn't remember what had happened... It's a form of hysterical amnesia...I didn't know a fugue was also a type of music.'

'Yeah, well, you wouldn't, would you, Ruby-baby? You're a musical philistine.'

She spits the words tartly picks up a lump of rosin and rubs it down and up the length of her bow's horsehair.

The seductive put-down. Part of her playful theatrical style.

Then she returns to infinity.

'Bach's mirror fugues were, in the composer's words, pieces

of *sublime music,* designed to be only *fully comprehended in the mind of God.* That is silently.

When you read the music certain notations in parallel bars appear to repeat—well, infinitely... It's an effect you can only get if you're reading the music, you can't actually hear it, except in your mind.'

She tells me, again, about Bach's numerology and his Unfinished Fugue.

'It was as if in attaining musical self reference, he had literally written himself out of this world, and 'into the mind of God,' as he might have put it. From the physical to the metaphysical. From life to the after-life, musical posterity...'

'Repeating to infinity?' I ask, unable to resist teasing her just a little bit more.

'How sublime, darling!'

She hits a discordant note. Her violin screeches in protest.

'It's not that funny, Love,' she says, shooting me a pained look. 'There's even a website about it.'

???????????????? the Mirror last week. In a state of psychogenic fugue a person forgets who they are, they lose awareness of their???art)

'It's not that funny, Love,' she says, shooting me a pained look. 'There's even a website about it.' /// The Unfinished

I can hear it again, even here now. Margarita's music. I can't stop hearing it. Can't push a button, turn it off. Twisting and turning around my head, screeching and echoing and crashing. A ghostly fugue that never stops. That never stopped. She was preparing to audition for the Adelaide Conservatorium. She played all day, all night. Shimmering like an apparition, a vision, in the semi-darkness of my room. Her practice, never-ending practice. Driving me away.

This is it, here it comes now and again... sweet high-pitched music—her pain, her sadness, her knowledge and her striving towards beauty—which, somehow, then, I could never take seriously...

Yes, now I see it. What I so glaringly failed to consider. I didn't take Margarita seriously enough. Never reckoned on her force, her power. Margarita. My 'satellite personality,' wasn't that what you, Raymond, called her, charmingly, yet aptly, I was happy to think, in those first crystal days—when she arrived, unannounced, bags in hand on my doorstep, 'Surprise, I've come to stay!' In the early days of summer. That hot and crazy time. Our only summer.

???n. An intellectual mind-game. In the Baroque, composers were fascinated by labyrinthine effects: mazes, mirrors…they were

att??together. Is the notion of 'infinity' an illusion, or can certain immaterial things, like number patterns, like certain musical

in the Mirror. In a state of fugue a person forgets who they are, they lose awareness of

'It's not that funny, Love,' she says, shooting me a pained look. 'There's even a website about it.'

E=5

I/J=9

O=14

L=11

U=20 V=20

= 79   7+9=16

6+1= 7

16 The Mayfair 1+6 =7

Margy Margarita—will not—mention Margarita

my closest friend my best friend must not mention Margy!

No, no, no, deep breath, calm down RELAX! paper bag over the head

take a pill

a swill

what a muted thrill-spill

sliding down the hill at the Farm on cardboard sleds

me Margarita screaming behind me

& rolling rolling rolling flying sliding

laughing-crying through the long grass   crying because it's scratched her legs her hands her face is swollen red with tears because she feels hot too hot   she has to stop

But I still see Margarita falling

The memories swirl into a kaleidoscope of rushing colour receding at a giddy speed away from me and I have to grab onto the solid frame of my easel to stop myself from falling.

For seconds I am overcome by vertigo. I close my eyes and see red, pounding in my eye-lids, red so dark it's bleeding into black, darkness, layers of darkness pushing against me so that for a few moments I don't know, I forget where I am. Until the voice of Chatterton, the beautiful boy, the art teacher from outside, cuts through my panic, connects me to the real world.

'Ruby, are you alright?' His solid hand descends gently upon my shoulder.

I jump, open my eyes. I am standing in E-Room, the education room in West Wing. It's a perfectly normal Wednesday afternoon in the middle of August. A thin watery light is washing through barred windows. Beryl and Cheryl—both husband-murderers, femmes fatales, like me, who are making papier-mâché plates—are looking with narrowed eyes, indecipherable expressions.

I gaze into the canvas I am working on. There is scarcely anything there. Just a sketchy roughed-in beginning of a portrait of a girl playing a violin. It's just a girl, playing violin.

That's all.

'I'm okay, thanks, Chats—just felt a bit faint. It's nothing.'

'D'you want to lie down? Go back to your cell?'

His warm brown eyes, classical features, long gold-flecked curling locks; his obvious concern and sympathy, suddenly make me want to smile… Sure, I'd love to lie down, baby! Go back to my cell with you…But I turn my gaze away from his and grasp more tightly onto my brushes.

'No, I'm okay now. I'd rather keep on with this,' I say. 'I have to get it finished.'

It's taken me a long time to be able to represent Margy so simply. To be able to see her clearly, in my memory, without her image collapsing beneath the weight of all my broken dreams, frantic explanations, words-words-words multiplying like cancer cells. Like the voices of the judge and jury, screeching around my head. GUILTY!! I can't do it…*like a figure in a painting by Caravaggio… phantom-beauty, horror movie, Medusa-locks*…Already I am overlaying memory-images with metaphors and similes, finding analogies to obscure the facts.

Shying away from the long-lost reality, the vanished truth of the banished moments, which I'm trying hard to conjure, hold steady within the inner eye of my memory and paint. Translate into colour and form, separate material reality, that woman who was my friend. Turn her into an object of art. To hang upon a stranger's wall.

I have to go deeper; remember Margy as she really was, as I saw her once, many times, when we lived together, so long ago. I have to go deeper and deeper into my mind, to bring up and paint the images that I hope will lead me, tap-tap-tap, towards total conscious recall. Take a deep breath, a diver about to descend into murky water.

The institution greens (mint; pea) and the chalky smell of E-Room, Cheryl and Beryl and their papier-mâché platters, Chatterton, the bored guard at the door; all disappear.

What remains is growing stronger. A ghostly luminescent skin. Shimmering time space. Ghost, apparition, vision. She is standing, quivering in rapt concentration, like an instrument herself, in the only patch of half-light in the room. Beside the dark wood table I am supposed to be using as my work-desk. On it, in my mind's eye, I see my things. Rimbaud—a selection. Paint brushes in a jar, my brand-new palette, immaculately shiny tubes of paint.

I am standing in the kitchenette, in the Haunted Castle. The floor slopes so steeply in here, at such an alarming angle, it sometimes feels like if you jumped the whole balcony-room would fall crashing into the overgrown garden, two storeys below. Everything is doll-size, scaled-down, miniature in the balcony-room. There's a shaky card-table and a one-ring gas camping stove. Concealed behind a ragged green and yellow curtain, at the end of the room, is Margy's tiny bed. Built into the wall, on a shelf, like a bunk bed in a nineteenth-century European gypsy caravan; she has to curl up her legs to fit onto it.

She had lost the toss when we moved in. With a flip of a twenty-cent piece, 'tails!' I had won the medium-sized room with no windows. Furnished with an ancient sagging double bed, carefully made-up on our arrival with yellowed sheets and a thin grey army surplus blanket (to be replaced immediately by my Hillary sleeping bag). A dark wardrobe loomed towards the ceiling, at the end of the bed. 'God, it looks just like the wardrobe in *The Tenant*,' Margy sniffed as we took stock of our new abode. After that, every time I noticed the wardrobe, uneasy images from Polanski's urban noir classic (Margarita's favourite film) flashed through my mind. I saw a deranged transsexual in garish make-up gibbering quietly inside its dark reaches, biding time, just waiting to leap out at us when we least expected it. As I went to sleep at night, I closed my eyes against the wardrobe towering ominously in front of me, holding our clothes, our shoes and hats, all mixed in companionably together.

With my lucky flip I won the large dark wood table in my room. I imagined arranging my painting things on the table, setting up an easel. Maybe even creating a studio. But as soon as we moved in, Margy started practicing in the big room.

'Can't you play in the kitchen?' I asked her. 'Couldn't you practice in there?' She curled her upper lip in ravishing expression of contempt.

'What are you talking about? I'm trying to get into the Conservatorium,' she hissed passionately. I looked at her in secret admiration. Margy was so attractive when she was disdainful. Head thrown back, full lips quivering with scorn. 'There's no room to sit down, let alone play violin in the so-called kitchen.'

She made mocking scare-quotes in the air. 'Why can't you take this seriously?' Her high-pitched voice rose until it was ringing, almost hysterically, in my ears.

I looked at her in concern. I knew how important this was for her. I thought about her grandfather. Her grandmother who had died in a gas chamber. Ghosts of tortures too terrible to think about hovered trembling in the stagnant air. At that moment nothing seemed more important than Margy playing violin, the Minski family instrument.

'Okay, then,' I said. 'That's cool.'

So for three weeks, I haven't been able to do any painting in the apartment. Neither have I been able to work on my second year Visual Arts essays, which I can see before me now. A guilt-trip of drifting papers, abandoned on the table, behind Margarita's metronome and self-help books. I kept my anxiety to myself.

I didn't want to upset her.

Carefully, reverently, I slide my brush along the angular length of pale arms, rolling in dots and streaks of white to make a ghostly luminescence. Painting from memory, I stroke edges of her pale heart-shaped face. Her high clear forehead. The outlines of her features, quivering with the excessive refinement and complexity of the music. She told me once it was 'Baroque' as opposed to 'classical.' But it was all the same to me. The kind of music my grandparents insisted on listening to as if it were an emblem of moral virtue. The music I liked was wild and unrestrained with an edgy, sexy soul-searching touch: vintage new wave, punk and post-punk rock 'n' roll. Patti Smith, Joy Division, P.J. Harvey, Nick Cave...worlds away from Bach. Not that I was getting much chance to play my CDs now. But at least one of us wasn't planning on taking out a retirement pension at the age of twenty-one, at least one of us was still in touch with the (post) modern world. And it wasn't my best friend.

Margy had recently renounced her electric violin, which I considered brilliant. Wild sweet improvised psychedelic mazurkas, which she played with her friend Siimon's punk band in Melbourne. I danced to her music in grungy nightclubs. I went busking with her on the inner-city streets.

I could sympathise forever over her family tragedies. But, try as I might, I couldn't understand why she'd chosen to give up her original inspired music. To try to join the faceless ranks playing pieces which had already been played a million times. It was so competitive; and she was doing so well with her electric violin. She called me a philistine.

'Margy, could you take a break please. I'd like to listen to *The Sisters of Mercy* while I'm working on my essay.'

'I've told you; I've got to get this right for my audition. No, I can't stop.'

'Okay then, I'm going out.' Slam!

As the days passed, my friend and I were fast becoming locked in a silent—or rather non-verbalised—battle of style wars. Unspoken divisions splintered between us on discords and squeaks.

Her eyes are large, heavy-lidded, iridescent blue, fringed with black curling lashes. 'I have my mother's Irish eyes,' she told me once. I thought that was a bit gruesome, as her mother had died with her father in a catastrophic car accident when Margy was three. I choose the deepest most intense cerulean. Add a touch of white to lighten it just a bit. Stroke in each dark lash with the delicate tip of my sable brush (I have very good brushes, sent from Hugo in London). Her nose is straight, Romanesque, was how she put it. A noble nose. A shadow of grey indicates its stately size.

And then, heart beginning to pound, I dabble my brush in the carmine and pink. Mix and test and approach the canvas.

I have plenty of time to paint and research now. Ironic that in all the years I lived in London, when I owned and ran the gallery (Ruby Love Gallery, my very own gallery!) I didn't even doodle. It's taken prison to bring out the artist in me again. Murder your best friend, go to prison and bring out your inner artist! You too can do a Jean Genet!!…I borrow books from the library, five per fortnight. I can even order in books through the inter-prison library system, which is linked to the university system. And I'm allowed to keep a small collection of my own books and papers in the cell. Every morning—after breakfast of stodgy grey porridge, sickly-sweet orange juice and instant coffee which tastes of cardboard, followed by a half-hour walk, fifty laps of the perimeter—I do my research.

I sit on the bed, leaning against the flat prison pillow, which I prop against the blonde brick wall behind my back. Before I start work I glance up at the clock bolted onto the wall above the door. 10:45 a.m. precisely. Every morning, since I was transferred here from Sydney, it's the same, with only minor variations on the positioning of the hand. 10.43; 10.46…

Tick tock, like a metronome. The most exciting thing that happens here all day is the movement of the hands around the clock face.

I've developed my own routine. Self-disciplined study habits to stop me going crazy here. Research and drawing in the morning. Painting in the Education Room in the afternoon. With the small rather philistine kind of satisfaction you get from sticking to a plan, starting to see results, I pick up my copy of *The History of European Art*. It's my own book. Hugo gave it to me in Sydney, after the trial, as I was being held in custody before being transferred here. 'Something to inspire and soothe your soul, my darling,' he said as he handed me his gift, wrapped in pale pink paper decorated with Botticelli cherubs. Hugo could always be relied upon for an elevated turn of phrase, and he had a knack for choosing an unlikely gift. Things that if you thought about it, you had probably always wanted (the red stilettos, and the black leather studded wrist-band which he asked you to wear for him with magenta nail polish). Hugo. My husband. Still on my side against the world despite all the evidence against me. He assures me in his frequent letters that he still believes in me. 'Venus in Furs! My Boadicea!'

His booming bass voice, his cutting laugh, echoes in memory like the fog horn on a big safe ship sailing away in the night, leaving me stranded here in my cell alone. Incarcerated in bushland of the Hunter Valley. Hugo. He wanted me to be his Ideal Woman. A cross between Cleopatra, Lucrezia Borgia and Minnie Mouse. But now I'm Lady Macbeth, washing my hands. The stain won't come out. Crimson blood stains snow-white skin. Scarlet lips on peach and ivory. Red paint drips through the canvas onto the floor of my cell.

I received Sir Hugo's latest letter from London last week. Brought to me by Jackson, the Sydney dealer he's appointed to show and sell my 'prison paintings.'

I read his letters over and over. Can't quite take it in. The words are written to someone else. Not me. 'You've become famous. Quite a cause célèbre in the London art world, my darling...'

Jackson brings me clippings from the British press.

SELL OUT SHOW FOR MURDERER-ART DEALER!

Does he really think I want to know? Does he think I'm ecstatic about such so-called 'success' as an artist? Can't think about it. Won't think about it. Reasons are fictions. The 'M' word. Falling. Thirty-two feet per second. The speed at which bodies fall… As if that means anything to me now. The art world, media glitz and glamour, the PR beat-ups, stunts and hype which I used to think I loved. A million years ago, in London.

Tumbling and falling. All things return into the ground. Crime of passion. The French defence. Into the ground. Bone meal for the next generation of falling joys.

Eurydice, deep inside the ground. Deep inside me. Guilty.

Ruby Love. Contemporary art gallery director. Married to Lord Sir Hugo Sir Hugo. It's not what I had that I miss. It's what I didn't have, what I never had. What I couldn't have. What was taken from me.

That collapses my soul, inner body, into an empty mausoleum of perpetual longing and grief.

The book falls open at the section Baroque in Flanders, Holland, Spain. It's to be faithful to the mood of Margy's obsession with the music of the Baroque, that I've chosen to paint my series of portraits of her, and Raymond, in a post-modern neo-Baroque style, incorporating elements which characterised the Baroque in painting.

A fascination with light, illumination; the juxtaposition of high and low elements, the grotesque and the sublime; the bawdiness and rowdiness of everyday life, which had never before been thus depicted in high art; ordinary low-life characters illuminated with the metaphysical brilliance of heavenly light. A fascination with tricks, labyrinths, mazes, mirrors which repeat and distort meanings to infinity. A love of lavish ornate embellishment which turned architecture into extravaganzas of whirling wings and curlicues. But the defining feature of the fine art of the Baroque was, always, what was out of frame, unseen, unstated. The unseen presence to which a sculpted figure turns; unseen source of light which transfigures in a brilliant ray the low-life barefoot tavern drinkers in Caravaggio's *The Calling of St Matthew*…

—What was it that was out of frame? What was it that I couldn't see? In that tangled intense time the three of us spent together. ??????????????????????????????????? That never stopped. She was preparing to audition for the Adelaide Conservatorium. She????? ??????????????????????'s

that's what Raymond called her, charmingly, yet aptly, I was happy to think, in those first crystal days—when she—

The page I want is book-marked by a photograph. Margarita and Raymond at the Farm. Snapped by me. High summer in the High Country. A time of dazzling light, intense heat, screeching cicadas and drought in the starkly beautiful rolling hills and plains; the foothills of the mountains. My best friend and my lover are standing outside the old red weatherboard farmhouse. Next to the rambling tea rose, wilted in the heat. It was a simple cottage with none of the comforts or conveniences of modern life. No electricity, gas, piped water or phone line. The property was bound on one side by the rushing river. On two more by a narrow creek which ran underground in summer. And, on the fourth side, by a small mountain. Mount Satyr was named after a dream. The family had often talked of owning angora goats. A plan which, like all the family's grand plans, fell to nothing when Harry left.

'The Farm' was an optimistic euphemism for the acreage

of stony, semi-wilderness that the parents bought after we returned from China. We'd lived in Beijing, in a luxury foreigner's compound, for three years, from when I was ten to thirteen, whilst Harry was employed by the Australian government in the Global Co-Operation—Economic Sector, international aid agency.

For a couple of years we went to the Farm every weekend and holiday. Harry, Aphrodite, my sister Lily, brother Alex, Margy and myself. All squashed into the family's suburban assault vehicle, our battered old four-wheel drive; the dogs, Russia, the red setter; and Rufus, the German Shepherd, panting in the back. Setting out on the two-hundred kilometre journey from our big almost-renovated terrace in Glebe. Driving down the Great Western Highway, as the sun set above us. Out through Sydney's sprawling western plain, up through the Southern Highlands, and beyond. Often friends—as well as Margarita—came with us. Or people dropped in to stay, and it was always a fun time, playing out a comfortable, middle-class version of Early Settlers. Stranded in the bush, many miles from civilisation, with huge roaring log fires at night, plenty of food and wine, long bushwalks and river swimming, painting, fishing, orchard planting, horse riding and reading in the daytime.

Then Harry ran off with his young, blonde, research assistant. And the family—which had stayed together throughout several moves around the world—fell apart. All that remained of the dream of goats running free was an allusive name which we'd long ago corrupted to Goat Hill.

Aphrodite didn't go to the Farm after Harry left. But I kept on going down with Margy and Wolfie, my boyfriend before Ray.

In the photo, Raymond and Margarita are both laughing at some long-forgotten joke. They are glowing in the full glare of the sun, as if they've been irradiated. It's almost as if they are haloed by light. I don't want to look at them now. I look at the page in the art history book.

Velázquez's *Las Meninas* takes up quarter of a page. It's in black and white; its wash of greys is grainy. But its magic still shimmers through. The image, saturated with so many forms of light, dances into my eyes. Little Princess Margarita, with her long blonde fluffy hair, surrounded by playmates and maids. In front of her, a dwarf and a large loose-jowelled Flemish dog. To her left and right are two older girls, curtseying in a display of avid attendance. The group is standing in the artist's studio, where it is assumed; we are informed by the text, the little princess has just been posing for Velázquez. The artist has included himself in the portrait. He is a long-haired moustachioed swash-buckling kind of figure, holding a brush and palette. Standing before a gigantic canvas, almost as tall as the high-ceilinged room. Its left edge is just visible on the left-hand side of the canvas, as if it is propped against and held up by the inside of the painting, *The Maids of Honour*, itself.

Two small figures are reflected in an illuminated mirror on the wall at the far end. The text reveals that they are Princess Margarita's royal parents, although it is impossible to tell this from the blurry indistinct image alone. Whether the images of the royal couple are reflections of images Velázquez has painted on his unseen canvas, or reflections of the couple standing out-of-frame in the open space (where the viewer is positioned) to which the group in the portrait are all looking, as if towards the viewer who is, in turn, gazing into Velázquez's portrait, is also unclear and unknown.

Beside the mirror is an open doorway, the vanishing point, in which a male figure stands on stairs which lead apparently into nowhere but a rectangle of brilliant light. This figure is turned towards the viewer. Although it was painted a couple of hundred years before the advent of photography, it looks as if the figures in the group (except the reflected 'royal parents') are turning to a photographer who captured them as they turn before a formal pose has been struck.

Velázquez opened a window onto a visible world created from light, challenging the viewer in the process to enter a labyrinth of reflections and optical tricks. What at first sight looks to be a straightforward group portrait is revealed to be a complex maze of shimmering mirage-meaning...

I have gazed for many hours at this reproduction and yet have not come any closer to solving the mysteries and paradoxes it sets up.

There's always more to do. More pictures to paint. I can't stop now.

At night, she whispers to me, softly-brusquely, telling me everything I need to know about fugues, their structure, their content, their history, their genesis...my inner ear tickles with her voice, my mind echoes with the sound of her violin. In my dreams she is standing in the room in her black slip dress, playing *The Unfinished Fugue for Three or Four Voices,* our voices, the music that once drove me crazy.

I can look at her but cannot touch her. I cannot reach her. I can paint her but I cannot make her see me, I cannot make her smile, or talk again. No matter how many pictures I paint, and words I write, I cannot make the blood flow back.

I cannot give her life.

Coda

George

CAME HOME TO FIND A MONSTROSITY.

I had always loved Margarita.

Of course she must stay in my apartment, when I was away in Portugal for my sabbatical.

All year, in the dusty squares of Lisbon, the blazing white maze of Costa da Caparica's seaside streets, I could not stop seeing her. Cooking in my kitchen. Eating at my table. Soaking in my bath. Sleeping in my bed. Wandering through the rooms of my apartment…I could see her reclining on my sofa, exotic and forbidden, the living ghost of my desire. She called to me as I sat at the wooden desk of my office in the Language School, wondering what I was even doing here.

Teaching English as a second language became a hollow joke. I had to see her, had to return to tell her that I loved her, in the primary language. I had to move back—in with her.

I decided I would surprise her with gifts of brightly-coloured wall ceramics. Patterned plates to hang on the walls of our home. Bottles of extra virgin olive oil. And the straw head of a donkey with long ears and a tasselled rope about its neck.

I let myself into my apartment.

Music was playing.

Something classical. The type of music Margarita liked. It was coming from the bedroom. I would surprise her with my special gift. The painted wooden statue of the sad Madonna.

I approached and saw that the door was open.

I've kept silent for so long. Almost two years.

But I can't keep it to myself anymore.

I see her everywhere I go.

Smiling. Looking sadly at me. Those beautiful grave downcast eyes. My Lady of the Sorrows.

The statue sits on the top of the wardrobe in my bedroom, gazing down so sadly, yet with such compassion. I washed the blood off under the kitchen tap. Let myself out quietly. The voices told me to.

Her eyes say everything, and today I have to do it.

Pray she will release me from the burden of guilt I feel. Those tragic eyes.

'Go to the Police Station.' 'Put on your shoes.' 'You have to do it.' I have to go now.

I have to tell someone.

I have to confess my sins.

Ruby

Cockle Beach, Sydney, November 2003

It's five weeks since the real murderer confessed, and I was freed. Wrongfully accused charged and convicted; there's a history of this here, and I was 'branded' behind the scenes, the victim of prejudice and false accusations. There will be a very large amount of compensation paid out to me soon. I have been on my own, trying to process everything that happened, in my writing.

I'm still in Sydney although I will leave soon. Fly back to my life. I'm staying in a dilapidated apartment near the beach, the empty holiday house of a friend. I write every day, and night the dark hours before dawn—which some call the small hours, but which I think of as the large hours as time expands then. I write overlooking the ocean, the crying of seagulls is the music of my daytime; at night, silence, and the hiss of my laptop rings in my ears. Now I see what this process has been: one of collecting myself. You can't remember something you didn't do. But you may imagine it in writing.

I'm almost at peace now.

The wandering journeys in my mind have ceased.

It takes a while to become used to justice, to believe I am free.

Acknowledgements

References to music and cultural history are from *The Writer's Fugue: Musicalization, Trauma and Subjectivity in the Literature of Modernity* (2007) Ruth Skilbeck's Ph.D. thesis held at the University of Technology, Sydney and published online.

Day Six:
1. p. 7. Wang Zhiyuan's *Beauties Captured in Time* is referred to with kind permission of the artist. The passage draws on Ruth Skilbeck's article 'From Mao to Now' in *(Not Only) Black and White* Issue 42, April 2000.

2. p.12. Ruby misquotes the first line from William Blake's 'The Sick Rose', in William Blake's *Songs of Innocence and of Experience: Showing the Two Contrary States of the Human Soul. 1789-1794*. 1794 (public domain). Blake's first lines are "O Rose thou art sick./The invisible worm,/ That flies in the night/In the howling storm:/ Has found out thy bed/"

3. p. 13. Ruby quotes from 'The Sick Rose' source as above.

Day Four:
4. p. 44. Hugo reads from: *Venus in Furs* by Ritter von Leopold Sacher-Masoch translated by Fernanda Savage (1921). First published as *Venus im Pelz* in 1870 (public domain).

5. p.47. This passage draws on Ruth Skilbeck's art research article 'Gazing Boldly Back and Forward: Urban Aboriginal Women Artists and New Global Feminisms in Transnational Art,' including her review of works by Fiona Foley. See R. Skilbeck in *The International Journal of the Arts in Society*, Volume 5, Issue 6, 2011: 261-276.

Day Two:
6. p. 66. Ruby misquotes/misremembers lines from William Blake's 'The Tyger,' in *Songs of Innocence and Experience:*

Showing the Two Contrary States of the Human Soul. 1789-1794. Blake's lines read: "What immortal hand or eye,/ Could frame thy fearful symmetry?"

Day Zero:

7. p. 76. Ruby misquotes the opening lines of 'The Night Before Christmas' first published Dec 1823, in *The Troy Sentinel*, newspaper, New York, the authorship of the poem has been disputed and it has been attributed to both Clement Clarke Moore and Henry Livingstone Jnr. The lines in the poem are: "'Twas the night before Christmas, when all through the house/Not a creature was stirring, not even a mouse."

Antipodean Space:

8. p. 113. Ruby's translation is of lines from Rimbaud's 'Les Premières Communions' (First Communions) in *Oeuvres de Arthur Rimbaud: Vers et proses: Revues sur les manuscrits originaux et les premières éditions mises en ordre et annotées par Paterne Berrichon; poèmes retrouvés* (1921) (public domain).

Margarita:

9. p. 130. The line is from Rimbaud's 'Vagabonds' in *Les Illuminations* (Illuminations): 'Je répondais en ricanant à ce satanique docteur, et finissais par gagner la fenêtre.' Margarita, or Ruby, mistranslated from Rimbaud's poem in *Oeuvres de Arthur Rimbaud, Vers et proses: Revues sur les manuscrits originaux et les premières éditions mises en ordre et annotées par Paterne Berrichon; poèmes retrouvés* (1921).

Margarita's Metronome:

10. p. 196. The story that Margarita retells of J.S. Bach's unfinished fugue is in Douglas R. Hofstadter's *Gödel, Escher, Bach: An Eternal Golden Braid—A Metaphorical Fugue in Minds and Machines in the Spirit of Lewis Carroll*, London: Penguin Books, 1979; and in Malcolm Boyd's *Bach*, Oxford University Press, 1983. Margarita paraphrases the words by Bach's son.

Calling Paintings into Being:

11. p. 214. Ruby misquotes/misremembers the opening lines of William Blake's 'Auguries of Innocence' which are "To

see a World in a Grain of Sand/And Heaven in a Wild Flower/ Hold Infinity in the palm of your hand/And Eternity in an hour". The poem was first published in 1863 (public domain).

12. p. 214. Ruby quotes a line, that she translates from Rimbaud's 'Eternity' (éternité). Margarita speaks the second line; Ruby quotes in translation, the remainder of the stanza of Rimbaud's 'Éternité' in *Oeuvres de Arthur Rimbaud, Vers et proses: Revues sur les manuscrits originaux et les premières éditions mises en ordre et annotées par Paterne Berrichon; poèmes retrouvés* (1921).

Unless otherwise stated translations are by Ruth Skilbeck.

Ruth Skilbeck is a British-Australian author living in Australia.